"Are you traveling alone?"

"Yeah. I'm heading to Flagstaff, Arizona. Do you need a ride?"

Stupid question. It couldn't be more obvious she needed a ride. She was hitchhiking. Fleeing her wedding, it would seem.

"Great," the woman said. It was more of a mutter, tinged with irritation.

Stepping back, she gave both directions of the highway a good stare. The old road, but for them, was deserted. She would have had better luck catching a ride on the main highway. Why would she come out here to hitchhike? Maybe someone was after her. Maybe she was in danger. His testosterone surged and pumped up his chest. He was a rescuer of damsels in distress.

****

He was probably a serial killer.

That's how her day was going. Day? No, that's how her life was going.

Previous releases:

The Marshal's Pursuit
The Darkest Sum
A Scandalous Request
A Bandit's Request
At Her Request
Blooms in the Fall

It Happened on Route 66

by

Micki Miller

It Happened on Route 66

Contact Information: info@thewildrosepress.com

Cover Art by *Tina Lynn Stout*

The Wild Rose Press, Inc.
PO Box 708
Adams Basin, NY 14410-0708
Visit us at www.thewildrosepress.com

Publishing History
First Edition, 2024
Trade Paperback ISBN 978-1-5092-5270-1
Digital ISBN 978-1-5092-5271-8

Published in the United States of America

Dedication

To Dinah Hafen, who encouraged me to finish this book. Thank you, for reading my unfinished pages with optimistic eyes.

Chapter 1

The Tyrannosaurus Rex of hangovers taught Joel Tyler two things. One, red wine and tequila don't mix. Two, heavy drinking with certain people leads to bad decisions, like mixing red wine with tequila. In the same glass.

If the green-faced emoji had a name, it would be Cabernet Sunrise.

Joel forced open his sandpaper eyelids, scraping them against the desert floor of his eyes. It had been a big mistake not closing his drapes before flopping into bed last night, or rather, early this morning. He squinted through the vicious aftereffects of last night and the nuclear-level sunlight of today. He should have gone to sleep wearing his sunglasses.

With caution, he twisted toward the plastic parrot alarm clock on his bedside table. Had the parrot's colors always been so bright? Had morning?

Next to the bird clock and reeking with curdled funk sat an open bottle of beer, almost full, and a white bag smashed down by a half-eaten burrito. Discolored filling wretched from the hardened flour tortilla. Joel's stomach roiled.

He could swear, just for one second, the plastic parrot with the clock in its belly was cringing like a cartoon come to life. Joel blinked. If he didn't get some eyedrops soon, he'd have grooves in his eyeballs.

His muddled state, along with the southern California sun blasting through his bedroom window, fuzzed the numbers on the clock. But he was still able to make out the time. It was *10:00 a.m.* Bad news. He should have been up and moving two hours ago. Why didn't his alarm go off? He really needed to get a clock made for grown-ups.

Hopefully, his saint of an older sister, Mariel, would notice him missing before his bosses, A.K.A. his parents, and cover for him. A heavy sigh huffed through his dry lips and swung upward to punch his aching head. A grown man of twenty-nine and he still had to answer to his parents. *Well, that's what working in the family business gets you, everlasting adolescence.*

And now, thanks to a broken alarm clock, a questionable friendship, and the misguided invention of the Cabernet Sunrise, he was going to be late for work, again. These last few days, fearing his career was circling the drain, had amped up his drinking. He couldn't have another failure.

A faint whiff of flowery perfume had him scanning his bedroom through a squint. Was it a remnant from a previous one-night stand, or did he have a woman here last night? He couldn't recall. *Oh, wait.* A memory emerged from the fog in his head.

Things were going well with a pretty brunette he'd met at the bar. He couldn't remember her name. What happened…? Oh, right. Roz had shown up flashing the ring he'd given her. She'd yelled at the brunette about being his fiancée before whispering in his ear how time was up because they were both almost thirty. The brunette had given him a scalding look before grabbing her purse and marching out.

Damn. He should have stayed home last night, watched some TV, and gone to bed early. But no. All it took was a call from Boone, and he was ready to party, hard.

Joel stretched his dehydrated muscles. Though he belonged to a gym, much of the credit for his toned body was due to his time spent working in the warehouse of the Tyler toy factory. It was the one place he was always competent. After this last debacle, he should surrender his nice office and make the warehouse his permanent workplace.

This afternoon he'd drive one of the company trucks to Flagstaff, Arizona, to pick up his most recent failure. Well, that's what everyone thought. In truth, his mission was to convince Mr. Hargrove, owner/operator of the store, to give his product more time. Joel knew it was good. A month on the shelf wasn't long enough.

Joel closed his eyes. If he failed this time, it *would* be the end of his career.

The parrot clock on his night table squawked and flapped its colorful wings. The clattering plastic was not softened by the mass of discarded clothes strewn about his room or the pillow he burrowed his head into, but instead echoed inside his throbbing skull. Where was death when you needed it?

Joel slapped his hands over his ears and curled into himself. He'd yank the covers over his head if he didn't fear the movement would cause him to lose whatever rancid mix was still in his stomach.

The clock squawked in its imitation parrot voice. "Wake up! Wake up! *Awk, awk!* Wake up!"

****

Maddy Hayden used the back of her wrist to shove

away a strand of her wheat-colored hair that escaped from the big clip on the back of her head. The hair stuck to the perspiration at her hairline. She glanced at the back door of the kitchen. Someone had closed it. After flipping the pancakes, she opened the door again and let some fresh air into the room.

She pressed both hands into the small of her back and arched. Her first break of the day gave her about thirty seconds to take a breath and see past the sink and stovetop.

The cream-colored appliances were almost two decades from new, but everything worked, and like the white linoleum floor and white tile counters, Maddy kept it all clean. Last year her dad had given the walls a fresh coat of summer peach. The kitchen pretty much looked the same as it had her whole life. Today, however, with her wedding just hours away, it was busier than it had ever been.

"Dad," Maddy said. She had to yell across the kitchen to be heard above all the voices. "Take your pill. It's next to your glass of juice."

He folded down the top corner of his newspaper, exposing little more than hazel eyes and thinning blond-gray hair, still wearing the military cut of his army days. His forehead, like the rest of his face she couldn't see right now, was leathered from his years of working in the sun.

Her dad scanned the crowded tabletop for his juice. After taking his pill, he ducked back into hiding.

The noise level swelled. Maddy grabbed a paper towel to dab the moisture from her forehead. She sucked in a breath, huffed out, and tossed the paper towel into the trash. Also sitting at the table was her sister Rachel, two years younger than Maddy's twenty-eight years. Rachel, already in full makeup, kept talking to their dad through his newspaper.

Her sister yakked about her family trip to Hawaii. Rachel, her husband, and the two kids had been back for a month, but her sister continued to tell the same stories. They were interesting and colorful the first time. Second time, too. Maybe even the third. If Maddy heard about grilled pineapple one more time, she was going to…listen again.

The voices of Jessica and Jennifer, Rachel's four-year-old twin daughters, and the cutest handful of trouble a person could have for nieces, almost overtook their mother's. At present, they were arguing over who could eat more pancakes.

"I can."

"I can."

"I can."

"Aunt Maddy," Jessica said. Her dark, ringlet ponytail, identical to her sister's, swayed with the swish of her head.

Maddy flipped pancakes onto a plate. "What, sweetie?"

"We're all out of pancakes."

In three strides, Maddy was at the table. She picked up the empty plate and replaced it with a plate full of fresh pancakes. "Enough with the syrup, girls. It's dripping over your plates and onto the table." *That was going to be a bear to clean.*

"Who opened the door?" Rachel said. "It's freezing in here." Maddy's sister rubbed her arms through her thin, floral robe and shivered as if she'd stepped into an ice cave.

Maddy crossed the kitchen to the sink and slipped on her rubber gloves. "It's hot by the stove."

"Jennifer," Rachel said. "Go close the door for Mommy."

Maddy fanned herself with her gloved hands but stayed at the sink.

Less than a minute after Jennifer had closed the door, it opened again. Cool air blew in like a gift, along with Grandma Sophie.

"Hello all!" Sophie said.

Grandma Sophie had forgone her usual animal prints and bold colors for the occasion and wore a simple pink dress. Her grandmother had to hate it, but she wouldn't complain, not today. Maddy smiled. Her grandma's compromise was to carry her giant, zebra-striped purse. It was almost big enough to hold an actual zebra. Her red hair was sprayed to a helmet, and her lips were brighter than her hair.

Sophie set her purse on the floor near the back door. "Hi, Sam, Rachel, girls, where's Mad…" Grandma gasped when she saw Maddy.

"Rubber gloves!" Sophie said. "You're cooking and cleaning on your wedding day!"

"It's just a few pancakes."

Maddy said the words, but they hadn't come from her heart. In her imagination, the day had gone a different way. She'd pictured her sister helping to get everyone fed, helping to clean up, the whole time talking about the excitement of the wedding. Or build some excitement. Maddy's nerves were too overwrought to enjoy the day. Was that normal? It must be. Still, she'd like to feel some happiness. She'd like to feel…special. *Stop being ridiculous.*

"Are you hungry, Grandma?" Maddy said. Grandma Sophie was a twig. A powerhouse, but a twig.

"No, sweetie. It smells delicious, but I already ate. I'll help you get cleaned up, and then I'll help you get ready."

"Rachel said she'd do my makeup."

Hearing her name, Rachel perked up and swung away from their dad, still hiding behind his newspaper from the barrage of grilled fruit stories. "You bet. Are you ready?"

Maddy headed for the table to collect the dirty dishes. "A few more minutes. Oh, girls!"

The twins were dipping their fingers into their plates of syrup and had drawn circles around each other's eyes. Their artwork had also left a sticky mess all over the table, the floor, and their princess-something-or-other pajamas.

Jessica laughed. "We made glasses out of syrup."

"So you did," Maddy said. "Rachel, didn't you see what they were doing?"

"I can't watch everything all the time. Girls, go wash up now."

As the twins giggled and skipped out the kitchen door, Maddy said, "Use soap! And don't touch anything on the way to the bathroom."

Maddy glanced at the clock. The kitchen was a mess. She hadn't even showered yet. At least she'd managed to stuff a few bites of food in her mouth while she was working.

"Is Joann here yet," Grandma Sophie said.

Joann, Maddy's best friend since high school and her maid of honor. "She should be here any minute." Sophie snatched up the dishrag and started on the kitchen counter while Maddy cleared the table. "Dad, are you finished eating?"

Without looking over his newspaper, he said, "I'm done."

With the two of them working together, Maddy and her grandmother had the kitchen cleaned in half the time it would have taken her alone. She glanced at the clock. Good thing.

Maddy had just put the bag of leftover pancakes in the freezer when the front doorbell rang. "That must be Joann now."

Rachel stood up. "I'll get it. I have to go check on the girls anyway."

"Don't strain yourself," Grandma Sophie said. Rachel either didn't hear or ignored their grandmother. Pure Sophie. Pure Rachel.

At footsteps, Maddy glanced toward the door, but it wasn't Joann who entered. It was her husband-to-be, Owen.

"Good morning, everyone," Owen said. He handed a fist full of yellow roses to Maddy and kissed her on the cheek. "And a special good morning to you, my bride." She smiled, as expected. Yellow was Owen's favorite color. She hated yellow. With her fair coloring, it made her look like the ghost of a summer squash.

Owen wasn't yet dressed for the wedding, but he was still dressed well in a salmon-colored dress shirt, black dress pants and shiny tasseled loafers. His blond hair was neat and styled, as it was every minute of every day, and his tart cologne cut through the smell of pancakes. He was a good-looking man, though a little less time in the tanning booth would be better.

"You're not supposed to see me before the

wedding." Maddy said it without ire. She wasn't superstitious and neither was Owen.

"I thought I'd drop off these pamphlets on campgrounds for your dad. Hi, Sam," Owen said. He set the pamphlets next to her dad's plate.

Campgrounds. Her dad had already given his notice of retirement, and he and his friend Hal were making plans to buy an RV and travel the country. They were so cute, taking turns highlighting places on their map they each wanted to see. They'd talked about taking the trip someday for a long time. Their plans solidified as soon as she got engaged, like she figured they would.

The day's pressure grew teeth.

For the first time since he sat at the table, her dad set down his paper. "Owen, come in, sit down! How about some coffee? Are you hungry? Maddy made pancakes this morning. You know what a great cook she is. Have you ever tried her pancakes? They're the best."

Her father sounded like he was selling Owen a used car, pointing out the serviceable engine so he wouldn't notice the dull paint.

Owen sat at the table across from her dad. "Smells like heaven in here. I'd love some coffee and pancakes."

Maddy glanced at the clock. She needed to get in the shower. Owen grinned and winked at her with a short nod. It was his way of telling her to get to it. She should tell him that annoyed her. Instead, she opened the freezer, reveling in the blast of cold air, and took out the baggie.

Owen scrunched up his face. "Ooh, frozen? I like them made fresh."

"I just put them in there," Maddy said. She bent the pancakes to show they were still pliable. "I'll heat them for you."

"Maddy," her father said. "Make the man some fresh pancakes."

Using baby talk, Owen said, "Pweez, Maddy."

That also annoyed her. It rattled her a little, too. Sometimes, when the baby talk didn't get Owen what he wanted, the man talk got a little mean. Maybe her nerves were making everything seem worse. It's not like he ever got horrible. Just…unpleasant.

Maddy glanced at the clock again. Shower, hair, makeup, get dressed, maybe a few minutes to catch her breath before she walked down the aisle.

Before she could answer him, Grandma Sophie snatched the bag of pancakes from her hand, tossed the bag on one of the plates she'd just dried, and dropped the plate on the table in front of Owen. "She's got to get ready, you know, for the wedding."

Maddy took a quick peek over her shoulder as she was shuffled out of the kitchen. Owen's hazel eyes fought to keep the stare from turning into a glare. He never showed that side of himself to her family. Grandma Sophie sensed it, though. It's why she didn't like him. But Owen's harshness only made occasional appearances. After they were married, he'd soften. Probably. Hopefully.

As they passed through the living room, the silver-framed photo on the end table next to the couch caught her eye. Her parent's wedding picture. They were so young, so happy. Rachel had their mother's beauty, but Maddy liked to think she had her mother's heart. Sixteen years since her mom had passed away. She still missed her.

They reached the stairs near the front door as

someone was knocking on the other side. Maddy opened the door and there was Joann. She had her bridesmaid dress on, bright yellow taffeta skirt, fitted bodice, cap sleeves, pale yellow lace trimming the scoop-neck. Low-heeled shoes dyed the same color as the lace.

Joann hugged her, all smiles and beauty with her auburn hair against the yellow. She was as happy as Maddy's father but better at showing it. "Big day!" Joann said.

"Big day," Maddy said. The big day already had her half worn. Her sister and the kids drove in yesterday, a day before Rachel's husband, who was at this moment making the hour-long drive from Rockport, and Maddy had been working hard ever since. "Look, I'm going to jump in the shower. Joann, would you get my small travel bag from the hall closet? One of Owen's friends is letting us use his cabin for the next couple of nights, and I need to pack a few things."

"Sure," Joann said.

"I think it's buried under some stuff, way in the back."

"I'll help her find it," Grandma Sophie said. "You get your shower."

Maddy let the steamy water hug her until it turned cold. She washed with her special lavender soap, hoping the calming scent would, well, calm her. These past weeks had drained her to sluggishness. She'd worked her job at the fabric store right up until yesterday and cried all the way home. When Owen told her she wouldn't be working anymore, he made it sound like a gift. But she loved working at the Yarn Barn, all the fabrics, the colors, the people she worked with, the customers, and her employee discount.

Why hadn't she fought for her job? She hadn't said anything. She sat there like a pin cushion and accepted it as part of her reality. Same as it ever was.

After her shower, Maddy wrapped her hair in a towel and slipped into her comfy old terry robe. She opened the bathroom door to laughter coming from her room. Even from Grandma Sophie, who'd called last night to tell her it wasn't too late to change her mind. Owen and her grandma would warm up to each other. Once the wedding was over. Once Maddy's life was set.

Her father could move on to his RV adventure with Hal because he wouldn't be worried about her anymore. Owen would calm down because their relationship would be solidified. She'd have a good life with Owen. She'd have a life with Owen. She'd have life with Owen.

If Maddy had her way, she'd live on her own for a while before settling down. A couple of years ago, she'd gotten her own apartment. It wasn't in the best neighborhood, but it was in her budget. She had it for a whole three days before someone broke in through a window in the middle of the night. She woke up when the man opened her bedroom door.

If asked the day before what she would do in such a situation, Maddy believed the answer would have been to curl in a ball and beg for her life. But she hadn't begged. She hadn't fainted, shivered, cried, or done any of the wimpy things she and everyone else would have expected.

The slats of moonlight slanting through the blinds lit on her knitting basket, only a few feet from her bed. She grabbed a knitting needle and jabbed at the intruder like a swashbuckling sea captain in piggy pajamas. *Swish, jab, swish, jab, jab.* She did it without thought, without hesitation. After a couple good pokes, one to his rear end when he spun, which drew blood, the intruder ran screaming from her apartment. It still made her smile with pride. That night, she was her own superhero.

She never should have told her father what happened.

He was so freaked out by the break-in he demanded she move back home right away. There was no arguing with him, though she did try. He was already packing her stuff in the boxes she hadn't yet thrown away. It was because he loved her. Still, she'd been so excited about her little apartment, the adultness of getting it, of having it, the thrill of advancing her life. The relief of knowing her father would live his dream, too.

Laying in her childhood bedroom that very night, it struck her how her father wouldn't take his retirement unless Maddy followed her sister's path and got married.

Not long after, she met Owen. He checked most of the boxes. Owen was a good catch. He was polite. He was a gentleman. He was attractive and had a good job with a respected financial institution. He had his faults, but who didn't?

Every so often, Owen got angry about something, but he was never violent. *So who doesn't get angry every now and then?* He could be bossy, a little controlling, sometimes more than a little. But he cared about her. She cared about him. Life wasn't a fairytale. Then there was the other factor. Her father.

He was farm-work strong and aside from high cholesterol, under control with a daily pill, he was in good health. But what if his health took a downward turn? What if he never got to live his dream? Her dad had worked at the Welch vegetable farm ever since she could remember, foreman for the last fifteen years. He'd worked hard his whole life. He deserved his dream of selling the house and traveling the country in an RV with his friend Hal. How could she block his way?

Maddy sniffed in her lavender-scented skin. Again. One more time.

She stood in the hall for a full ten minutes before entering her bedroom.

Chapter 2

Joel picked up the keys to one of Tyler Toy's trucks from Natalie. The stout woman with a tight, gold perm and copper lipstick had been his mother's secretary since he was ten years old. She handed him the truck keys, attached to a small rectangle of wood with a screwed-in chain and key ring. Natalie also gave him a smile. A sad one. Like the sympathetic smile people share at a funeral.

Today was kind of like a funeral, as far as anyone at the company knew. His best idea had died, and he was going to collect the toys for return. Let the pity party begin.

His hangover danced a jig in his skull, making time for an occasional dip in his sour stomach. A long, hot shower and several glasses of water carried him part way back to normal. Then he dressed in a clean, white T-shirt, his soft-worn jeans, and an old blue hoodie. He shaved and took a nice jacket to put on for his meeting with Mr. Hargrove at the toy store.

His hangover helper, C.A.G.E.—Crackers, Aspirin, Ginger ale, and Eyedrops, took him a little farther. But his drinking kicked him around with cruel after-effects, and there was only so much his remedy could do.

Joel glanced from Natalie, seated at her tidy, walnut desk, to the key chain's other side. The number three was burned into the block of wood. He'd be driving the smallest and oldest truck the company owned. "Thank you."

"You're welcome, dear," Natalie said. The weight of her sympathy dragged her voice down an octave. Natalie tipped her drooping face to the right, giving emphasis to her pity.

His hangover laughed at him.

The reception area to his mother's office was tasteful. Lavender walls with blurred landscapes, a long, pale green, tufted couch, and a pair of matching chairs all positioned just so on a stone-colored carpet. Several white teddy bears sat beside white vases. A light, flowery scent drifted in from a source he had never found. The door to his mom's private office was maple, shiny, and closed.

The proper show of respect would be to pop in for a quick hello before hitting the road. But he wasn't ready for a conversation with his mother. He had to speak with Mr. Hargrove first, had to convince him to carry the toy for at least another month.

The soft scrape of a tissue leaving the box drew Joel's attention back to Natalie. She wiped a tear from the corner of her eye. From her desk, she lifted a beveled glass bowl of candy-covered chocolates.

"Have some candy, Joel," Natalie said. She tilted her head and gave him another one of those funeral smiles, then she dabbed at her eyes some more.

Before he ended up comforting her about his own impending doom, Joel gave her a quick "No thank you'," turned around, and walked away. He took with him the keys to the truck and left a little of his dignity behind.

His journey was off with the start he had earned.

Yahoo.

****

Joel stepped out of the bright fluorescence of the company garage, leaving the smell of gas and oil, of tires, sweat, and other various garage standards for the fresh air.

He crossed the parking lot at a slow but steady gait. A mass of strung-out clouds, gloomy and low, crept across the sky in what had a real feel of symbolism. He tipped his head down toward the blacktop so as to not meet eyes with anyone he might pass. He wasn't up for talk today.

He tossed his old duffle bag and hoodie behind the canvas seat of company truck number three, laid his nice jacket on top, and climbed inside. The old girl, a ten foot box truck with a creaky cab, had a standing appointment for repairs. It couldn't be more than a trip or two away from retirement. He crossed his fingers that it would make it to Arizona and back without breaking down.

The company logo was painted on both sides of the turquoise blue truck, teddy bears forming two Ts beneath a bright rainbow. 'Tyler Toys' was painted in yellow on the cab doors and on the back roll-up door.

Joel took a sip of strong, hot coffee from a steel tumbler. He set the tumbler in the cup holder, plugged in his cell phone, and secured it in the clip mount. Before leaving his apartment, he'd chosen his route. It was an easy decision to forgo the highway and travel Route 66. He wanted the solitude of the low-traffic road so he could run his speech through his head until it was its best.

He tapped on his app and hit go. The security guard gave him a wave and a smile as he passed through the gate. Joel forced a smile and waved back. He made a left at the Tyler Toys sign and was gone.

Once the city was behind him, the relief of getting

away from the business helped him think. For the rest of the day and tomorrow, there would be no one to pity or disparage him. At the toy store in Flagstaff, he'd make his case to Mr. Hargrove to keep the dolls a little longer. He had the speech written in his head, and he'd go over it a hundred times before he got there. Joel's entire future rode on a yes.

****

Joel rumbled along the old road, hard rock music rasping through the truck's pitiful speakers. Even with upping the volume, the music struggled to be heard over all the creaks and rattles of the company truck. But the music gave him a positive vibe, even with the static, so he kept it playing.

A few minutes earlier, he had turned onto Route 66, and some of his tension eased. Like when he was a kid playing hide and seek and found a good place to hide. The trip would take longer on this route, but he could make it fit.

The historic desolation offered an odd sort of comfort, like he shared a connection to the far-spaced structures whose youth and good times were on an old calendar. He fit in here. But like the life that used to run through these once pleasant and necessary places, he couldn't stay.

After a brief glance at the fickle sky, Joel took off his sunglasses and tossed them on the spider-cracked dashboard. When he'd rolled out of the parking lot of the toy factory the clouds had shifted enough to allow the sun to pour its warmth on him, giving a momentary feeling of hopefulness. Thirty seconds later, dark clouds swallowed the light again.

Joel's mind drifted back to the place of his

employment, the place he'd known since birth. He had worked there after school since the fifth grade and then his entire adult life. Growing up, it was the best place in the world. He and his sister, Mariel, were the envy of the neighborhood kids. Their family owned a toy factory! Every kid's dream was his reality.

An endless array of toys decorated each room in the building. Teddy bears of all sizes and colors smiled their fuzzy comfort at every turn. Soldiers in assorted uniforms stood poised and ready to defend dump trucks and baby dolls from dinosaurs, dragons, and battery-operated attacks.

In the factory area, molding machines and vats of vibrant colors made from plastic pellets waited along the assembly line for their turn to shine. Toys rolled on conveyer belts in an everlasting parade. In the warehouse, packaged toys stretched out as far as a little boy could see from atop the shoulders of his loving grandfather.

Often, toys were prototypes, and many of those would never see the inside of a store, but Joel and his big sister got to play with all of them.

At the end of their week's work after school and over the summer, sweeping, emptying waste baskets, delivering messages, etc., Joel and his sister had a choice of modest pay or their pick of a new toy. Life was great.

After graduating with a degree in business, Joel still loved Tyler Toys. He had an office on the top floor, though, much like his father, he spent plenty of time in all the departments, keeping up with every aspect of the business. His older sister already worked for the family business full time. It was natural for him to follow suit.

The production of a new toy continued to thrill him.

His family was pretty cool to work for, at least back then. That was before he decided to make his mark in the creative department. Oh, to go back in time.

He was so sure creating new toys was his calling. He loved working in the design room, the use of new technologies, and the bud and bloom of it all. He believed with all his heart it was where he belonged. By the time he realized how wrong he was, his numerous failures had made it impossible for him to regain his standing.

These thoughts were picking at Joel when the clouds shifted, and a fat ray of sun shot down to the ground. Centered in the sunbeam spotlight was a sight so peculiar, so outlandish, he turned down the radio so he could see it better.

Joel waited for the vision to come into clear view. When it did, he was close to certain his night of reckless drinking had left him brain-damaged.

Standing on the side of the road, almost afloat of it, was a goddess. No, she was an angel, complete with a flowing white dress and a white halo on her head…and she was hitchhiking.

As he got a little closer, it became clear it was not an angel beckoning him with her thumb but a woman in a white gown. Nearer and the halo made sense. The gown she was wearing was a wedding dress. On her head was one of those things brides wore, like a princess crown with white lace flowing back on the breeze. What were those called?

A travel bag, the size for a weekend getaway, sat next to her , and she had a look of desperation obvious even from this distance. What the hell was she doing way out here? The woman stretched her arm out farther into the road space, thumb up and wiggling as if her thumb would be what drew his attention. He didn't have time for extra stops today, didn't have room for someone else's drama, but what else could he do?

Joel hit the brake and the clutch and downshifted.

Chapter 3

Joel had someplace to be and only so much slack, which he was using to drive the old road. He didn't have time for any side adventures. But he sure as hell couldn't leave her standing there all by herself. A lonely road, abandoned buildings, she was a horror story waiting to happen. He rolled to a stop not far past the hitchhiking bride.

He got out and walked to the back of the truck as she was walking toward it, dragging her bag on its rollers.

"Hi," he said.

"Hi."

Her face had a pleasant, heart-sort-of shape, with emerald-green eyes, a dainty chin, and delicate ears with small, sparkling earrings. Her wheat-colored hair was twisted fancy and bulged through the ring on her head with the lace hanging down her back. A veil. *That's what it's called. A veil.*

She might be kind of pretty, but it was hard to tell with all the makeup the woman was wearing. Between those ridiculous fake lashes weighing down her lids and all the dark gunk around her eyes, the too-red cheeks, more powder than a donut, and lips so glossed they reflected the sun, there was no way to tell what she really looked like.

The woman, he guessed her to be in her late twenties, passed him without a pause. She trudged all the way to the cab of the truck and stood on her toes to look in the passenger window. He followed her.

"You're alone?" she asked.

Her tone held concern and maybe a little frustration.

"Yeah, I'm headed to Flagstaff, Arizona. Do you need a ride?"

Stupid question. It couldn't be more obvious she needed a ride. She was hitchhiking. Fleeing her wedding, it would seem.

"Great," the woman said. It was more of a mutter, tinged with irritation.

Stepping back, she gave both directions of the highway a good stare. The old road, but for them, was deserted. She would have had better luck catching a ride on the main highway. Why would she come out here to Route 66 to hitchhike? Maybe someone was after her. Maybe she was in danger. Joel's testosterone surged and pumped up his chest. He was a rescuer of damsels in distress.

****

He was probably a serial killer.

It's how her day was going. *Day? No, that's how her life was going.*

After a hopeful stare down both sides of the empty road, Maddy glanced down at herself.

The bottom of her wedding dress was soiled and ragged, the hem coming loose and sagging in places. Dirt and road grime caked her pretty shoes, ruining the white lace over the toes. She was tired, hungry, and grouchy. The last thing she should be doing right now is getting into a truck alone with a strange man. Then again, this whole day had been full of things she shouldn't be doing.

What she *should* have been doing these past few

hours is laughing and dancing at her wedding reception. Instead, she'd hiked across dirt, gravel, and road, escaped a snarling dog on a precarious leash, ran screaming from a snake (or maybe it was a stick, she wasn't sure), dodged her family, her friends, and the man she was supposed to marry. Her head hurt. Her stomach growled. Blisters were having a party on her feet, and her legs had been cursing her for the last couple of miles.

The fiery surge of energy that whisked her through the back exit of the chapel had lost much of its verve. Even after her long, long walk, she still couldn't believe she had done it. It was either the bravest thing she'd ever done or the most foolish.

Now what? Continue walking until dark, curl up in some abandoned building for the night, and hope no wild animals come in to dine on her? Or get in the truck with this possible serial killer. She didn't even have any knitting needles with her.

She couldn't go back, at least not until the commotion settled, and that wouldn't happen for a while. So, what to do? She had no place to go other than away. The truck was headed away. More walking wasn't much of an option at this point. Digging a hole and lying in it for a month or so was appealing. Too bad she didn't have the energy or a shovel.

Maddy scanned the road again, hoping for a minivan carrying a nice family who would stop for her. If she was very lucky, they would like her and invite her to live in a corner of their basement, a domestic troll of sorts, cooking and cleaning to pay for her keep. She'd had plenty of practice.

There was not another car in sight, and according to the sun, it was way past noon. She looked back at the truck driver guy, dressed in jeans and a white T-shirt. He was attractive, appeared to be friendly. It's how they always describe the truly evil bad guys, the ones nobody ever suspects of murder.

He was such a nice guy! Quiet, polite. Who knew he was driving around with a bunch of dead bodies in the back of his truck?

One of the cable channels had just run a series of documentaries about serial killers. She never should have watched them. Now, everyone looked suspicious.

Maddy took a deep breath and let it out. Exhaustion was playing with her. So was hunger. She didn't have so much as a breath mint in her bag. She stretched out a cramp in her leg and glanced at the guy who was bigger than her, stronger than her. Her tired legs wobbled on her sore feet.

Really, how many serial killers could there be out here? If he wasn't one, the next guy might be. She was going to have to take a chance. On the bright side, it would be the last of her screwups if she was murdered while hitchhiking.

She lowered the handle of her paisley weekend bag until it clicked.

Maddy shook her head before she opened the passenger door and tossed her bag on the floor. She then tugged up her dress and gathered its masses in her arms so she could climb into the truck. Halfway in, the weight of the dress shifted. She lost her grip on the seat and slow-slid backward. The maybe serial killer caught her by the waist.

"Hey, hey, I can do this," Maddy said. She slapped at his hands, in no mood to be pleasant. He was probably going to murder her and dump her body on the side of the road anyway. Or add her to his collection in the back of the truck. Until then, she was calling the shots. For once in her life.

"Just lending a helping hand," he said.

"Well, keep your hands to yourself. And you should know, my friends are tracking me by my cell phone." It was a big lie. No one had a clue as to where she went. They couldn't even call her because she'd turned her phone off hours ago. But he didn't need to know that.

"Hey, relax. It's not like I'm a serial killer or anything."

Maddy plopped onto the seat and did a slow head rotation toward the truck driver. Those are the words a serial killer would use, reassuring her, worming his way into her trust by making such a joke, something he could laugh about later. And here she was, getting into his truck. She must have lost her mind.

Maddy scooped in the rest of her dress. "Well, if you are a serial killer, do me a favor and kill me now. It's already been one hell of a day." Without waiting for a response, she slammed the truck door. Half a minute later, they were rolling down the road.

"I'm Joel."

Maddy yanked bobby pins from her hair until her long-laced tiara was free. She gazed at the thing as if it was an offense. "I'm Maddy."

She inspected both sides of the tiara, crown-like in the front with the veil sewn on halfway around in the back. A tiara. How ridiculous. Who wears a tiara? She certainly hadn't chosen it. The tiara, like everything else about the wedding, had been Owen's idea. Whatever she had chosen somehow never made it to the final plan. Not one thing. The realization sparked another rebellion.

Maddy grabbed the crank and rolled down her window. Warm air blew through the cab of the truck, and she squinted against it. Then, she flicked the veil-draped tiara out the window like a flying disc.

From the corner of her eye, she caught Joel's glance. At least he didn't tell her not to throw out her veil. Or worse, tried grabbing it to stop her from doing something she wanted to do. If he had, well, she'd be tempted to start her own killing spree.

"Is Maddy short for Madeline?"

She nodded. "When we were kids, my little sister couldn't say Madeline, so everyone started calling me Maddy."

Throwing out the veil felt so good that Maddy took off one of her wedding shoes with the ruined lace across the toes and tossed it out the window. The other shoe followed. Looping a finger under the garter, she slid it off her leg, pinched and stretched it back with the fingers of her other hand like a slingshot, and sent it flying out the window.

While keeping herself covered with the skirt of her dress, she squirmed out of her white stockings and threw them out, too. Maddy wiggled her sore toes. Raw blotches on her feet shone angry and red. The truck driver peeked over at her feet and winced.

She reached under her dress and wiggled out of her giant, ruffled slip. The whole getup was absurd. Her sister and her fiancé loved the overdone look. She did not.

After some maneuvering and one good shove, the white mass of undergarment whooshed out the window.

Joel, the truck driver, kept quiet. He was either baffled by her behavior or plotting her murder.

Whatever.

"So where are you heading?" he asked.

Maddy took some sneakers out of her bag and tossed them on the floor. After rooting around in the bag for a moment, she took out a pair of white socks. She stared out the truck's big front window, half huffed, half sighed. "Flagstaff, apparently."

Maddy put her socks on and rubbed her sore feet through the fabric.

"Why didn't you change into your socks and sneakers earlier, save yourself all the foot pain?"

Maddy paused, rolled a sideways glare out the passenger window, and shook her head at herself. Great idea, three hours too late. *Thanks for pointing out my mistake.* She yanked some jeans from her travel bag and slipped them on underneath her dress.

She took a pink T-shirt from her bag. The neck and the sleeves were lined with tiny butterflies, each of which she'd sewn on herself. She laid the shirt between them on the seat. Then she reached around to the back of her dress, one hand over, one hand under, and managed to get it unzipped. With one hand on her chest holding up the front of her dress, Maddy worked her arms out of the long, lacy sleeves.

She slid a glance over to the truck driver. Yeah, he was looking. The perv. She whipped her head and sent an icy stare his way. He jerked his face toward the road again.

"Sorry," he said.

Her clothing rustled, but he kept his eyes on the road while she got her T-shirt on and her wedding dress off. Once she shoved the dress out and rolled up the window, Maddy peeked over at him again. His head kept shifting to the long side mirror outside the truck. Curious at the sight it must be, Maddy looked at the side-mirror outside the passenger window.

Against the glow of the late afternoon sun, her wedding dress rolled down the road, like a giant, white tumbleweed.

Chapter 4

When ten long minutes of silence passed, Joel turned the radio up a little. He and his psycho bride passenger stared out the front window of the Tyler Toy's box truck.

After the last of her bridal attire was gone and literally blowing in the wind, he'd made an attempt at conversation. She wasn't into it. Fine. He had his own troubles to think about.

With a few more miles behind them, he glanced over. She didn't look crazy now, just low and lost. All the makeup gave her a kind of sad clown look. Joel resisted an urge to comfort her, to reach over, take her hand, and tell her everything would be all right. Even in his own head, it sounded corny. Besides, he wasn't very optimistic about things these days. Maybe it *wouldn't* be all right. He didn't know her or her situation.

She was a stranger. She was a strange stranger.

Joel questioned the sanity of picking up an attractive yet disturbed hitchhiker. She had accused him of being a serial killer. What about her? *She's* the one who could be a serial killer. *It's happened before.* He'd just watched a series of documentaries about serial killers.

One of them had been a woman who'd murdered a bunch of men and ended up on death row. She let the men pick her up in bars or…hitchhiking.

As sly as he could, Joel slid a peek her way.

Goosebumps popped up on his arms. This woman beside him could have a gun in that bag at her feet. Or a butcher knife, maybe stained with the blood of her previous victims. She might be waiting for the right moment to start carving into him, just like the woman in the documentary. *Shit.*

Not like he didn't have a clue something was off about her. She was hitchhiking in a wedding dress. *Who hitchhikes in a wedding dress?* And where was her new husband? Dead, his body rotting in a shallow grave? Maybe that's what she does, marries men and then kills them right after the wedding like some black widow psycho killer. He'd seen such a story in one of the documentaries. Maybe someday she'd be known as the 'Black Widow of Route 66.' It could happen.

How embarrassing. Driving this old company truck painted with teddy bears and rainbows on the way to fight for a load of dolls, and then murdered by a crazy, hitchhiking bride he'd been stupid enough to let in his truck. *Shit.*

Another ten minutes passed with nothing but the static-littered music from the radio and the creaks and rattles of the truck. From the corner of his eye, he caught the hitchhiking bride giving him a sneaky sort-of glance. Then, *she reached for her bag!*

Joel stared at her hand with the pink, painted nails, moving slow like a stalking cheetah. She unzipped the bag… His heart pounded, his breath tightened, and his wide-open eyes stared at the bag like the prey he was. He should slam on the brakes and make a run for it before she drew her weapon. He should do it now.

His stare flicked from the bag to the road, from the road to the bag.

Crazy lady was in her bag almost to her elbow.

Her arm stopped, and then retreated, slow, snake-like. She had, oh God…it was…it was a book. It was just a book. Okay, no more serial killer documentaries for him.

****

Maddy examined each page of her design book. There was no reason for her to have packed it in her bag. No reason in the world. She hadn't planned to show her drawings to Owen. At least not until she had a bit of success, or at least some interest in her work. Why risk getting shot down before she even took flight? And what made her so sure her fiancé would shoot down her dream?

Because he would.

Owen wanted her to be what she'd been to her father and sister for so many years—planner of meals, maker of home, and also a docile attachment to his arm for business affairs. She was suited for it. Except for the business affairs, it was what she'd known for most of her life, what was comfortable.

Then she lay in bed awake most of last night. Not with wedding jitters, but marriage jitters.

Quitting her job at the Yarn Barn had hurt. Every day she worked there, she got new ideas for clothing designs. Her younger sister, Rachel, had some of Maddy's fancier items. Maddy preferred a simpler look, and she'd drawn and sewn a few things for herself. They were the seeds of her line of casual wear, the line she dreamed of creating.

It was Maddy's dream to make her passion her profession. Working at the fabric store, handling the home finances, taking care of the house, her father, and babysitting her sister's twin daughters every time Rachel needed a break didn't leave much time for her own pursuits. In the back of her mind, Maddy had thought about working on her career after she was married. But she never told anyone. Not even her fiancé, Owen.

Well, she *did* tell Owen.

Okay, she should have said something to him sooner than twenty minutes before the wedding. She didn't find her voice until then, until her bridesmaids had all gone to attend to one thing or another, and she stood alone in front of the full-length mirror. Instead of seeing a woman about to blossom into a new life, she saw her wimpy old self falling into the same life she was leaving.

It scared the hell out of her. It scared her the hell out of there.

She hadn't considered anyone else, not her family, not her fiancé, not the hundred and eighty guests. She hadn't given two seconds of thought to the uproar she would cause. Panic had blurred everything but her future as it stood.

While she walked by assorted businesses, meandered through an upscale neighborhood, and crossed patches of vacant land, Maddy kept an arrow's vision. Nothing behind her. Nothing to the side. It was the only way she could keep going. Even now, she forced herself to stare at her book so she wouldn't think about the mess she'd made. It was a struggle.

Maddy studied one of her earlier designs for a minute or so, a fitted, cap-sleeved T-shirt done in blended pastels, before returning the book to her bag and zipping it shut. A thought from the back of her mind raised its hand. If she had an actual career instead of a job, she could afford a better place to live. Maybe then she could convince her father to retire and go on his RV adventure with Hal.

A career. Her. Uneducated past high school. No experience beyond her tiny world. Off her feet and having caught her breath, reality crept up on her.

Foolish dreams, foolish decisions, and foolish acts. When for the first time in her life, she jumped the tracks of normalcy, she leaped like a gazelle…over a cliff. Must be all the years of holding back, of pretending her needs didn't matter, of her own aspirations smothered to silence beneath the laundry, the cooking, and the cleaning. Today, the facts of her life lit a fuse, and she'd gone off…Boom!

Running out on her own wedding had been so outlandish everyone must think she'd had a mental breakdown. Maybe she had. She didn't make spur-of-the-moment decisions. Beyond her domestic duties to her family, she didn't make decisions at all. A sigh whooshed through her head. Maybe there was good reason she didn't.

Maddy assessed her situation. She was sitting in a truck with a man she didn't know, who may or may not be deadly dangerous, heading to Flagstaff, where she knew no one, with less than a hundred dollars in her bag. Not only had she thrown away a secure future, but she'd delayed her father's retirement dream indefinitely. She glanced toward the bag holding her precious book. Maybe she should have designed a straitjacket.

When she'd snuck over to the groom's quarters to talk with her fiancé, Owen must have thought she was having a simple case of wedding day nerves. He had no way of knowing it had been her long, secret dream to design clothes. Dreams. Dreams were for a fantasy life.

What Owen had offered was tangible. What she had thrown in the garbage today was solid reality, traded for silly nonsense.

What were they all doing now, the families, the friends, and of course, the groom? Were they searching for her? Were they worried? There must be a dozen messages on her phone. She should have at least left a better note than scribbling in lipstick on the mirror saying, *I can't*. She wasn't thinking when she ran away. She wasn't thinking at all.

Maybe everyone was so busy consoling poor Owen they had forgotten about her. Maybe Owen had sent all the guests to the reception. Everything was paid for, food, music, etc. She should call and at least let them know she was all right.

No, she wasn't going to call anyone. Not yet. Not her father, her sister, her best friend, or even her grandma. She'd have to explain herself. She had no good explanation for what she'd done. On a bright note, this could be a fresh start. Anything was possible now. Anything could happen for her now. The thought lightened her burden a little.

An instant later, an obese reality rolled over her again. Anything could happen *to* her in this truck. Maddy slid a glance to her left.

Maybe she was being paranoid. Or maybe good sense was flagging her down. She knew nothing about this man, yet she had gotten into his truck as though he was a trusted friend. No one knew where she was. My God, she had hitchhiked! What was she thinking?

A stream of nervous energy surged up her spine, making her sit a little straighter.

She was like a character in one of those scary

movies she enjoyed, except she was playing the part she hated. The part where people kept getting killed for doing stupid things, like walking into the woods late at night, alone, like swimming in dark water away from the group…like hitchhiking…like getting into a truck with a man who was driving alone on a desolate road.

She'd wandered here not knowing where she was going. What about him? What was he doing on Route 66? This wasn't an industrial road. He didn't look like a tourist out here all by himself. And what was with all those teddy bears painted on the truck? What kind of a man drives a truck with teddy bears and rainbows painted all over it?

The truck looked pleasant enough on the outside, but who knows what might be back there, locked away. A nice collection of murdered bodies, perhaps?

Maddy shivered at the recurring thought, feeling more real now as the sun was setting. He hit the headlights. On they rolled.

Night gobbled up the day with shocking speed. Dusk swallowed the last sliver of orange. Slate clouds muffled the full moon. Streetlamps were sporadic. Lighted buildings were few and far between. It was as if the whole world had left her alone with a stranger.

She slid him another quick glance before peering through the windshield. A minivan approached from the other direction and zoomed by before she could see who was in there. Probably the nice family she'd been hoping for.

Maddy nibbled on a cuticle. It was all too easy for her to picture herself as a tragic headline on the evening news. Commentators would crinkle their brows while they told the sad story of the little fool who didn't know any better than to stand alone on the side of a lonely road with her thumb out. *Oh no.*

Mothers would hold her up as an example to their daughters of what *not* to do. Reporters would shove microphones in the faces of teary-eyed friends and family on the front lawn while her father watched from the window, cursing his daughter's stupidity. Well, at least she'd be dead and wouldn't have to get a 'what were you thinking?' speech from her father or her sister. Now there was a tarnished silver lining.

They hit a pothole, and Maddy bounced from her seat and slammed against the passenger door.

"Sorry," Joel said. "Are you okay?"

"I'm fine." Maddy rubbed her right arm. She yanked the harness across her body and shoved the tongue into the buckle.

Today was the first time she had gotten into a vehicle and not automatically put her seat belt on since…since she could remember. All her safety senses were jammed.

She took another peek at the driver.

Okay, before giving in to hysterics, she should talk to him, try and get an impression of what he was about. "What are you hauling in this truck anyway?" she asked. The question was innocuous enough. If he stumbled for an answer, then she would worry.

"Nothing right now."

Okay. No hesitation there. Good. "So, you're going to pick up something?"

"My assignment is to pick up a load of toys."

Was that a pause? Maddy peered across the cab of the truck, reading what she could of his face through the faint light of the dashboard. "Toys?"

"I work for the Tyler Toy Company. We have a new doll out, and she's not selling very well."

That explains the teddy bears and his reluctance to talk about a company failure. She relaxed a little. If he was a real pick-up and delivery driver, people knew where he was. He had a schedule to keep. It was unlikely the man was out cruising for victims if his whole company knew where he was going.

At least, she hoped it was unlikely. Hard to say. Her good senses had taken a vacation. Right now, they were probably lying on a sun-soaked beach somewhere, sipping umbrella drinks and laughing at the mess she'd gotten herself into during their absence.

The truck rolled by the bleak skeleton of a gas station long ago closed and a small antique store with a neon *open* sign glowing in the window. One dusty car sat in the parking lot.

"What kind of dolls are they?" Maddy asked her question out of more than politeness. She was still getting a feel for this guy, seeing if he'd stumble for an answer. It was hard for her to care about some unwanted doll with her own troubles pounding on her.

"It's a…it's a concept doll. She's designed to be a reflection of a lot of today's women. That was the pitch. You know, she takes care of the kids, holds down a job. She's attractive, but not perfect looking. She's realistic."

Maddy twisted toward him. "Sounds like a great idea for a doll. Why didn't she sell?"

Joel flicked a glance her way. Even in the dim light of the truck cab, his surprise was obvious. "You really think it sounds like a great idea?"

A memory flashed through Maddy's mind. She had been nineteen, her sister Rachel, seventeen. They were standing side by side in front of the bathroom mirror, about to leave for their cousin's wedding. Her sister, who had spent no less than four hours getting ready, looked fit to grace the cover of a magazine.

Rachel had spent the day giving herself a facial, doing her nails, her hair, and her makeup. The previous week her sister had shopped the malls until they closed, trying on, and finally choosing the perfect dress. Well, it was almost perfect.

Rachel had run into Maddy's room the day of the wedding in tears, crying about how her new shoes required the dress to be hemmed up two inches. By the time Maddy had it done, after serving lunch and cleaning the kitchen, she had less than twenty minutes to get herself ready. And it showed. She was clean, combed, and dressed. It was the extent of her grooming.

Everyone fawned over Rachel's beauty. In all fairness, her sister was gorgeous. She worked out every day. She ate dainty little lady meals and never snacked. Even without makeup, styling, and fashion, her sister had a better body, better facial structure. Rachel did give credit to Maddy for the hem job, for which Maddy received her due compliments.

"Sure, it's a great idea for a doll," Maddy said. "Little girls should learn to accept women come in all shapes and sizes. We are imperfect. *That's* what normal is. But we grow up thinking we should look like pageant queens, or something is wrong with us. It's about time there was a doll reflecting reality."

"I…well, that's what I thought. But I didn't know if others would see it the same way. Thanks."

"This doll was your idea?" Maddy gave him her full attention. He was tall, well-built, and very masculine.

This guy invented a doll sensitive to women's realities?

"Yes, the doll was my creation."

"Wow, I'm impressed," she said. "Don't take this the wrong way, but I'm a little surprised the idea formed in a man's head."

"My sister has always been a little on the heavy side. Several times when we were kids, some bully picked on her, then I'd have to go and beat the bully out of him. Mariel acted tough, like it didn't bother her. But when she was home in her room, sometimes I heard her crying."

"You two are close."

"Very. My sister has a heart as big as the world. She's smart, sensitive to others, beautiful. But I don't think she ever felt very good about her appearance. I was at work one day, and I started thinking about when we were little kids and how Mariel used to play with this doll. It didn't look anything like her. I figured the same must be true for lots of little girls."

Maddy nodded. She didn't say her childhood had little room for things like dolls once her mother got sick. At ten years old, she'd stopped being a kid. By age twelve, she'd taken on all the domestic duties.

"You made this doll for your sister?" she said.

"For her, because of her."

"That's the sweetest thing I've ever heard." All she could do was stare at Joel. *What guy thinks about such things? Wow.* For the first time, Maddy looked at him with complete regard. What stood out gave a little heat to her face.

The soft glow of the dashboard light illuminated his face, the planes of masculinity with a rascal's boyishness highlighted by a dimple when he smiled. Hair the color of dark chocolate, with a slight wave, lay back on his head except for the loose lock at his temple. His white T-shirt stretched to cover his broad chest, the sleeves taut around prominent arm muscles. This guy was in calendar condition.

And, he thought and cared about a woman's feelings, about her self-esteem. *Wow.*

Joann, her best friend, would flip for him. Maddy took a peek at his left hand. No wedding ring. If he didn't turn out to be a serial killer, maybe she would introduce them.

Something her fiancé once said drifted through her mind. Joel looked like what Owen would refer to as a worker bee. "These kinds of people," Owen would say, his opinion rolling down his lofty nose. "Must always have someone telling them what to do."

Though she hadn't spoken up and said so, Maddy never did see anything wrong with being a worker bee. The world needs worker bees. Otherwise, the suit and tie bees would be lost at sea in a luxury sailboat with no sail, an engine that wouldn't turn, and a radio that wouldn't transmit. The world couldn't stay afloat without worker bees. Besides, she was as worker bee as anyone. Maybe more so than average, considering her job at the Yarn Barn and all her domestic duties at home. What was Owen saying?

"So, do you have any brothers or just the one sister?" Joel asked.

"Just the one younger sister, Rachel." Maddy chuckled. "She's probably having a raging meltdown right about now."

"Do you want to call your family? I can stop and take a walk, give you some privacy."

As much as she didn't want to, she *should* call someone and let them know she was all right. At least send a text. It was beyond inconsiderate to make everyone worry about her. *So* not her, which would make them worry even more. The thought of opening that door, though. She wasn't ready.

What to do? What to do?

Her stomach made a grumble so loud he had to have heard it. Maddy placed a hand on her belly to muffle any more embarrassing sounds it might make.

"I have an idea," Joel said. "Why don't we stop somewhere and eat?'

Ugh. He'd heard her stomach making hungry noises.

"We'll order, then you can step outside and make your call."

Her stomach had been nudging her for hours. The mention of food propelled her hunger to the front of her attention. And, as much as she dreaded it, she needed to call and let everyone know she was all right. By now, the shock had turned to worry, and not calling was cruel.

"Whenever you're ready to stop is fine," she said.

Over the miles traveled together, they'd passed a couple of restaurants and motels still open for business, catering to the tourists who liked traveling the old road. Several more were gloomy and boarded, relics of their glory days. A few were just bones.

They rolled by a brick building painted beige, with an excess of colorful graffiti; random symbols, a caricature of a clown, *R + M* was spray-painted inside a giant, cockeyed red heart. Someone had spray-painted a few feet of cartoon daisies along the bottom of the wall.

They passed a little café, long closed. Tall weeds sprouted through cracks in the parking lot. The front window was busted out, exposing a thick darkness inside. Faded green shutters hung askew on opposite sides of the window, giving the illusion of droopy eyes. A yellowed notice was still taped to the door.

Silver speaker boxes and menu boards stood beside most of the front parking spots. The menus were cracked, some with large chunks missing, and one of the speaker posts leaned at a sharp angle, bulging a mound of broken parking lot at its base. The lot lines were faded to near invisibility. Maybe this was one of those drive-in restaurants. The kind with roller-skating waitresses. Maybe, at one time, this was a happy, busy place, and everyone wanted to be here.

The historical vision was almost tangible. It was easy to picture vintage cars with vintage music streaming from single-speaker radios. Women in A-frame dresses, men in hats, kids with toys instead of devices. The smell of French fries everywhere. Maddy blinked. The images paled. How long would she have to be gone before she faded to memories?

Wasn't there a saying about old soldiers? Something about how they never die, they just fade away? Maybe it was the same with old highways and runaway brides. After a while, they're just ghosts.

Maddy gazed ahead, past the headlights. Road and sky blended into one dark, gaping mouth. Maybe in the daylight it would look different, but cloaked in the night, sparse-lit by a partial moon, Route 66 was a scene from an end-of-the-world movie.

They approached a building on the right outlined in lighted pink neon. On the edge of the lighted sign at the street glowed a neon waitress in a white blouse, a short, pink skirt, and a blonde, beehive hairdo holding a tray.

The thought of food made her stomach growl again.

Joel steered the truck into the parking lot of Daisy's Diner.

Chapter 5

The old-style jukebox blasted out fifties rock music. The music filled all the empty space in the restaurant. Maddy and Joel were the only customers.

The whole place was done up like an old-style diner. Large black and white tiles covered the floor in a checkerboard pattern. Empty barstools with red vinyl seats on shiny chrome stands lined the counter along the back. Swinging doors to the left of the counter had square windows in the tops showing a kitchen behind the doors. The place was sparkling clean, with a faint aroma of pine cleaner and coffee.

Tables sat in neat, staggered rows across the rectangle floor. The wall to the left near the front door had a glass case of candy bars and a tall desk on which sat the cash register. Along the right wall and the front windows were red vinyl booths. They chose one of the booths by the front windows and waited.

One bouncing song finished, and with a few clicks of the lighted jukebox at the end of the counter near the restrooms, another song began. It was upbeat, very danceable, if one was in the mood to dance.

Maddy had her hands on the cool, laminate tabletop, left hand resting on the right. Sitting in a booth with a stranger, in some empty retro-diner in the middle of nowhere, she stared at her empty ring finger. Had she made the biggest mistake of her life?

As Maddy wandered around her head, wondering if she should pick up the pieces of her life or sweep them away, she caught Joel staring at something in the back of the restaurant. She followed his direction toward the square windows at the top of the swinging doors leading to the kitchen.

At first, it was just a flash of movement, then the window showed a head with a white, boat-shaped hat bopping across the room on the other side. A muffled voice singing along with the song on the jukebox accompanied the movement.

The head bopped by the window one more time before the swinging doors burst open, and a skinny, fair-faced young man in his early twenties, wearing a white apron, danced through the doorway.

His head was tipped down as he sang into a giant metal spoon at top volume. He did an impressive rock-and-roll spin, stopping so his back was to the counter, and he was facing the two customers, head still down. He swung his hips in a convulsive hula sort of movement. Maddy covered her mouth to muffle her laughter. Joel managed to laugh in silence.

The young waiter spun around again and while singing loud enough to be heard across the street, raised his head. He froze stiff as though winter had blown through the diner and turned him into an ice sculpture. His eyes were as big as the end of his metal spoon microphone, and his lips were round, still forming the high-pitched "Wooo." Surprise and embarrassment stifled his voice.

Maddy and Joel stared back, flicked a smile to each other, and gave the guy a round of enthusiastic applause. The red-faced waiter tipped his head in a partial bow. He rounded the counter, tucked a couple menus in his apron pocket, filled two red plastic glasses with ice and water, and carried it all to their table.

"Can I get you something to drink besides water?" the waiter asked.

"Water is fine for me," Maddy said.

"Me too."

The waiter walked away without saying a word. As soon as he was in the kitchen, Maddy and Joel met eyes and burst out laughing.

At the tail end of her laughter, Maddy sat back and sighed. For a couple minutes, they looked over their menus.

"I'm sorry I was rude back there," Maddy said. She stared at her hands, once again folded on the table next to her menu. "Like I said, it's been a bad day."

Joel rubbed a hand down the light scruff on his face and mumbled as he stared at his menu, "Forget it. I know what a bad day can do to a person."

The gruff sincerity of his tone caught her attention. "Are you having a bad day, too?" Of course, she didn't want him to be having a bad day, but the old adage of misery loving company was feeling kind of true.

Joel studied his menu in silence and shifted in his seat a little.

"Well, I'll bet you didn't spend the afternoon hitchhiking down Route 66 in a wedding dress."

Joel chuckled. "No, I didn't."

Maddy's smile was small, self-deprecating, finding a bit of humor in the sight she must have been.

The waiter returned and wrote their order on his pad. His fair skin still had a tinge of red.

"Well, I guess I'll go make my call," she said.

Maddy walked out and wandered toward the end of the building. The white block was dyed pink by the bright, neon trim. She turned on her phone and waited for it to come to life. The night had cooled, and she considered going back inside to make her call. Instead, she paced.

Since her first cell phone, she'd rarely had more than one message. The number thirty-seven had her staring in disbelief. She didn't even know thirty-seven people, which meant the handful of people she did know had been making repeated calls. She had thirty-seven texts and forty-two voicemails. Oh boy.

She didn't have time to listen to forty-two voicemails. Even if she did, who wants to hear 'Where the hell are you?' forty-two times?

Maddy scrolled through the texts. They were essentially the same as what she imagined the voicemails were. A long string of texts were from Owen, her jilted fiancé, wanting to know what was going on, where was she. The man deserved an explanation. The problem was, she didn't have one. At least not a clear one.

There were quite a few texts from her sister wanting to know where the hell she was, what the hell she was thinking, and when the hell she was coming back. There was one from her best friend, Joann, asking if she was okay. At least she didn't push for the marriage again.

One text was from her grandmother. Grandma Sophie told her to have a good time and to call if she needed a ride, a few bucks, or some condoms. Maddy couldn't help but chuckle. God, she loved that woman.

Grandma Sophie was a character and a half. She tended bar her whole adult life until three years ago when she turned seventy and finally retired. She was the best listener in the world. If no one else, Maddy should call her. Grandma Sophie was always on her side.

No, she should call the groom she'd abandoned. Owen deserved an explanation. But she'd have to take some time first and figure out what to say.

She should call her dad, who was either furious, worried sick, or some combination of the two. She should call her sister, who was definitely furious. Maybe she should call Joann. Her friend's words made a return visit to her head. Joann meant well, wanted her to be all right, but like everyone but Grandma, Joann wanted her to marry Owen.

Although no one outright said it, they believed she needed someone to take care of her. Like she was a child. Like she needed some sort of guardianship. Had it slipped their minds she was the one who took care of everybody else? Didn't all her efforts count for anything?

So what if she never lived outside her family home? Well, except for the very short and disastrous three days. She'd taken care of her dad and sister since she was twelve years old when her mom passed away. Earlier, really, since her mom had been sick for two years before.

She'd been an adult before she was a teenager. So what if she rarely dated or went out with friends? It's not like she had no desire to do something besides go to her job all day, then come home to do the cooking and cleaning, maybe go online after cleaning up the dinner mess and pay a couple of the household bills while a load tumbled in the dryer. She wasn't reclusive. She was tired.

None of them got it. To them, she was a timid homebody still living under her dad's roof. They acted like she couldn't survive a life between her father's house and a husband's. What was this, the eighteenth century?

Maddy tapped on her contacts, swiped out, then tapped back. This time, she chose a number.

****

Joel glanced back at the jukebox. The song had finished. Another one didn't begin. He considered putting some money in to play more music, maybe something calming. No. He needed a few minutes of quiet so he could think.

He sat back in the booth for a recap and some forethought. He chuckled at himself, how he'd thought Maddy might have been a serial killer. Watching a series of documentaries on serial killers and picking up a hitchhiker the same week was a bad combination. The hangover didn't help.

Sliding his phone from his back pocket, Joel checked his messages. He had a text from Roz wanting to know where he was and when he was coming back. Another problem on his already full plate. Did he have some kind of quality, making him attractive to crazy women?

The waiter walked over with two rolled paper napkins with silverware inside and told him their dinner wouldn't be much longer. Joel thanked him, then grinned a little at the young man's back before glancing out the window. Maddy had her phone against her ear, but her back was to him, and he couldn't see her face.

It was obvious Maddy didn't have a plan other than to run away from her wedding. What was he going to do with her? And why'd she run away in the first place? Was her fiancé cruel? Unfaithful? Maybe she realized she didn't love him. It wasn't his business or his problem. He had enough troubles of his own. Like his place in the family business, like keeping the desperation from his voice while convincing Mr. Hargrove to carry the dolls for another month. Like what the hell he was going to do if Mr. Hargrove said no.

He shifted his attention to Maddy. She had her phone to her ear and was pacing the sidewalk. Pink neon lit her face when she turned his way, but between the pink lighting and all the makeup, he couldn't make out her expression.

She might want to stay in Flagstaff, start over. Or he'd give her a ride back to Santa Monica if she wanted. Then, she was on her own.

Less than ten minutes after she'd gone out to make her call, Maddy was back inside. She and her tight expression marched straight to the ladies' room. A moment later, a short scream had him on his feet. He'd taken a single step when she popped her head out the door.

"It's all right," she said. "I just saw my face in the mirror. I'm not used to wearing so much makeup. It…caught me off guard."

With a soft chuckle, he slid back into the booth. The waiter set down their plates a few seconds before Maddy returned to the table. Joel almost dropped the ketchup bottle. His lungs forgot how to function, and his heart skipped around in search of its rhythm.

She'd scrubbed her face clean. Her fair skin was a little red from the washing, but…wow! She was gorgeous and without a speck of makeup on her face. To stare at her the way he did was rude, but it couldn't be helped. It would be like standing on the beach with your back to the sunset.

High cheekbones, a few pale freckles across her dainty nose, full lips made for kissing. The biggest draw were her eyes. Without the fake eyelashes and the caked-on makeup hiding them, they were stunning. Emerald green, huge, captivating, the kind of eyes a man could stare into for hours without losing interest.

She'd let down her wheat-colored hair and brushed it out, so it hung in loose waves a little past her shoulders, framing her stunning face. Joel could say in all honesty, she was the most beautiful woman he'd ever met.

"Come on," she said. "You've seen me at my worst."

Oh, she was talking. What did she say?

He shook off the shock at how great she looked without all the junk on her face. "Um, what?"

"Tell me about your bad day."

Joel cleared his throat. "You first."

Maddy tapped her fingers on the table a couple of times, then squirted a dab of ketchup on her plate next to her French fries. "All right. Fine. Well, I was supposed to get married today."

"You're kidding."

She grinned at his jest. Then it bloomed. A sunburst of a smile joined forces with those bewitching eyes. She could own him.

Her smile faded, and she huffed a sigh. "A few minutes before the wedding, I realized it was a mistake, a big mistake. Definitely a mistake." Maddy glanced out the window and chewed her bottom lip. "Probably a mistake. I mean, it could have been a mistake, or maybe not. There's a chance I might have thrown away my happily ever after and wrecked my life."

"Did you decide right out of the blue you didn't

want to get married?"

"I snuck over to the room where Owen was with his groomsmen, to tell him something. He stepped out into the hall, looking all handsome and so happy." She sighed again and hung her head. "God, I'm a horrible person."

Did she tell her fiancé she didn't love him? Had she screwed around with another man? Did she tell him she was in love with someone else?

Joel bent toward her and placed his forearms on either side of his plate. "What did you say to him?"

"I told him I wanted to pursue a career after we were married."

Joel leaned back and stared at her. "He got mad because you want to get a job?"

"I have a job. Well, I did until yesterday. Owen doesn't want me working outside the home. I thought it would be fine. It's what was…comfortable. I've worked my whole life in one way or another. My mom died when I was twelve. Cancer."

"I'm sorry."

"Thank you. She deserved better. After she passed away, my dad was a wreck. My sister is a couple years younger than me and couldn't do much more than cry. My Grandma Sophie is a strong woman, but losing her daughter took the wind out of her sails for a long time."

"It had to have been hard on you, too."

"Of course. I was devastated. No girl of twelve expects to lose their mother. But wallowing in grief doesn't get the laundry done, the house cleaned, or the meals cooked.

"You stepped up and took care of everyone."

"There wasn't anyone else. I was already most of the way there anyway since my mom had been sick for a while. By the time she was gone, I'd been taking care of the house and everyone in it. The pattern was set."

She swirled a French fry in the spot of ketchup but didn't eat it.

"My dad eventually went back to work. He had to. Mom's illness ate up what little savings they had. When I was fifteen, I got a job at a fabric store, The Yarn Barn, working on the weekends. After I graduated, I worked at the store full time and still took care of the house, my dad, and my little sister until she left for college."

"That's a lot for them to put on a kid."

Maddy shook her head. "You don't understand. I wanted to do those things. I was glad to keep busy. Kept the grief from overwhelming me. Taking care of the house and my family gave me purpose, you know, made me feel needed. It's just, well, I always thought someday I would travel a different road."

"Owen wanted you on the same road."

"He did. He saw the kind of woman I was, very…domestic. I was exactly what he wanted. It's not his fault. It's all mine. I kept my mouth shut until the last minute."

"How did he react when you told him you wanted to work outside the home?"

"At first, he thought I was having wedding day jitters. When he realized I was serious, he didn't like it. He didn't like it at all. He made it clear that was not how our marriage was going to work. He wanted the woman he thought I was. Then, when I was alone in the bride's room and looked in the mirror, it struck me hard how my future was a continuation of my past."

"So, you ran."

"I freaked out and left…ran…quiet and quick.

There's always the chance it may very well have been the right thing to do. Then again, maybe not. Owen's a good guy. He was up front with his feelings. He didn't deceive me. I'm the one who misled him, and for a career I don't even have. Maybe I threw away the best thing that ever happened to me. I can't decide. Besides, my dad has been waiting for the wedding to be done before he takes his retirement and goes on this big RV trip he and his friend had planned for forever. I screwed up a lot of lives today."

She dropped her French fry and squirted more ketchup onto her plate.

"What about a compromise, like you going back to work at the fabric store part-time instead of full-time?"

"I'm not talking about the Yarn Barn."

"Oh. Then what?"

She sighed, then shook her head. Her hair floated around her shoulders. "Never mind. I don't want to talk about it. I ran out on my own wedding today for something that's never going to be anything anyway. I had no plan, no thorough thought. I hitchhiked. I threw my wedding clothes out the window. Something's very wrong with me."

"I take it you're not normally a spur-of-the-moment kind of woman."

She huffed a chuckle. "No. I plan out the meals for the week, laundry days, grocery shopping days, bathroom cleaning days, etc."

Joel smiled. "You picked quite a day to turn over a new leaf."

Maddy laughed. Then she laughed again, harder this time. A wild belly laugh, edging toward hysteria. "Yes, I did. I certainly did. My grandmother must be swimming in joy."

"She doesn't like the guy?"

Maddy bit half her French fry, chewed, and swallowed. "She says Owen isn't any fun, which means a life without fun."

"Is Owen fun?"

"*I* think so."

There was a hint of defensiveness in her tone. Guilt, maybe. Reluctant to say anything bad about the guy she jilted.

"What matters is if you think he's fun," Joel said.

Maddy shifted to stare out the window. "Right. What I think."

She took a bite of her sandwich. Joel did the same. More questions wandered through his mind, but she'd given him so much already. More than he planned on giving her. At least she had some thoughts about her future. Everything for him depended on what happened when he met with Mr. Hargrove the next day; a career-saving yes or the no that would end it.

Joel changed the channel on his thoughts before his stomach tightened too hard to eat. He picked up a French fry and glanced across the table. Who did she call? What was said? The questions were nothing more than a distraction from his own problems. It's not like he cared.

They ate the rest of their meal in silence.

Chapter 6

"This is just too much," Rachel Hayden-Lupine said.

Joann glared at Maddy's little sister again. The woman was some piece of work.

Rachel paced the kitchen, waving her almost-empty glass of red wine. She still wore her sunny yellow bridesmaid dress and matching, low-heeled shoes. A few strands of dark hair had escaped her updo and swayed in the breeze her pacing created.

Joann, Maddy's best friend since high school, tapped her sheer-pink fingernails on the kitchen table where she sat wearing her identical bridesmaid dress. She did her best to ignore Rachel. The woman was impossible. Spoiled, bossy, and fuming because her day to glow as the bride's sister, to show off her beauty in a flattering dress, had been taken.

Joann glanced down at her yellow dress. The color was great on Rachel. It flattered her dark hair and trim waist. It wasn't bad on Joann, either, with her olive-toned skin and auburn hair. However, with Maddy's light coloring it was a poor match, washing her out, giving a yellow tint to her fair skin.

Maddy had always hated yellow. Yet, it was the color for her wedding.

Rachel had tried compensating for Maddy's fair coloring with extra makeup. All she'd done was make a mess of Maddy's pretty face. A different color for the bridesmaid dresses would have been better. But Owen's favorite color was yellow. He loved the way it looked against his tanning-bed skin. So, yellow was chosen.

"Unbelievable," Rachel said.

The slur to Rachel's words matched her unsteady hands as she refilled her stemmed wineglass. A splash of her pinot noir sloshed over the rim and onto the white-tile countertop in the Hayden family kitchen. Rachel ignored the mess like she always did. Everyone knew Maddy would come along and clean it.

Rachel rolled around and leaned back against the same counter where this morning, the morning of Maddy's wedding, Maddy had cooked breakfast for everyone. The aroma of pancakes still lingered.

Rachel downed a gulp of wine. "Two hundred people are consuming thousands of dollars worth of fine food and champagne, and we're sitting here in the house waiting for my selfish brat sister to realize she's too old to run away from home."

Joann slid a narrow-eyed glare toward Rachel and held it until the woman saw her.

"What?" Rachel said.

"You're calling Maddy selfish? Talk about too much."

Rachel stiffened and lifted her chin a notch. "What's that supposed to mean?"

Joann folded her arms and ignored her. She should have known better. Rachel would not be ignored.

Rachel waved her wine glass. "All the work everyone put in so this day would be perfect for Maddy, and she takes off without one bit of consideration for anyone but herself."

"It's her life, her marriage, her decision," Joann said. She hoped to relieve her guilt by throwing some anger at Rachel. It didn't help.

Self-loathing had been oozing through Joann ever since Rachel had walked into the waiting area and announced to the bridesmaids and to Maddy's father that Maddy was gone. Minutes before, Maddy had turned to her closest friend for support, and Joann had denied it.

It was for Maddy's own good.

Yeah, keep telling yourself that, Joann. She stabbed a hand in her purse, hanging from the back of the kitchen chair, and snatched out her pack of gum. She unwrapped a stick, shoved it into her mouth, and chewed hard while staring at the tattoo of a grinning full moon on her left forearm. It was a counter to the grinning sun tattooed on her right forearm. She hated both of them. She and her ex-husband had gotten the matching tattoos the day they got engaged. What made her think she knew what was best for someone else when she couldn't even get her own life right?

Poor Maddy wasn't looking for someone to calm her doubts. She was all but pleading for Joann to support what Maddy's instincts were telling her; she didn't want to marry Owen. Joann did everything she could to convince her otherwise. God, she was a rotten friend.

The weight of it squashed her, how she had treated her friend with the same lack of faith and respect Maddy's father and sister always had. Maddy wasn't having wedding day nerves. Her friend knew in her heart this marriage was a mistake, and she took a drastic step to escape. Now Maddy was out there somewhere, alone. The poor woman must feel like she had no one to turn to, not even her closest friend.

Rachel separated her forefinger from her wine glass to point it at Joann. “Now you listen here, missy.”

“No, you listen!” Joann jumped from her chair. “Maddy is who you should be concerned about, not how you’re missing out on the reception!”

Rachel raised her voice louder than Joann’s. “It’s not a reception without a groom *and* bride! *I* know that. But what else should I expect from a woman whose personal experience with a wedding reception consists of a few beers at whatever bar is closest to the Justice of the Peace!”

“That’s it, Rachel!” Joann lunged, clapped her hands on the sides of Rachel’s face, and squeezed. Rachel’s eyes opened wide with shock, and her lips were forced to purse as though she was about to give a big kiss. “Focus, Rachel,” Joann said. “Let’s focus here. I know how difficult it is for you to put your attention on someone other than yourself but try.”

Joann continued to pinch Rachel’s cheeks together so that when Rachel spoke, her lips looked like a fish at feeding time. “You’re overreacting.” Wine rolled in the glass she was still holding. Joann squeezed a little harder, and Rachel’s face took on a Claymation appearance.

Rachel whined through her fish lips. “All right, fine, I’ll focus on Maddy. Now let go of my face,”

“Enough!” Sam said. Rachel and Maddy’s father stiff-walked into the kitchen and crossed the room.

Maddy’s father still wore the dark blue suit and shiny hard shoes he’d dressed in to give away his daughter. His face was clean-shaven, and Joann could swear there were more grays in his neat-cut blond hair now than there had been this morning.

Sam was a scarecrow of a man. Farm-work strong,

though. He was only in his mid-fifties, but between working outdoors, the grief of losing his wife, and raising two daughters on his own, his face bore the deep lines of a longer life.

Sophie, Rachel and Maddy's grandmother, was right behind him. Sophie had forgone the animal prints and bold colors she normally wore and had dressed for the day in an appropriate pink dress. It was odd to see her fit-from-jazzercize body clothed in such an ordinary manner. At seventy-three years old, the woman still dyed her hair bright red, could hold her own in any argument, and could outdrink most people half her age.

Sam's face bunched with tension. His eyes reflected a tense mix of anger and misery. Joann drew back her hands but maintained serious eye contact with Rachel for a few more seconds.

Rachel massaged her perfect facial features back into place. "She started it."

"Give it a rest, Rachel," Sophie said.

"Oh, Grandma!"

Rachel crossed the kitchen on unsteady legs and plopped down in the chair Joann had vacated. Her head swiveled, and with an obvious longing, she gazed at the bottle of wine she'd left on the kitchen counter. She rolled a peek at Joann, then whipped away when their eyes met. Rachel gently patted her face before draining the little bit of wine left in her glass.

Joann crossed her arms around her middle and squeezed. Maybe she could ring out some of the guilt knocking around her insides. She'd been a terrible friend to Maddy, unsupportive, unreceptive, without faith in the most decent person she had ever known.

"Where could Maddy be?" Joann said. "Where

would she go?"

Rachel tipped back her glass and then glared at its emptiness. Again, she eyed the wine bottle on the counter next to Joann.

"I don't know," Rachel said. "But she has a lot of explaining to do."

"I'm sure she's fine," Maddy's grandmother said.

Sophie's tone was calm, but she had to be worried, too. Maddy didn't do things like this. Maddy was stable and sedate. She held everything, and everyone, together by way of her consistency. Whatever craziness was going on in the world, you could count on Maddy to be there with some kind words, a needle and thread, a pot of homemade soup, or whatever was needed. Maddy was a young woman with an old, nurturing soul.

Joann snatched a napkin from the bamboo holder on the table, spit her gum into it, and tossed it in the trash. "I just wish she'd call and let us know she's all right."

With a casual motion, Sophie smoothed out her dress. "Maddy needs some time to think."

"Think about what?" Sam said. He was leaning against the back door, arms crossed, face hard. His words were like a German shepherd's bark. It gained him the full attention of the three women in the room.

"Owen proposed," Sam said. "Maddy agreed to marry him. Her life was all set. What more does she need to think about? What's wrong with her?"

Sam scowled, shoved away from the door, and slammed his fist on the table, making everybody jump. From his point of view, Maddy had thrown away a golden opportunity. Maybe he was right. Joann cringed inside. Maybe not. Maybe they were all equal in their guilt of underestimating Maddy, of thinking they all knew what was best for her.

Like Sophie and Rachel, Joann stared at Maddy's father. The man was a bit of a curmudgeon, but he really didn't have much of a temper. Not most days, anyway.

Joann had been there when Sam told Owen Maddy was gone. It about killed him to say what his daughter had done. Then, after a period of waiting and hoping she'd return, Owen had to announce to a room full of people there would be no wedding.

"I can't believe she did this," Sam said. "The girl never gave me a minute of trouble her whole life until now. She's always been agreeable, meek. Hell, Maddy wouldn't say boo to a bug. Now all of a sudden, she decided to turn into her grandmother and stir up the world."

Sophie slid a glance his way and raised her chin. Not angry, though. Proud. Joann suppressed a grin.

Sophie was a live wire. You never knew what she was going to do next. Sometimes she volunteered at the local animal rescue. Sometimes she had a couple of drinks and called radio shows to give her opinions on topics they may or may not have been discussing.

Less than a year ago, Maddy had bailed her grandmother out of jail after she'd gotten into a heated argument with a guy over a parking spot at the mall. The guy's first mistake was thinking he could intimidate Sophie with his size—more than double her hundred and ten pounds—and his loud, angry voice. He'd leaned over her, yelling and waving his arms.

Sophie had hit the guy with her big, heavy purse, scratching his jaw with the clasp. The twenty-something man called the police, filed a report, and had Sophie charged. That was his second mistake.

The poor guy didn't know what he was up against.

Sophie showed up in court looking like a frail old woman in a flower-print dress and thick-souled shoes. She'd used a walker she still had from hip surgery a few years ago, wore a gray wig over her red hair, and smiled kindly as she handed out hard butterscotch candies to everyone in the courtroom.

During her testimony, Sophie dabbed at her eyes with a lace handkerchief when she spoke about being afraid of this angry young man who'd bent his bulk her way. After all, she was in her seventies. The judge so embarrassed the guy he ended up apologizing to Maddy's grandmother. Sophie, Maddy, and Joann had gone out for drinks after court, and Sophie toasted the advantages of age several times.

Rachel raised a brow and gave the room a hard nod. "I'll tell you what's wrong with Maddy. She's lived under this roof her whole life with Dad taking care of her and now she doesn't know how to be a grown-up."

"Oh, I have *so* had it with you!" Joann said. She jetted toward Rachel. Panic filled Rachel's eyes an instant before she slapped both hands on her own cheeks in a protective motion.

Sophie snatched Joann's arm. "Come on, Jo," Sophie said. Then she lowered her voice and leaned close to Joann's ear. "Let's take a walk before somebody gets hurt and her lawyer husband sues you."

Joann laughed. She couldn't help it. Sophie was a handful, but she had good people instincts, even with family. Rachel was Sophie's blood, her own granddaughter, and they did love each other. But unless you were one of Rachel's special friends, she could be a hard person to like.

****

Rachel glared at the backs of her grandmother and Joann as they left the kitchen through the back door and outside. Joann was a troll with a total lack of class. Violence! No wonder Sophie liked her. Rachel loved her grandmother, but she didn't much care for her. The woman was absurd, the way she dressed, the way she was always causing trouble somewhere. It wouldn't surprise her if she'd helped Maddy run away.

Rachel glanced at her father. Well, at least she was still Daddy's little girl. She was the good one. The one who'd been popular at school, who married well and had two babies, who knew to show up for her own wedding. She picked up her wine glass. It was empty and sad.

Oh, Joann was gone. The wicked woman. Rachel made a direct line for the wine bottle on the counter and filled her glass. The fading sounds of her grandmother and Joann's laughter made it through the door as they walked around the house, heading for the front.

They weren't out the door more than a minute or two when the landline on the kitchen counter rang. Rachel downed a swallow and answered the phone.

Chapter 7

Maddy ate her sandwich while the phone call she'd made played back in her head…

Her chest had tightened when the phone rang on the other end, the landline her father insisted they keep.

What could she possibly say to excuse or explain her terrible behavior? Cold feet? PMS? Temporary insanity? That's it. Her pre-wedding jitters swelled beyond her control, and she'd flipped out of her head. Most of her family already thought she was weak-willed anyway. They might believe nerves caused her to act without thought.

Not a person who knew her would have guessed her to be the type to run out on her wedding if she was in her right mind. She was solid. She was reliable and predictable, lacking any trace of spontaneity. She was dull as dirt. She was the kind of person most people didn't even notice. God, she was elevator music.

Another ring. Her mind drifted to a particular part of the conversation she'd had with Joann, her best friend since high school, a few minutes before she'd bolted.

Joann had been right about at least one thing. Owen would take care of her. Well, he would have. Everyone thought that was something she needed as if she wasn't a grown woman and had to have someone to guide her through life.

Hmm. Running away, getting in a stranger's truck,

and her wedding dress blowing in the wind many miles back, maybe they were right.

Would Owen take her back? Did she want him to? How could he still want her after what she did? He deserved better. He could certainly do better. The man was good-looking, had a good job, a fine home, and a solid future. Of all his many choices, she was the one he wanted. And she'd humiliated him.

She could beg for his forgiveness. With a boatload of luck, she could go home, get married, and live happily ever after; whatever that means. What it would mean for sure is her dad could live happily ever after. Maddy took a deep breath, tapped on her home number, and then disconnected before it rang. She tapped her contacts again, but this time she tapped Owens's number.

Poor Owen. Was he staring at his phone, waiting for her to call, tears brimming his eyes? She tried imagining Owen in tears. Where was he right now? After being jilted by the woman he loved, he would be too depressed, humiliated, and worried sick to be anywhere but home, likely sitting in the dark with a bottle of brandy. She really was a horrible person.

After six rings, Owen's voicemail picked up, and she disconnected. Was he not near his phone, or did he not want to talk to her? Maddy wouldn't blame him for ignoring her call.

He'd had the ringer off for the wedding. Maybe he forgot to turn it on again. Maybe Owen was at her house, talking to her family, trying to figure out where she might have gone. She tapped on her home number. The phone was picked up on the second ring. Her sister answered, and the harsh tone of her hello made Maddy's heart pound even harder.

"Hi, Rachel," Maddy said.

"Where the hell are you!"

"I'm all right. I got a ride with a truck driver. Is Owen there?"

"No. Last I heard he was at the reception. I don't know where he is now."

"He went to the reception?"

"He figured it was better to face them all at one gathering than go through a hundred individual pity parties. Can you imagine what it was like for him, Maddy?"

She hadn't thought about it before just now. Everyone there would want to offer condolences like she died or something. For Owen, it would be worse than her dying. He had to explain to everyone why his bride changed her mind at the very last minute. And she'd left him there to deal with the mess all by himself.

"No, I can't imagine." She was a horrible, horrible person.

"What truck driver?" Rachel didn't wait for an answer. "What do you think you're doing, Maddy? Were you drinking with Grandma, or did you just lose your mind?"

"Well, you see, what happened was…" Think, think, what was the story? Terrific, now she couldn't even remember her excuse. Maybe she really had lost her mind. Oh, right. That was the cause she'd decided to use. For a reason she couldn't grasp right now, she didn't want insanity to be her defense. "Is Grandma there?"

"No, she's out with Joann. Knowing them, they're at the closest bar and won't be back for hours." Then Rachel's voice took on a snideness, setting Maddy's teeth on edge. "But Dad's here."

"No, no, no, no. Don't put Dad on. I don't want…"

"Madeline!" Her father yelled into the phone so loud she thought Joel might have heard from inside the restaurant.

"Hi, Dad."

"Don't you hi Dad me after what you did today. Are you all right?" Like Rachel, he continued without giving her a chance to answer. "No, of course you're not all right. Do you have any idea what you've done? You've shamed yourself. You've shamed this family, and you've shamed a good man, a man who wanted to marry you."

Maddy cringed at his string of accusations. Especially since they were true. Though she'd already berated herself with the same, to hear them from her father cut a fresh slice into her.

"Where are you, Maddy?" he said.

Concern softened his tone. As much as he was worked up right now, he really did love and care about her. She'd taken care of him all these years. She did his laundry, kept the house, fixed all his meals. She promised she'd still come over a few times a week after she was married to tend to the house for him and leave some meals in the freezer. She and Owen would have him over for dinner at least a couple times a week when he was between RV adventures.

It had all been worked out until she…

"Maddy, I said, where are you?"

"…Not too far. Dad, please just listen—"

"Owen's the one you should be pleading with," Sam said. His anger caught a second wind, and he wasted no time making use of it.

"I plan to talk with—"

"I'll tell you what you better plan. You'd better plan

on getting yourself home right away. Believe it or not, I think that blessed man still wants to marry you. So, you get back here and make things right with him. Men like Owen don't come around every day. Especially…"

Especially for a wallflower who still lives at home with her father.

Her dad didn't say it, but they both knew. Maddy hadn't had more than a small handful of dates her whole life, and none of them had ever blossomed into anything. Maybe if she'd had time to get fixed up and go to parties and clubs the way Rachel had, time to get out and meet people. She met very few men at the Yarn Barn. Fewer still at home.

And why does everyone think she needs to get married? The question kept at her, like a buzzing fly.

These weren't olden times. Just because thirty was only a couple of years away didn't mean it was too late in life for her to start hacking her own path through the world. It's not like she had a *sell by* date stamped on her forehead. Women managed just fine on their own and at all ages.

Joann did. Her friend had survived a few rough patches, one divorce. It didn't stop her from living a good life. Grandma Sophie, too, and she was one of the happiest, most independent people Maddy had ever known. Sophie didn't just enjoy life. She squeezed every drop out of it, and she savored it. Maddy could be independent. She could savor life.

Sometimes her family made it sound like she walked around the house in a domestic haze like she didn't want anything in life other than to be what she'd always been.

Did she give them reason to think about her in such a way?

"Do you hear me, Madeline!"

"…I hear you, Dad."

"Do…do you need me to come and get you?"

His voice softened once more, care dulling the edge. He became Daddy again, the man he'd been before Mom passed away. Being crusty on the outside was her father's way of dealing with his emotions. Maddy understood. It's why she didn't get upset when he snapped at her for reminding him to take his pills, or when he barked at her for more coffee. Dad was getting through life the best he could.

But she was, too.

Taking care of everyone filled the time she used to spend with her mother, time grief would fill to consumption if she hadn't kept busy. She'd never meant it to be a way of life for the rest of her life.

"No, Dad. I don't need you to come and get me. I've got a ride."

"Then, we'll see you soon," he said. His voice was less than grouchy, but he hung up the phone without saying goodbye.

Maddy wished her grandmother had been there. Though, she could guess Sophie's advice would be to keep going, have a good time, and call us when you get there. It's what Sophie would say because it's what Sophie would do. But that wasn't Maddy. Of course, today she had acted the anti-Maddy.

So, which one was she— the good girl who followed all the rules and did what was expected of her, or the rebel who ran away and stuck her thumb out on the highway? Neither skin fit well. Option one was more comfortable, but option two was new, and made her life interesting for once.

A worrisome thorn dug deeper.

Had all the years of being a good girl, of blending into the background so everyone else had what they needed, created a poor impression of herself? Had it created *her*?

Maybe Joann was right. Though her best friend had never come out and said so directly, would never want to hurt her, Maddy must come across as a bland blob of putty, a malleable mass fit for nothing better than picking up what was pressed into her. Damn it, no!

Maddy rubbed her temples.

Images of other women ran through her head, Joann, Rachel, and Grandma Sophie. Sophie. Now there was a woman who knew how to take charge of her life. Oh, to be like her. What would it feel like to have that kind of assertion, to tell off a rude customer or some guy at the grocery store who made a crude remark instead of shying away? To go after her own future?

Maybe after all the years of making sure everybody else's needs were met, she missed the boat on developing her own needs. Was it too late?

No!

Be honest.

Yes. It was probably too late. She was set and not in the mold of her dreams. What's more, she lacked the wherewithal to get somewhere else. She was weak tea. She was a neutral color. She was plain oatmeal in a sugared cereal world.

As much as Maddy yearned to burst out of what she was and be somebody else, it wasn't going to happen. Today she had lost her mind for a while. Maybe that happened to people like her every so many years. Like a cicada, her backbone made an appearance and annoyed everyone, then disappeared again.

Tipping her head back, Maddy stared at the stars and fantasized about riding one like a motorcycle, twisting the throttle, circling the earth, sprinkling stardust, and granting wishes, her own as a finale.

She breathed in the fresh air, huffed it out where it belonged, and blinked herself back into reality. The night's breeze was mild but with enough chill to make her shiver. Still, Maddy stayed outside another minute or so before trudging to the door. Once inside the restaurant, she headed straight to the ladies' room. The ghoul in the mirror scared a scream out of her.

Oh. It was her.

After telling Joel everything was okay, she peeled off those ridiculous false eyelashes. What a relief! She hadn't realized how heavy they were, how they weighed down her eyelids. She scrubbed her face with the harsh soap from the dispenser, twice. Then she dug in her purse and found a small bottle of lotion to soothe her skin.

Joel was squeezing ketchup onto his plate next to his French fries when she slid into the booth. He paused and looked at her with an odd expression like he was surprised to see her looking so plain. Or maybe he was appalled by her plainness? Ah, yes, inside and out.

They talked for a while. Well, she did most of the talking. He asked questions and listened.

Joel set his napkin beside his plate and leaned back. "If you need to get home, I can turn around and take you back before I go to Flagstaff."

"No, no. You have a schedule to keep."

"It's not a problem."

****

It *was* kind of a problem. He did have a schedule to

keep. Whatever slack the trip allotted, he'd used up taking Route 66 instead of the main highway.

He already had enough screwups for one lifetime, and Maddy was a burden he couldn't take on right now. Between teetering on the verge of losing his position in the family business, not to mention the growing problem with Roz, he had enough troubles of his own. The last thing he needed was someone else's troubles mingling with his. They might breed.

He stared at her from across the booth, at how she'd sunk into the vinyl, looking so alone and…vulnerable. There was something else, though, some foggy reason he was reluctant to take her back home right away, even though he knew he should.

She seemed so lost, even worse than him. Then it hit him, the reason. Having Maddy around was making him feel capable. It had been a long time since he'd felt that way.

She'd been in a dangerous situation out on the road. There were all kinds of crazies out there. What if he hadn't come along? Joel puffed up his chest, all manly for getting her off the road. Yes, he was manly—forgetting, of course, how he almost leaped from his own moving truck when he thought she was taking a weapon from her bag. *Shh.*

"You're not driving all the way back there just for me," Maddy said. "Absolutely not. I won't hear of it."

She had family at home, people who were worried about her. No matter how masculine she made him feel, keeping her with him to boost his own sorry ego was pathetic. "Well, maybe a bus comes through here," he said. "I think they have tours."

Maddy sank deeper into the booth. She chewed her

lower lip in a sad, adorable way, while staring at her empty plate. The dejection on her face, the hint of panic in her eyes, hauled Joel into her truth. He was in command of a vehicle driving away from her circumstance. Whatever conversation she'd had on the phone didn't inspire her to get home anytime soon.

"Actually," he said. "If you're not in too much of a hurry, I'd appreciate the company."

The smile of her obvious relief had Joel puffing up his chest again. Yes. He was manly. So manly.

****

Owen shifted his eyes from the road to the cell phone in his hand again. When he looked up, he had to slam on the brakes because some damn minivan with one of those idiotic *Kids on Board* signs tacked up inside the back window had come out of nowhere, pulled right in front of him, and not gotten up to speed in a timely manner.

"Asshole!"

He wiggled in his uncomfortable tuxedo and glanced back at the phone for the millionth time.

When he first snuck the tracker app on Maddy's phone, he'd done it for good reason. His plan was to surprise her when she was out somewhere, solidifying proof they were meant to be together. Plus, he could make sure she was always where she said. But Maddy rarely went anywhere besides work, home, and the grocery store. Good. Just the kind of woman he wanted for a wife.

He'd meant to delete the app before she found it tucked away in one of her folders, but he forgot all about it. Thank goodness.

The downside of having an airhead for a wife, okay,

still a fiancée, was that she was, well, an airhead. Nothing wrong with that, mostly. In her case, it was an asset. He'd be in charge, and she wouldn't question his decisions. She'd cook his meals and clean the house. Maddy was everything he wanted, pretty, sweet, docile, domestic. She was perfect.

When Maddy had slipped over to the groom's dressing room twenty minutes before the wedding to tell him she wanted to pursue a career, he figured it was just the pressure of the day. She wasn't used to being out of her tidy little comfort zone. He should have hired someone to keep an eye on her. But how could he have guessed she'd go so wacko on him and actually run away?

She couldn't handle pressure. He could. He'd handle this like he handled everything. With competence and intellect.

Traffic slowed. Owen got right on the tail of the blue minivan and glared into their rearview mirror. The minivan made a right at the next corner. He kept going straight.

Within minutes of being told Maddy had run off, leaving nothing but an *I can't* scrawled on the mirror in lipstick, Owen got her family out of there. The last thing he needed was their interference. He didn't tell them about the tracker, lest he look like a creep. Instead, he told his future in-laws Maddy might call the landline they still had at the house—what kind of people still had a landline?—and they should go wait there in case she called.

He didn't know if it was his insistence or his conveyance of worry, but they left without question.

Next, he announced to the crowd who'd come to see

them get married there'd been an illness in the family. He didn't say which family, figuring each side would think it was the other. Then he told them the wedding would be rescheduled and they should all go down the hall to the reception room and enjoy the feast so it wouldn't go to waste. A feast he'd paid a fortune for, by the way.

Owen ground his teeth together.

He inched his way toward the door, but people kept stopping him to ask questions he hadn't the time or inclination to answer. It added another layer of bullshit he didn't need today. It took all his effort to maintain a smile and a calm façade when he needed to plan his next step.

His pasted-on smile was hurting his face by the time he got the hell out of there, more than an hour after he'd made his announcement.

For a while he drove the area, looking for a woman walking around in a wedding dress. Nothing. She must have called a ride share. Driving to her house, the only place he could think of she'd go, Owen had called Maddy's cell, again. He'd already left three messages saying he was worried, please call him. Her family and friends must have been doing the same thing because the fourth call he made to her got him an automated voice telling him her damned voicemail was full.

Owen poked the button on his steering wheel and disconnected the hands-free call.

That's when he remembered the tracker app he'd never gotten around to deleting from her phone. He slipped his phone from an inside pocket and scrolled until he found the app. He was punching in his different passwords without success when the blue minivan had almost caused him to have an accident.

Damn minivan. Damn passwords. Damn this whole damn day!

Owen pulled into the lot of a grocery store, parked crossways in a broad patch of empty parking spots, and tapped the app for his password safe. Half a minute later, he had the right password. As soon as he got into the tracker app and tapped the right buttons, he realized the app wouldn't work if her phone was turned off, which apparently it was. After turning on the notifications, he threw his phone onto the passenger seat.

Alone in his car where no one could see or hear him, Owen pounded the steering wheel with both fists and cursed a blue streak.

How dare she? He'd offered her a dream come true. She wouldn't have to work at the Yarn Barn anymore. All Maddy had to do for the rest of her life was take care of him and their home. What woman wouldn't jump at such a chance?

It was the pressure of the day. It had to be. He just had to find Maddy, calm her down, and take those vows. He had to.

The last thing he wanted to do was get out in the dating world again. He was sick of it. Nothing but greedy, self-centered bitches out there. He got so lucky with Maddy. She'd been sheltered her whole life and had very little experience with the outside world. Not even with her job. A fabric store. Who knew those things still existed? He was getting her out of a nothing job and upgrading her home. She should be jumping for joy to marry him.

Maddy would have a good life with him. He cared about her. Even kind of loved her. She was pretty and sweet. She kept a clean house and was a great cook. A little tame in bed, but he could work on improving her, given the time.

Focus, Owen. Okay. Make a plan. What to do, what to do? The question no sooner stalled in his head when his phone dinged. He snatched it from the passenger seat and held the screen in front of his face.

Maddy had turned on her phone.

Chapter 8

"There's something I should tell you," Joel said.

Ten minutes had passed since they'd rolled out of the diner's parking lot. He'd opened his mouth to tell her at least that many times before he managed the words.

"What?"

Joel shifted in his seat. She'd been so open with him. To hold back seemed low, sleazy even. Besides, maybe once he said things out loud, they wouldn't seem so bad.

"I'm not really a driver for this company," Joel said. If only he was one of the drivers. He could be proud about being a driver.

Her head shifted halfway toward him. Her eyes, however, wide and wary, rolled until they pinned him.

He paused and took a breath before continuing. "You see, my last name is Tyler."

"Tyler?" She blinked, swiveled her head, and faced him with her brows drawn together. "As in Tyler Toys? It's your company?"

"No. My grandfather started it. Now the business belongs to my parents. I work for them. At least for now."

He glanced at her. The worry was gone, replaced by curiosity.

"Are you quitting?"

Quitting the family business. It would be like quitting his soul.

"…I don't know."

His mother was tough, but his leaving would hurt her. Dad was an old softie. His father might get teary-eyed. The thought tightened Joel's chest. Mariel, his sister, was equal parts both their parents plus her own special love for him. She'd be hurt most of all. A big part of him would die, too, if he were no longer part of Tyler Toys.

He gathered his resolve. He wouldn't have to think about leaving if he could get Mr. Hargrove to carry the dolls a little longer. With some more time on the shelf, they'd sell. He felt it in his gut. They *had* to sell.

Maddy shifted her body in his direction. She accompanied her question with hand gestures, palms up, hands bouncing. "Where do you find your courage?"

Joel was too taken aback to answer. He wasn't courageous. He was tired of failing. Quitting wasn't courageous. It was chickenshit. He couldn't keep falling on his face in front of his own family, in front of the entire company. It was no secret that his creations kept falling flat. The thought of swimming through a pool of pity yet again had him ready to dive into a bottle.

Maddy sat back and stared forward, out into the night. "I could never just throw away my past and start all over."

Joel couldn't help the burst of laughter. "I picked you up on the side of the road, hitchhiking in your wedding dress."

Maddy blew out a chuckle on a puff of air. "Oh, right."

Joel's laughter faded, but his smile lingered for a while. They were quite a pair, the two of them. Not funny, really, but if misery loves company, they were well suited for this trip.

Joel stared at the road ahead.

In the darkness lit only by the truck's headlights, low shrubs whooshed by, their outlines indefinable as they blended together. Someday they'd separate from their root and tumble down the road, rolling on the wind like a puppy off-leash, unless and until a fence or a building stopped the fun.

Joel shook his head. He must be losing it, pondering the fate of tumbleweeds.

"I'm going back to marry Owen," Maddy said. No inflection. No sadness, no joy. "If he'll still have me."

"You're going in the wrong direction."

The corners of her lips lifted with one of those soft chuckles she did when she found something he said funny. Making a strange girl laugh shouldn't give him a feeling of accomplishment, but it did. Then her words sank in.

"So you want to get married after all." His tone also lacked variation. It was hard to work up a happy vibe for her when her doubts about marrying this guy had been so big she'd run away from the wedding.

She ruffled her hair with her fingers. "I'm going back *in a little while*. For the time being, I'm keeping you company." She smiled again, sad and happy at the same time. "I'm having an adventure."

He glanced over as Maddy stared at the dark road ahead. Her smile wilted, but it didn't go away. She was like one of those tumbleweeds, rolling down the road at her leisure. *Until she hit a fence or a building, or a husband.*

Fifteen minutes passed before Joel had to downshift and stop the truck. He glanced at Maddy to take in her reaction and smiled at her bafflement, at the way she leaned forward and stared out the window.

"Is…is that a burro?"

"Yes, it is," Joel said. "We're passing through Oatman. They're all around here."

He grinned at Maddy, who stared at the burro like it was an alien. The animal stood in the headlights without a care or a worry.

"He's so cute! Are they friendly?"

"They're used to people around here. Do you want to pet him?"

She swung toward him, eyes wide, lips slightly parted in excitement. "Can I?"

"Come on," he said.

He was already petting the burro's head by the time Maddy finished her slow approach. She used her fingertips to stroke the burro's long ears, then felt her way to his mane. "What a sweet animal."

"Lots of them wander around here during the day. Usually, they head for the hills at night. This guy must be running late. When the stores are open, you can buy burro food."

"You've been here before?"

"Made a couple of road trips here."

She continued to pet the burro but glanced around. There weren't a lot of lights, but there were enough to make out the scenery.

"It's like an old west town," she said.

"It is. Look, those are wooden sidewalks. See that hotel over there? It's the one with the big board of a sign hanging like a shingle. I heard Clark Gable and Carol Lombard spent their honeymoon there. I don't know if it's true."

The burro made a half circle and walked off into the night.

"I guess he's ready to call it a day," Joel said.

Maddy smiled at him. "Thanks for stopping. I never pet a burro before. Never saw one. It was a treat."

"You're welcome. We'd better get going."

When Oatman was about twenty minutes in the rearview, Maddy leaned her head back against the headrest and closed her eyes.

The old truck rolled through the darkness. Joel kept the volume of the radio down so it wouldn't disturb Maddy. He glanced over at her again. She was the first person he had ever met who was more displaced than he was. Or maybe not. Maybe she really does love the guy, and she'd had a momentary lapse in judgment. He could relate. The Cabernet Sunrise he and Boone had invented last night still crusted him.

At least Maddy had some possibilities. He was on the verge of ousting himself from a successful business (though no thanks to him) and falling into a whole lot of nothing. A year from now he could be living amongst the tumbleweeds. He had no prospects. No career alternatives. The only work experience he had was with his family's toy company.

Maddy thought he was courageous. Could she believe such a thing? No, probably not, but it was good-hearted of her to say so. And it was a nice thought to hold. The nicest he'd had since…since Maddy told him she liked his idea for the doll, even though she didn't know it was his idea. Hmm.

Joel slid a glance at her for the third time in as many minutes. She may be a bit of a nut, but she was a beautiful nut with a flair for saying what he needed to hear.

Joel forced his attention back to the road.

His sister, Mariel, was always good for a kind word and a pat on the back, bless her big heart. But it was impossible for her to hide the pity. He didn't know which was worse, his sister's sympathy or his parents' disappointment.

Joel glanced over at Maddy again.

Waves of wheat-field blonde hair lay around her clean face. Her lips parted a tiny bit in her relaxation. She'd drifted off to sleep.

Joel covered a yawn. He'd had a late start today. The plan was to stay at a motel near the toy store and drive back the next day. In accordance with his plan, he should get some more miles in before calling it a day. But the abuse he'd done to his body last night was dragging him down, fast. A bed and a pillow sounded like heaven. He'd stop at the next motel.

Joel's eyelids drooped. He shook his head and opened his eyes wide. He had no idea how much sleep he had gotten, but it wasn't enough. A good blast of night air might help keep him awake.

He grabbed the crank to roll down the window. With a click and a sudden loosening, the handle broke off in his hand. Tired and punchy, all he could do was chuckle and shake his head. He wiggled the handle back in the hole. He managed to catch the mechanism and get the window rolled down.

The temperature had dropped with the sun. At least something was going his way. Cool air chilled his lungs and rushed across his face, through his hair. In just a few seconds, he was awake and alert, ready to be responsible. Such an adult.

The cold breeze roused Maddy too. She stirred,

shivered, and then opened her eyes. Sitting up, she rubbed her arms with her hands. "Did I sleep through till winter?"

"Sorry," Joel said. He took hold of the window crank . "The cool air was helping me stay awake."

"Oh, well, then leave it down."

"We'll compromise halfway." He turned the crank twice, rolling the window up about a third of the way before it busted off in his hand again. This time, some piece inside the door broke off and tumbled down. He tried reinserting the handle again, but it was no use. The piece it was supposed to latch on to was gone.

Joel burst out laughing. He didn't know why. The cab of the truck was cold, and it was only going to get worse. Maddy laughed too. Maybe they were both punch-silly from a long, crappy day and not enough sleep. Following Maddy's earlier example, he tossed the handle out the window. Laughter exploded in the cab of the truck.

Joel dug his arm behind the seat and tugged out a hoodie. "Here," he said, handing her the hoodie.

"What about you, you'll freeze?"

"That's the reason I rolled down the window in the first place, so the cool air would keep me awake."

Maddy maneuvered into the hoodie without taking off her seatbelt. "I can drive for a while."

"Do you know how to drive a stick?"

Maddy glanced down at the gearshift. "Oh, right. No, I never learned how. Is it hard?"

"No. It just takes a little practice. You could learn it in no time."

"You think so?"

"Sure. Here, I'll teach you." Joel downshifted and

steered the truck onto the shoulder.

"Now?"

"Why not? Then I can catch some Zs while you drive."

****

As Maddy slid behind the wheel, doubts slid into her. Memories of her father teaching her to drive flashed bright and harsh in her mind. He hadn't the patience for such things. Grandma would have taught her, but the bar where Sophie worked was short-handed, so she was working a lot of overtime, and as Maddy's birthday approached, she was too excited to wait.

She'd never forget her dad, sitting in the passenger seat, tapping his hands on his thighs, back stiff, blurting out orders at the least infraction. The lesson lasted six blocks before her dad mopped his brow with his forearm, ordered they change places, and said she wasn't ready to learn how to drive.

In all fairness, she *had* almost taken out a mailbox. Stupid dolphin mailbox. Who wouldn't be freaked out by one of them staring at you as you drove by? Damn thing looked like it could jump in the window, dopey smile turning into an evil sneer full of fangs as it made the leap.

She really shouldn't watch horror movies.

A couple weeks later, Grandma Sophie taught her to drive. But by then, Maddy had developed a driving phobia, like the car would be infused with an evil spirit and race wherever it wanted as soon as she started it. *Wasn't that in a movie?* It took quite a few deep breaths for her to get behind the wheel again, but she did. Sophie was patient, laid back, and taught her well. Maddy got her license on her first try.

Her nervousness clung, however, and to this day, Maddy had to calm herself every time she drove somewhere. Lucky for her, the few places she had to go were close to home. Her job, the grocery store, Grandma Sophie's, and Joann's, were all within seven miles of her home. Her sister, Rachel, lived farther. But she drove there, too, as it was familiar.

If she was feeling adventurous, Maddy would drive all the way to the Sand Dollar Mall, fifteen miles away.

She almost never drove on a road she didn't know. Same for driving at night, though not because her nervousness got worse at sunset. By evening she was in the kitchen cooking dinner and then cleaning up the mess. From there her exciting life left her time for a little TV, then she climbed into bed to read a few pages before turning off the light at exactly ten o'clock. Yeah, she was a wild woman.

When Maddy settled into the driver's seat of the truck she sunk so low she had to stretch her spine in order to see over the steering wheel. She had an image of a beer-bellied man holding a cigarette in his mouth with a long, drooping ash and a cowboy hat on his head, spending many, many hours crushing the seat springs into uselessness. The image didn't describe Joel.

The interior light brightened the cab when he opened the door. Maddy glanced over at him as he climbed into the truck on the passenger side. This guy was out of her league attractive.

She liked the way his dark hair was careless but not sloppy. There was a fine line there and he managed to stay on the right side. And what a smile! Whenever he turned it on her, it was like sinking into a warm tub, all cozy and comforting. It made his already handsome face even more so, with his pale blue eyes and a dimple showing through a trace of dark growth. Peering at him, she figured he must work out. Joel had muscle-toned arms and no fat on him she could see.

The visual was great, but it was Joel's manner she found most attractive. The way he thought of her without overwhelming her. Like giving her his hoodie when she was cold, without scolding her for not thinking to pack one of her own.

Maddy liked how he was ready to come to her rescue when she screamed in the ladies' room. Of course, she was able to rescue herself from a situation, as she'd proven today. *Okay, so running away from her wedding might have been a huge mistake, but whatever.* The point is it was nice to have backup.

She had to be crazy, letting Joel teach her to drive a stick shift. Right now, he only thought she was peculiar, not inept. He would see her in a different way once he tried teaching her to drive a stick. Okay, okay, she could do this, probably. At least she hadn't seen any dolphin mailboxes, so far.

The steering wheel was bigger than the one in her car. Along with a windshield the size of her living room window, it cursed her with a sense of puniness.

Get over it.

Okay. She buckled herself in and took a breath.

She looked to Joel for instruction, and he grinned down at her. There was that warm tub again.

"How does it feel so far?" he asked. He closed the passenger door and the interior light dimmed to gone, leaving them with just the light from the dashboard.

When Joel was in the sunken driver's seat, he was only a little taller than her. Now Maddy had to tilt her head back to make eye contact. She must look like a toy person beside him. Glancing at the stick shift, at the extra pedal on the floor, all of it out of her reach, she sank even farther.

Joel leaned over, and his hand disappeared under the bench seat beneath her legs, brushing the backs of her calves. The warm cab got warmer.

Maddy caught a whiff of his soap, something spicy and masculine. She stole another sniff before he nudged the seat forward and backed away.

"Better?" he asked.

She caught her breath and assessed the situation. This was more than she could handle. What was she thinking, learning to drive a manual? She didn't do new things. She didn't expand her horizons. She liked to keep her horizons short and simple. *So why are you here? Why aren't you married to Owen right now?*

"Yes, this feels fine, thank you." Maddy smiled up at him to help the lie.

Okay, you can do this. Countless people have learned to drive a stick shift without any catastrophic occurrences. Besides, she had an advantage because she'd seen it done. Her friend Joann had a stick for a couple of years. Maddy had a general idea of how it worked. So, what could happen? A missed gear here or there, a bumpy ride. A horrible crash. Death and/or dismemberment?

"Okay," he said. Joel spoke in a casual tone like he wasn't putting his life in her hands. "Put your right foot on the brake and your left foot on the clutch. Good. Now, release the parking brake, the long, flat lever over there. Right. Now shift into first gear. It's the first one up."

The clutch and brakes were easy enough, but first

gear was playing a game of tag, and she was *it*. The gear shift wobbled in her hand as she searched for first. The muscles in her neck tensed, and she waited for Joel to let out an exasperated breath, followed by aggravation, maybe anger. Instead, he put his warm hand over hers and helped her shift into first gear. He then moved their hands together and he showed her how to find the rest of the gears.

"This is an old truck, and it's a little tricky. There, you feel it now?"

"Yes. Thank you."

"Your hand is freezing," he said. Joel opened a compartment, took out a pair of black gloves. "Here, put these on."

There he goes, being all considerate again.

"Just take your time getting used to the gears. You'll get the hang of it."

His mood was calm, his tone soothing. Maddy slipped the gloves on and wondered how long it would last once she started driving.

Joel continued to instruct her, and she paid attention. Her left foot lifted a bit off the clutch while her right foot gave it some gas, just as he told her to do. Nothing happened, so she gave it a little more gas and eased back on the clutch some more.

The truck rolled. Just when Maddy thought she was doing it right, she let off the clutch too fast. The truck lurched forward before it stopped as suddenly as if she'd hit a wall, rocketing Joel, who'd forgotten to fasten his seatbelt, forward with brutal force.

He flew like a baseball struck with a bat by a pro. For those two seconds, Joel was kind of a blur. His head made a loud thud against the dashboard before he crumpled into the footwell.

"Oh my God!" Maddy yelled as she dove for him, forgetting about her own fastened seatbelt. She bounced back against the seat, crying out as her hand gripped her left shoulder.

Joel stared up at her from the footwell of the passenger seat. Maddy couldn't decipher his level of anger. Very little of the dim glow from the dashboard light extended to the nether section of the truck where she'd sent her hapless host.

For a moment, they stared at each other. Maddy rubbing her shoulder and waiting for the torrent of fury, Joel staring with shock and holding his battered head. Then, to Maddy's utter surprise, Joel burst out laughing. Three beats later, Maddy followed suit with a laugh inspired more by relief than by humor.

He massaged the right side of his forehead. "Are you all right?" Joel asked.

"Um, yeah, I'm fine," she said. A dull pain pulsed in her shoulder. "How about you? Are you hurt?"

Joel climbed back up on the seat. "I'm fine. I rarely use that part of my brain anyway."

He was sitting there injured because of her, and still, he made her laugh. Kind of amazing. "I'm so sorry," she said.

"Don't worry about it. It was my own fault for not putting on my seatbelt. I should have known better. I must have done the same thing a dozen times when I first learned how to drive a stick."

"Really?"

"Really. I never sent anyone through the windshield, but I stalled out enough times."

Maddy smiled, grateful for his kindness. "Well, it's

going to be impossible for you to get any sleep while I keep this truck jumping down the road like a drunken kangaroo."

He grinned and laughed a little. "Good point. Look, I got a late start today, and I should call it a night soon anyway. How about we stop at the next motel?" He cleared his throat. "Um, I'm sure we could find a couple of rooms for the night."

"Sure," Maddy said. Of course, they would have to stop somewhere for the night. In accordance with her new and awful habit, she hadn't thought that far ahead. At least he'd said, a couple of rooms. He wasn't having any thoughts of the two of them sharing.

"Probably a good idea." She unbuckled her seat belt.

"What are you doing?" Joel asked.

Maddy looked at him without a clue.

"You're driving," he said.

"You still want me to drive, after that disaster?"

"If that's what you consider a disaster, then you must live a pretty tame life."

Pretty tame. It was a polite way of saying her life experiences had been dull and lacking. And damn it all, it was the truth. Well, not today. This day was hers. She re-buckled her seatbelt.

Okay, she was doing this. She was going to drive a stick shift.

"Now," he said. "Take a breath, relax, and we'll start again." Joel drew his seatbelt across his body and plugged it into the latch. She tightened her lips to stifle a laugh. He was trusting her, but not overly.

Maddy made the truck lunge and stall two more times before they rolled down the road again. Joel never lost a speck of his patience. He was right, too. Once she got the hang of it, driving a stick wasn't so difficult.

It was because of Joel. Her nervousness about doing it wrong dissolved, and she could just think about driving and not the aftermath of a mistake. It was…nice. Very nice. She flicked a quick glance at Joel.

Twenty minutes after Maddy had gotten the truck into high gear, she was downshifting. The two-story motel with gold stucco, turquoise doors, and two window boxes of pink and purple petunias on either side of the office door was the only lighted building in sight. With caution and a bit of confidence, Maddy steered the truck into the Last Chance Motel.

The name didn't sit well with her. It had an ominous ring, like the title of a horror movie, like it was the last stop of many a tourist before the maniac appeared and slaughtered them.

She really needed to quit watching scary movies.

Chapter 9

Joel bopped the little silver bell. They both had their eyes on the orange-curtained doorway behind the counter.

Maddy slid a glance toward Joel. In the light of the motel lobby, the red bump on his forehead was obvious. She dragged her stare from her handiwork.

The place was old, probably from the fifties, with a pink ceiling and aqua-blue walls. The paint had been redone over the years. She was guessing the same colors. A vase of plastic daisies sat on the counter beside a stuffed dog and a little sign telling customers they were *Pet Friendly.*

From the curtained doorway wafted warm aromas of home cooking and the familiar clattering of dishes as someone washed and rinsed. It made Maddy think of her life at home. Her father. Dad had his moods, but they weren't all bad. Sometimes he smiled. Sometimes he looked content. Every now and then, he even gave her a compliment, meaningful because they were rare.

Her sister dropping in at random times, hungry, or needing a babysitter, or surprising her with a box of cookies. Grandma Sophie coming over for dinner and sharing stories from the bar. She missed it all—for a moment.

For this little bit of time, she wouldn't think about her obligations, her past, or even her future. She'd be back to it all soon enough. This was her great adventure, her time to make a memory, one good enough to last her the rest of her life. She glanced at Joel. *Hmmm.*

No, don't even think it.

But really, just look at him.

His white T-shirt was snug against his chest and around the muscles of his arms. He had a strong, masculine look about him on the outside and a kind of sweet cuddliness on the inside. It was a heady mix. Just the sight of him made her feel…adventurous.

He probably has all kinds of girlfriends.

But not tonight.

She wasn't a one-night stand kind of girl. Never had been.

This is your special time. All for you. Do you want to make a memory or what?

I'm engaged.

But not yet married.

Now you're justifying.

So? Other people sow wild oats before they settle down. You never have. Not one single oat. Didn't even think you had any wild oats until today. Besides, are you really still engaged? I think you pinpricked that balloon this afternoon.

She scanned Joel from top to bottom. And a fine bottom it was.

No, Maddy, don't even think about it.

Too late. She *was* thinking about it.

Maybe Joel could be her wild oat. Could she take what she wanted, just this one time? Could she be one of those women who indulged in a man for pure pleasure and nothing else?

The thought was too alluring, the imagery intense

enough to flood her with heat. She was on the verge of utter sin. And kind of liking it.

Come on, girl, this could be your last chance to be naughty.

Maddy opened the hoodie Joel had given her and flapped some cool air inside. She was a little stunned at meeting this lustful side of herself. Had it always been there, waiting for the right moment to rip off her clothes and seduce a guy? She focused her attention elsewhere before Joel asked her why she was flashing waves of heat like a flaming tornado.

Maddy strolled the small lobby, willing her body temperature to cool.

The welcome mat was inside the door instead of out, and it looked brand new. In opposition, the long, oval rug in front of the counter was worn but clean. So was the bleached wood floor and the windows giving a view of the parking lot, dark, except for the white porch light near the door where a group of tiny bugs was having a party.

Along one wall was a rack of pamphlets with information on things to see and do along Route 66. In the opposite corner was one circular clothing rack with some T-shirts and blouses, a couple of sweatshirts, and tropical-looking skirts. Over the rack, hanging from the ceiling by two thin chains, was a 12" x 12" board with the words *Last Chance Boutique* burned into it.

Joel tapped the little bell again.

An elderly man wearing denim overalls and a red flannel shirt emerged from the curtained doorway. He was thin with a slight belly bulge. Sparse gray hairs bore comb lines across his head. A warm smile crinkled his eyes.

"I'm here. I'm here. Takes me a little longer to get moving these days. Welcome to the Last Chance Motel. I'm Ted, the owner and operator of this place." He poked a thumb toward the orange curtain through which he'd come. "Well, me and the Mrs." His eyes crinkled some more with a broader smile.

"I'm Joel. This is Maddy." Maddy smiled and gave him a little wave as she stepped over to the counter and stood next to Joel.

"Good to meet you folks," Ted said. He laid a hand on a giant book. No computer. Just an old-fashioned sign-in book. "You're lucky to get a room tonight."

Joel and Maddy stared at him before making a simultaneous shift toward the front windows overlooking the parking lot. They hadn't seen more than a dozen cars on the road, and there was only one other car besides theirs parked in the lot. They rotated back to Ted.

Ted tipped his head toward the side window next to the clothing rack he called a boutique. "We got a full busload of tourists in for the night."

A silver and blue bus was parked so close to the window it could have been mistaken for a wall. No wonder they hadn't noticed it.

"They come through here two or three times a month," Ted said. "Visiting the old sights and so forth."

Joel turned back to Ted. "I didn't realize there were enough tourists to fill a bus."

"Oh, yes. The tour buses are what keeps us going anymore. If this place hadn't been paid off years ago, we wouldn't have survived. This used to be an ideal location to have a business when my grandad opened this motel; busy all the time back in the day. Now, an occasional tour of historical sites is mostly what we get. And a few folks like you passing through."

"Wow, long time to be in the same place," Maddy said.

"You bet. Had a great time, too. It was really something, once upon a time. Should have seen it when things were hopping. Back in its prime, this motel was called The Lucky Cuss. After so many places went bust, we changed it to Last Chance. Seemed a better name."

Ted leaned forward and lowered his voice as if some competitor might be listening for his secret. "Gives people the impression there might not be another motel for quite some time." Ted stood straight and spoke in a normal tone again. "Fact is these days the name's not far off the truth. We can't complain, though. We're grateful for every one of those things pulling into our parking lot." He jabbed a thumb toward the parked bus. "They took most of the rooms for the night, but I have one left."

"One?" Maddy and Joel said at the same time.

"Yeah," Ted said. "And I know the Stop Inn a few miles down the road is full tonight. A lot of snowbirds take the route this time of year, soaking up the sun. They got a tour bus full down there, too."

"You don't understand, "Joel said. "We're not married."

Ted chuckled and opened his big old-fashioned sign-in book. "It's been a long time since motels cared about such things."

"No," Maddy said. Panic stirred her insides. No matter her earlier thoughts/fantasy, she really wasn't one to hook up with a guy and share a motel room. It was a daydream, meant to stay in a fantasy life. "What he means is we…we need two rooms."

Ted looked up from his book, first at Maddy, then at Joel. His chin lifted a notch, and his brow furrowed as if suspicious of something. Then, as though he'd come to some sort of conclusion, Ted's suspicions faded away, and he smiled again.

"Well, I'll tell you what I'll do," Ted said. "When I said you were lucky, I meant in more ways than one. You see, the room I have left is the Presidential Suite, and tonight I'll let you have it for the same price as a regular room."

"What's the Presidential Suite?" Maddy asked.

"It's our finest room. There's a first-class living area, a kitchenette, and a separate bedroom. One of you could sleep on the couch. It's the best I can do."

Maddy glanced over at Joel. He stared back at her. It was either this or sleep in the truck. She nodded at Joel. He nodded back.

"We'll take it," Joel said.

Joel took out his wallet. Maddy opened her purse. "It's okay. I've got it," he said.

"No, I'll pay half. It's only fair." And not being obligated means not being obligated. The fantasy in her head a few minutes ago was not made for reality. Who was she fooling? She wasn't a seductress. She could never be so bold. She should have told the little troublemaker in her head to shut up when she first suggested leaping so far out of her comfort zone.

"It's all right, really," Joel said. "The business is paying for my room, so don't worry about it."

Maddy returned her wallet and closed her purse slowly, like she was closing a casket. Was she really about to spend the night in a motel room with a man she barely knew? Her sex fantasy mutated into the more possible reality she'd considered earlier. This guy could be putting up a front. Yes, Joel was gorgeous and sweet. Isn't that what women said about the famous serial killer Ted Bundy?

A spine-tingling sound, faint because it was in the back of her mind, was no doubt background music from some horror movie she'd watched. The kind shrieking a crescendo right before someone gets axed.

She really needed to stop watching those movies.

****

Owen pounded his steering wheel for the second time. If he kept this up, he was going to bust the damn thing. Of course, at this point, he didn't care. Something was about to break, and it was looking more and more like it might be him.

He fiddled with his bowtie, yellow, like his vest, and checked the tracker app once more before lifting his head toward the mess in front of him.

All he needed was to get down the highway to the next exit, then he could get off and hop on Route 66. What the hell was Maddy doing on Route 66 anyway? He'd find out later. Right now, all he could do was sit in the stopped traffic, middle lane, second car back from an overturned manure truck, stewing in the stink.

If he'd been on the road just a few minutes sooner, he would have been past here before the truck flipped. Owen pounded the steering wheel again, both hands, in a simultaneous pow, pow, pow.

The beast of a truck still lay on its side like a dead dinosaur. Its tarp had peeled back, which had allowed the reeking contents to spread all over the highway. The road crew was taking forever to clean up this shit, literally shit. In the meantime, Owen was trapped there along with everyone else, breathing in the putrid, stomach-churning stench. Could nothing go his way today?

Since it was dark, the crew had to truck in portable light towers. That took forever. It took almost as long to get the lights up and running. And don't get him started on the officials!

Orange-vested or uniformed people stood around with bandanas tied around their faces to help with the smell. Good luck. His car windows were rolled up tight, and he'd set the air to internal circulation. It didn't help. The stink still got inside, powerful enough to leave him gagging. He'd have to get his car detailed. The tuxedo would probably have to be burned.

The crew and first responders drifted around the site in slow motion, acting as if all these people sitting in their cars for hours had no place else to be, like this was a party no one wanted to end.

Police vehicles and various other authorized cars and trucks flashed red and blue lights, yellow lights, and orange lights, in a mass display of public service, by appearances. Mostly what he saw were people standing around, talking, pointing here and there. *Get to work!*

Owen lifted his phone to see the screen, and the tracker app, though nothing had changed. Maddy had stopped somewhere for about forty minutes before heading east once more. Had she stopped to eat? Do some shopping? She'd turned on her phone, so she must have made a call. Or maybe she just checked her messages, which meant she got all of his. And didn't call back.

Well, he was done calling. Now he was a man of action.

According to the tracker, Maddy wasn't on the road

very long before stopping again. That was more than three hours ago. The tracker hadn't budged since.

Her car was still at her house. Owen knew because he'd hired a limo to take Maddy and her family from their house to the wedding/reception hall. So did she catch a ride from someone? She wouldn't have hitchhiked. The girl was afraid of her own shadow. She'd never get into a car with a stranger. Maybe she rented a car. Or gotten on a bus.

Or maybe…ah! That smell! His empty stomach spasmed. This was intolerable.

He rummaged around in his console until he found some breath spray. He pumped out what was left in the small can a few inches in front of his face. It helped, for about ten seconds. He covered his mouth and nose with his hand while staring at the phone again. Why Route 66? Did Maddy have a destination in mind?

The revving of a big engine drew Owen's attention to the disastrous scene outside. He sat up and pressed his head against the driver's side window for a better look and nodded with a little grin. A bulldozer scraped the road, shoveling the manure from the highway. Finally!

Chapter 10

Joel, duffle bag in his grip, flipped on the lights and entered the motel room. Maddy, rolling her weekend bag behind her, followed. Ted's description of the room had been overblown, to say the least. The first-class Presidential Suite had a bit of a tenement feel.

Maddy stood still and took in the place.

The tiny living area contained one threadbare couch. The thing might well be as old as the motel. There was a matching chair so butt-sunk you could set a basketball in it and only half would show, and an antique television set the size of Joel's box truck.

Against the far wall was the kitchenette consisting of a small, faux-wood table and two ladder-back chairs, a fairly new miniature refrigerator, a small sink, and a two-burner gas stove. Although the room appeared clean, a musty smell clung to everything like an old-timey cologne.

Joel crossed the room. "I'll take the couch," he said, tossing his bag on the floor near the sofa.

"No. You paid for the room."

"I didn't pay for it. The company did. I don't mind the couch. Really."

"No, I want to be fair about this," Maddy said. "I'll flip you for it. Have you got a coin?"

When Joel did nothing but stare at her, she said, "I insist."

Joel dug a quarter from his pocket. "I really don't mind sleeping on the couch. Besides, I wouldn't feel right…"

"Flip it. It's only fair."

"Fair is a big deal with you."

She'd never given much thought to fairness before today. Maybe because it would have been too depressing. It wasn't fair she had to be a grown-up at age twelve. It wasn't fair she hadn't the freedoms and opportunities of other young women. Tonight, she'd strive for fair.

"I guess so," Maddy said. "Indulge me and flip the coin."

"Okay. You call it," Joel said. He tossed the quarter in the air.

While it was spinning, Maddy shouted, "Tails! No, heads. No, tails. I want tails!"

She caught Joel's smile. Was he laughing at her or amused at her indecision? After he caught the coin, he slapped it on the back of his hand, lifting his fingers so only he could see.

"Tails, you win," he said. Before she could see the coin, he stuffed it back into his pocket.

Maddy doubted she won, but she let it alone. Fair or not, she appreciated the give. It awarded her more privacy. She rolled her small weekend bag into the bedroom, which consisted of one veneer dresser and mirror, a queen-sized bed with a green and gold nylon bedspread, and a picture of a sailboat hanging over the wicker headboard.

Since she'd never been inside a motel room before, she had no idea if it was standard décor or not. Nor did she care. It was clean and free, and the bedroom was hers.

She lifted her bag onto the suitcase stand and cringed at the pain in her left shoulder. With her right hand, she gave herself a little massage.

A small laugh escaped her as an image of them flashed in her mind—her being yanked back by the seatbelt designed to protect her while Joel sat on the floor of his truck, holding his bruised head.

His head had been battered because of her, and he didn't get angry. It's what she remembered most. Joel hadn't even been irritated. In fact, he'd laughed.

She stepped out of the bedroom with her hand still rubbing her sore shoulder. Joel was slouched back on the couch, using a gentle touch to probe the red orb over the outer edge of his right eyebrow. They looked at each other and chuckled.

"I'm so sorry," Maddy said.

"Stop it. I should have been wearing my seatbelt. Do you have any aspirin?"

"No, I don't. I'll go down to the lobby and see if they have any. I'll ask for some ice, too."

"I'll go. I could use a little walk after driving all day. Be right back."

After Joel left, Maddy took his place on the couch and took mental snapshots of all of her surroundings. She should get out her phone and take some pictures for her own personal remembrance, but she was too tired to go back into the bedroom and get it.

How many lovers had stayed here back in a time when such things were scandalous? No doubt, quite a few. Grandma Sophie would love it. Maybe she *had* loved it.

How did Sophie manage it? How did she cut loose

and have fun without worrying about a thousand different things?

It must be something a person is born with, like a good sense of direction. Either you had it, or you didn't. Maddy worried about everything all the time. But was that really such a bad thing overall?

There was a lot to be said for caution. Unlike her grandmother, no one ever had to come get Maddy out of jail. She'd had to bail out Grandma after she hit some guy with her big, zebra-striped purse. It was a whole ordeal for the family. It also gave Sophie a favorable reputation at the bar. Whenever someone acted up, they'd threaten to sic Grandma and her purse on them.

Fifteen minutes after he left, Joel returned with two shot glasses, a round box of salt, some lime slices in a plastic bag, and a full bottle of tequila.

Maddy raised a brow and a half-smile. "New and improved aspirin?"

"Compliments of Ted. He still thinks we're a couple. The old guy thought we wanted two rooms because we had a fight. He saw this knot on my head and figured you gave it to me."

"Well, I did give it to you. It just wasn't on purpose. I don't see any ice."

"Ice machine is broken. I think the swelling is going down already. It's really not that bad. At worst I'll have a little bruise."

"Why did he give you a bottle of tequila and the other stuff?"

"A customer gave the bottle to him, and he told me he and his wife don't drink anymore. He said if the two of us shared this, it would make us or break us. Either way, it was best to find out if our relationship was meant to last while we were still young. I tried explaining the situation to him, but he said again it wasn't any of his business, so I gave up, thanked him, and left."

By the time Joel had finished his explanation, he'd put everything on the small coffee table in front of Maddy. He then fell back into the stuffed chair. "He didn't have any aspirin. He said there's a gas station/convenience store down the street, but it's closed for the night."

Maddy stared at the little party in front of them. Shots of tequila. *Wow.* She wasn't much of a drinker. Good thing, too. Joann liked to have a few drinks, and Sophie enjoyed her scotch. Somebody had to be the designated driver. Someone had to be the responsible one. Somebody had to be the good girl. Maddy was always, *always* the good girl.

Maybe she would like to have a drink sometimes? Did anybody ever think of her? No. They all treated her like she was a nun. Okay, she did kind of live her life that way, but she had to. Someone had to make sure everyone got home safe.

So, why not try something different tonight?

What would it prove? What would it change? Besides, the liquid in that bottle didn't look tempting. Well, not too tempting. Well, not extremely tempting.

"I'm pretty tired," she said. "I should call it a night."

Yeah. You're a wild woman.

Well, she *should* go to bed, get a good night's sleep and take a fresh look at her situation in the morning. Yet, she stayed where she was, staring at the bottle of tequila and thinking about numbers.

The number of parties she didn't go to. The number of guys she didn't meet, didn't date, didn't kiss, didn't sleep with. The opportunities she never knew because she was busy taking care of everyone. The drinks she'd never had because she was the designated driver.

But she wasn't driving tonight.

"Do you want some?" Joel asked.

Her grandma danced through her mind. Sophie was carrying a big sign reading, *YES!*

Oh, come on! For once in your life crack your crappy, practical shell and have a little fun.

"Well, maybe just one," Maddy said.

Hehe.

Joel waved a hand toward the bottle. "Help yourself."

Maddy swirled the liquid around in the heavy bottle, then twisted and tugged on the cork until it popped out. She filled one of the shot glasses, slow, careful, like it was a ceremony. It did feel like a ceremony, a sort of celebration of flight, a hailing of the youth she'd missed.

After setting down the glass, she opened the baggie and took out a lime slice. She picked up the shot glass, paused, and then set it down again. Then she stared at the box of salt while confusion threatened her shell-cracking moment.

"What's wrong?" Joel asked.

She should go to the bedroom, get her phone, and do an internet search. But this wasn't a night for doing what she should. So, she overcame her embarrassment and asked her question. "Which comes first, the salt or the lime?"

"Did you forget, or have you never done tequila shots before?"

"I've *seen* it done," she said.

Joel raised an eyebrow. "I once saw a magician

make a car disappear. Doesn't mean I know how to do it."

He scooped up the bottle and filled the second shot glass. "Like this," he said. Joel snagged a slice of lime and held it in his left hand. He then poured a bit of salt on the web of the same hand between his thumb and finger. He licked the salt from his left hand, downed the shot with his right hand, and bit into the lime he held in his left all in one impressive, poetic, sweep.

"Ah," he said. He leaned back in the chair. "Hair of the dog."

"Oh, did you have some last night?"

"Some."

Maddy picked up her glass with uncertain determination. Then, remembering what she was supposed to do first, she set the glass down, picked up a slice of lime, and poured salt on the web of her left hand between her thumb and finger. Lots of salt. Enough to form a nice little pyramid. This prompted a chuckle from Joel.

"I like salt," Maddy said. This wasn't altogether true, but it was a good save. She'd do better with the next shot.

The next shot?

Woohoo!

Joel kept his eyes on her like he was watching a mystery movie.

You can do this, party girl.

Where the hell did that inner voice come from? It sounded an awful lot like Grandma Sophie.

Maddy picked up the shot glass and licked the mountain of salt from the back of her hand. She lifted the small glass halfway to her lips, but her face pruned at the soggy ball forming in her mouth. Instead of waiting like a good little pile of salt, the beast took on a life of its own. How could it be dissolving and growing at the same time? The stuff hardened and perspired on her tongue, creating a salty river rushing down her throat.

Her glass clunked on the table next to her dropped slice of lime, and she ran to the bathroom to spit out the salt. *Yuck! Spit. Spit. Yuck!* Maddy rinsed her mouth five times before leaving the bathroom.

After casually covering his laughter with a series of coughs, Joel said, “So, you like salt.”

Maddy said nothing, though she did give him a look, causing him to disguise another chuckle. He wasn’t very good at it. Screw him. She was doing this.

She lifted her chin, crossed the room, and sat on the couch, ready to try again.

This time, she sprinkled a *little bit* of salt on the back of her hand, the same hand holding the lime. She licked the salt, then flicked her wrist, and tipped her head back to down the tequila.

And all the air disappeared from the world.

The liquid was a toxic bomb. Her stomach teetered on the verge of tossing it back up while her lungs begged for a breath. Lost in the panic of imminent death, Maddy forgot all about step three.

“Lime! Don’t forget the lime!” Joel grabbed her lime-holding hand and stuffed the slice into her mouth.

The room quivered. Well, what she could see of it through the blur of her watery eyes. Her stomach pulsed and threatened a full rebellion, and Maddy readied herself for another run to the bathroom.

Where was the bathroom? She forgot. No, no, no! Don’t you dare throw up in front of Joel! She pinched the lime from her mouth. Maybe she was sitting still. Maybe she was swaying. Something was moving, but she couldn't tell if it was her or the room. After a minute, or maybe an hour, her lungs managed to drag in some air. Her stomach calmed. Her vision cleared, and then the world settled on a soft, jolly cushion.

Joel honored her with a hearty round of applause. "There you go! Not bad for a first time. Are you okay?"

Maddy nodded as warm excitement flowed through her body. "I've had tequila before."

"Really?"

"Well, I once had a margarita with my grandmother."

"Ooh, margaritas with Grandma. Party girl."

She glared at him. Okay, he couldn't know the comment would get under her skin. It shouldn't. So what if she'd lived a dull life? Some people in this world had to be the grown-ups. Without people like her doing all the work, everyone else would be sitting in filthy rooms while wearing stained sweatpants and eating pasta out of a can. People like her took care of the minutia of life so everyone else could have fun.

Well, not tonight. Tonight, it was her turn to cut loose and have some fun of her own. It's just, well, this was all so foreign. She didn't do shots. She didn't stay in motel rooms with men she didn't know, or any men, ever. The truth is, she'd never done much of anything.

After her workday at the Yarn Barn was finished, there was dinner to cook and chores to be done. By the time everything else and everyone else was taken care of, Maddy was too tired to get fixed up to go out. An hour or so of sitting in front of the television drawing designs, maybe a little reading before going to sleep, was her treat.

Looking back from this last year and a half of her twenties, it was as if her years had lived without her. Like she was late for the party, arriving just in time to help clean up the mess.

Well, her past may be bland, and her future might be an uncertain mess, but tonight was hers. Tonight, she'd live. She glanced at Joel. He was a little cocky. Sweet, too, and fine as hell, with his athletic build, his sexy smile, and a face she had no doubt turned many a female head.

Was she actually thinking about seducing him, for real, not just a fantasy? Maddy almost giggled at the thought. Could she? No. *Yes.* It's not like she'd ever see him again after this trip was over. It would be her little secret memory to keep. She had to grab this night with both hands and shake it until every drop of fun spilled out on her.

"You handled that well," Joel said.

"Yes. I *did* handle it well."

It was silly, shining pride because she downed a shot of tequila without throwing up, but she couldn't help it. Yeah, she could party. And damn, it felt good!

You're not done yet, girl.

"I think I'll have another," Maddy said. "How about you?"

Joel reached for his glass, then sat back without it. "Nah. You go ahead, though."

Two shots later, her thoughts of seduction blended with curiosity. She had a hard time picturing this masculine guy designing a child's doll. Was that a sexist thought? Maybe. She'd think about it tomorrow. Tonight, she had questions.

"So," she said. "Tell me what other ideas you had, besides the doll."

A look of discomfort, maybe even disgust, crossed his face. Or maybe her vision was playing tricks on her. Everything did seem a little…distorted.

Joel poured a shot into his glass and tilted the bottle toward her. "Another one?"

"Yes."

"You sure? This stuff has a kick to it."

"I'm sure." He poured for her, and she thanked him. "I'm sorry. I didn't mean to touch a sore spot."

"It's all right. You already know I'm going to pick up the dolls. You might as well know my other creations were a flop."

Maddy used the salt and passed it to Joel. He held the bag of limes. At the same time, they licked, shot, and sucked.

Joel leaned back in the chair. "Well, there was the toy dog. It walked and wet so children could walk their toy dogs just like a real one."

Maddy smiled. "Sounds cute. It didn't sell very well either?"

"It never made it past a prototype, much less a store shelf or the website. My mother, did I mention my parents were my bosses?"

She nodded.

"My mother pointed out it would be walking and wetting all over the house. Just what every mother wants, a toy dog to soil the carpet."

Maddy winced. "Oh, right. I didn't think of that."

"Neither did I."

Maddy picked up the bottle and poured another shot in each of their glasses. They performed the ritual together, salt, shot, lime. She was downing them like a pro.

"Then I created a toy soldier whose gun really worked," Joel said. "He or she could shoot tiny pellets up to ten feet. Soldiers could fire at each other, creating a more realistic battle. My dad looked at the plans for about ten seconds before pointing out the obvious."

Something was obvious? She gave her head a little shake. No, nothing clicked, but her brain sloshed a little. "What was obvious?"

"The toy was a lawsuit waiting to happen."

"Oh. I guess I could see a disaster coming."

"I should have. Now, the doll…"

A slow smile widened across his face, a mixture of pride and sadness. It urged her to hug him, and maybe do some other stuff. But she stayed where she was. How does one go about becoming a seductress? Maybe she needed some more tequila. What were they talking about? Oh right, the doll.

"The doll is your favorite design?"

"Yes," he said. "She was inspired by Mariel, my older sister. Mariel is a great mother to two boys, holds down a managerial position at the factory, and still finds time to worry about me."

"She sounds awesome."

"She is."

"Why does she worry about you?"

"She worries I party too much, thinks it's affecting my job."

"You produced the doll."

He smiled again, but it was still sad. "I really thought my doll was going to be the one. My family thought so, too. It was the first time my parents backed me. One hundred dolls were made and delivered to a store in Flagstaff, Arizona. The owner owed my dad a favor. He called it in for me. The guy agreed to carry the dolls for thirty days. That was twenty-nine days ago. Not a single doll has sold."

"Crap."

"Yeah. Crap. My mission now is to try and convince the store owner to carry them a little longer."

Maddy nodded. She had something to say here, but it got lost on the way to her mouth. She squinted around her head at all the meandering thoughts. At last, she managed to snag one.

"Have you ever been married?" The intrusive question flowed through her lips with ease because her filters had gone for a swim in the tequila. For a moment, she thought he looked uncomfortable with the question. She couldn't tell for sure. Whatever.

"No, but I'm not opposed to it, for someday. I want to wait until I'm more…occupationally grounded."

"Do you like working for your parents?"

"For a long time, it was good. Thought I'd be there forever. I get along well with my family, for the most part. I love the toy business. There was a brief time when I thought I'd have a career in sports. I played baseball in college, have a closet full of trophies and awards."

"Wow. I'm impressed."

"I doubt I would have made it."

"Why not?"

"I love the game, but I never had the passion for it like I do the factory. Seeing a project go from idea to design, that's where I most loved to work, in designing and then into manufacturing, it's the best. Watching a new toy roll off the conveyer belt always gives me a goodtime feeling, like when I was a kid. My mistake was coming up with my own ideas. I should have stuck to working with others."

Joel leaned sideways, resting his chin on a fist, and rubbed the backs of his fingers of the other hand against his facial scruff. He stared at her with interest. "So, what about you? What gives you the feeling of being a kid again?"

"I don't remember ever feeling like a child," Maddy said. She told him about her family. Then, about her fiancé, Owen. Owen had been her first real boyfriend and the only long-term relationship she'd ever had. And as her father pointed out, he was the only man to ever propose.

"So, your dad is real old-fashioned, huh?"

"He is. He worries about me more than he lets on."

"Why?"

"He worries about me being alone after he's gone. My life being what it was, I never had much time for friends or activities, not like my little sister."

"He's just now realizing it?"

"He was lost in his grief for a long time, and raising two kids by himself couldn't have been easy."

"Doesn't sound too easy for you, either."

"We all got by as best we could."

Joel nodded. "How'd you meet Owen?"

"His dad and my dad were old friends. They'd tried setting us up a couple of times before it happened. Over dinner on our first date, Owen told me if he had known I was as attractive as I was domestic, he would have made an effort to meet me sooner."

At the time she'd taken it as a compliment. Thinking on it now, she had to wonder if he was attracted to her as a person or attracted to what she would contribute to his home. And was that terrible, or just honest?

"He wants a domestic woman, and that's not what you want for your life."

"Don't misunderstand. There's nothing wrong with being a housewife, raising the kids, taking care of the home, keeping the family running. Those women keep the world turning. It's respectable. It's important."

"But it's not for you."

"It's been my life since I was a kid." Were her s's blending into the other letters?

"You're ready to branch out."

"I've been ready. I've been waiting. My little sister is grown and settled into her life. My dad is ready to retire."

"So, what's your dream?"

Maddy poured and downed another shot. Probably a bad idea at this point, as she was fairly certain she was already drunk. Oh, right. She didn't care.

"Designing clothes," she said. "It's silly. Ridiculous, even."

The thought sailed around in her head on a wave of tequila, and it didn't seem so ridiculous.

"Owen works in finance," she said. He never really explained his job. Did he think she wouldn't understand? "Fashion designing is too artsy for him to take seriously. Besides, he wants me to be home, to be to him what I've been to my family."

"So, are you going to marry him?"

Maddy danced another round with the salt, tequila, and lime. She had the pattern down quite well now. "Maybe I'll marry him. Or maybe I won't. Things can happen. Besides, he might not even want me after what

I did today." There go her s's again. Now her d's were sticking. She could hear it but couldn't control it. Did Joel notice?

Maddy had lost count of how many shots she'd done. Several. Good. She had a lot to make up for, and it's not like she was driving or anything. Tonight, she had no tasks, no duties. When was the last time she had a night where she wasn't responsible for anything? Never.

Shifting on the couch, Maddy made an effort to get up, but since she couldn't remember what she was getting up for, she sunk back into the worn cushions. Maybe she was going to brush her teeth and put on pajamas. She wasn't sure. The messenger traveling between her brain and her body had gone missing. Maybe he too had gone for a swim in the tequila. The visual made her giggle.

What were they talking about? Oh right, Owen.

Owen, Owen, Owen. He had nice hair. Blond, with a little bit of a wave to it. Good teeth, too. Aren't horses supposed to have good teeth? Um, husbands. Husbands should have good teeth. Why was she thinking about teeth? Or horses? Who knows? Maddy gave her head a little shake. Whoa! Don't do that again!

She would have to go back to her life, be a good girl, and marry Owen. He wanted her for a wife bad enough she could ask his forgiveness and most likely get it. Somewhere in her saturated mind, she was sure there were arguments against marrying Owen, but they were all enjoying a dip in the tequila pool. Party, party.

"Owen's a really is a good catch," she said. After consoling Joann through her marriage to the no-good bum she had taken vows with and then divorced, Maddy knew Owen had some very good, very important qualities. She bounced her hand with each sentence. "He's reliable. He's stable. He's sensible."

****

"You just described a good minivan," Joel said.

He heard the attitude in his voice but couldn't help or explain it. He had no reason to disparage Owen. He didn't know the guy. But she'd run away from the man once already, fleeing in her wedding dress to avoid the marriage. And when given an opportunity to go back, Maddy gave him some flimsy excuse about not wanting to disrupt his route.

It wasn't his business.

He had enough of his own troubles. Like a career on the rocks. Just because he loved the toy business didn't mean he should stay there. At some point, a man has to accept he's in the wrong line of work and move on to a new one. But leaving the family business, it hurt his heart to think of it. Maybe not facing the facts is what set him on a downward spiral.

He partied too much, true, but not as much as his sister thought. Okay, so he'd come into work hungover a couple of times. A few times. Several times. All right, so Mariel made a good point. Over the last couple of years, he'd partied more than he should. It wasn't always like that. The increase had been gradual, escalating with each failure. He eyed the bottle but didn't pour another shot.

Joel glanced over at Maddy. A gloss covered her eyes, and she listed to the left. She was going to feel like hell in the morning. He should put away the bottle before she did any more shots. She wasn't used to drinking like this. But who was he to curb anyone else's party? In his circle of friends, he was King Party All Night. Damn. His sister was right.

He eyed the bottle again. He should put it away for both their sakes.

Across the table, Maddy twirled a lock of wheat-colored hair around her finger and stared at the bottle of tequila. He knew that look. Somewhere in the back of her mind, she was telling herself drinking any more was a bad idea. But the front of her mind was giving the back of her mind the finger. He'd been there. More than a few times. He felt for her.

He held a certain degree of respect for her, too. She wasn't getting married out of greed, like some of the women who'd pursued him due to his family money. Maddy was sacrificing herself so her father would retire and take his RV adventure. How many people would do such a thing?

What Joel couldn't understand was why it had to be this Owen character. A nice woman like Maddy, with her looks, must have all kinds of men lined up at her door.

Maddy was hot as hell, from the top of her face, pretty without even a drop of makeup, down to her full breasts and narrow waist, long legs, and a rounded ass just made for her snug jeans. He'd hooked up with a woman night before last, but the way his body reacted to Maddy ever since she'd washed all the gunk off her face, it was like he'd been celibate for a year.

Oh boy. Joel rubbed his eyes with the heels of his hands. He might be in trouble here. Hot and sexy, and a little bit crazy was his type. But he drew the line at women who were spoken for. Of course, since she'd run away from her wedding, was she spoken for? Didn't matter. He also drew a line at women who were too drunk to make that decision. Didn't stop the erotic fantasy from playing out in his head, though. He was only human.

Maddy burst out laughing.

“Owen’s not a minivan,” she said. “You’re not being nice. You don’t even know him. He’s a good guy.”

“If he’s so good, why did you run away from the wedding?”

Maddy popped back up, and momentum flopped her head to the other side. Her eyebrows rose, and she straightened, sort of. Her neck was a little rubbery. “You know what I used to love?”

“What?”

“Fruity-Fruit candy.”

Joel couldn’t hold back his chuckle. Yeah, he should have put the bottle away. The lady was wasted. “Fruity-Fruit candy?”

“Yeah. Don’t you remember that candy? The commercial had a little song: Fruity-Fruit, Fruity-Fruit, Fruity-Fruit candy. Fruity-Fruit, Fruity-Fruit, wouldn’t some be dandy.”

It was an effort not to laugh out loud. She didn’t hit one note right on the simple jingle, but damn, she was cute. “Oh, right. Yeah, I remember. Wasn’t there a singing rainbow?”

“Yes! It danced, too. Each little ball of candy in the pack was a different color and flavor.” Maddy got a faraway look in her eyes. “Do you know if they still make it?”

“No idea.”

“It was *so* good.”

He peered at her across the low table while she chatted about candy like it was a precious memory. His smiles kept coming.

Maddy's voice took on an elongated singsong rhythm as she reminisced about the flavors. "Lemon, strawberry, grape, orange, cherry…and another one, I think. No, no, there aren't any more. The flavor was *excellent*."

Joel's grin widened. Somehow Maddy managed to be hot and adorable at the same time. The combination was more intoxicating than the tequila.

"I have to go to the bathroom," Maddy said.

Two seconds after she stood, she was swaying. A little to the right, and then so deep to the left, she couldn't correct herself. Joel caught her before she hit the floor or crashed into the coffee table.

****

Maddy stared deep into his captive eyes, the same blue as those popsicles she used to like.

Why did she keep thinking about childhood treats? Forget about them. Joel. Look at Joel. This was all so romantic. A private room, drinks, and a guy so good looking, she wouldn't have the nerve to talk to him in any other situation. Where would she ever meet someone like him anyway? He didn't look anything like the very few men who shopped in the Yarn Barn.

They were face to face, lips inches apart. Dramatic, like some old black-and-white movie seconds before the big romantic kiss. His arms were strong on her back. She arched into him.

I could kiss him. I could kiss him right now. And then he'd pick me up and carry me into the bedroom.

Her toes tingled at the thought.

Was he thinking the same thing? Yes, yes, he was. Just look at the passion, intense on his face. Her breath deepened. Her heart beat faster. Attraction simmered hot in his eyes, boiling with desire. His lips parted. He was making his move! Maddy's eyes fluttered to slits, and she tipped her head back a little more, offering her lips.

"Are you going to throw up?"

Oops. Embarrassment threw a sopping blanket across her fervor. Her eyes snapped open, and she backed off of the intimate pose. Well, as much as she could in his solid grip.

That wasn't desire in his eyes. Joel wasn't having lust-filled thoughts about her. He was watching to see if she was going to lose her lunch on his T-shirt. Did he have a clue as to what she'd been thinking? She hoped not. *Scrub it all from your brain so he can't tell. Now!*

"…No, I'm fine. I just stood up too fast."

Joel grinned. She frowned. What's so funny about standing up too fast? It could be dangerous. A person could fall and get a serious injury. And it lingered. The room had a tilt, and it was slow to straighten.

"Excuse me," Maddy said. Her c and s in the word excuse blended to make a long s. She tried again. "Escuse me." *Ahh!* "Accuse me." *What the hell?*

Maddy backed away and rounded the coffee table, then aimed herself in the direction of the bathroom. Her forward lean gave her momentum. Too much. Uh oh. Did she look like she was running? She straightened her spine and her steps. There. Now she was in a groove. She was doing it. Great! Everything looked normal.

Halfway across the room, Joel took her arm. "Do you need some help getting to the bathroom?"

Could drunk people blush? She hoped not. And she didn't need any help. Just because she stood up too fast and got a little dizzy. Jeez!

"Of course not," Maddy said. With a huff, she

yanked her arm back and made it the short distance from the bedroom door to the bathroom door just fine. She swung her head back toward Joel, standing in the bedroom door, to give him a gloating smirk and rammed her shoulder into the door jam.

"Ow!"

When she glared back at Joel, he held his hands up, palms toward her, lips pressed together, and stepped back. Good. She was in no mood to…to what? She really had to pee.

Maddy had no idea how long she was in the bathroom. After she'd washed her hands, she sat down on the floor. Probably a mistake. Now she'd have to get back up again. Please, please don't let him come in looking for me and find me like this. He might be on his way right now, all worried about her. She was getting worried about herself.

Did she swallow a carnival?

Thoughts bounced around the inside of her head like they were on the Scrambler. Her head spun like the Zipper. Her balance had the stability of someone who'd just stepped off the Tilt-a-Whirl, and her stomach roiled as though she'd eaten three of those giant buckets of French fries all by herself.

While she stared at the door, the Fruity-Fruit tune jingled through her head again. It made her giggle.

Okay, stop laughing and get up. The simple command took an army's effort. Up on her knees. Hold onto the sink. Hope it doesn't come off the wall. Okay, she was standing. Maddy faced the mirror, then leaned over to get a closer look. For a second or two, her eyes spun around like pinwheels. She held onto the edge of the sink.

"Oh yeah," she whispered to the tanked-up woman facing her. "It's time to go to bed…I mean, go to sleep."

Maddy made a good effort to walk like a sober person to the living room. Joel stood, and she leaned back against the wall.

"I saw a blanket in the bedroom closet," she said. The words were a little soft around the edges, but the centers held. "I'll get it for you. Then I'm going to bed. To sleep."

She glanced down. The floor had an angle to it. It threw off the entire room. Must be because the motel was so old. Ted really should get it fixed before the whole place collapsed. Maybe she should have Joel run down there and tell him right now.

"Are you all right?" Joel asked. He was walking toward her, a little crooked because of the floor.

"Oh sure, I'm just taking a break here before I go to bed."

Stupid crooked room made her dizzy. Time to hit the sack. She peeled herself away from the wall but kept going in a slow, rather elegant forward sway. Uh oh. Here comes the floor.

Then she tilted backward, and her feet left the ground. Joel held her in his arms like Rhett held Scarlett. So romantic.

Oh, don't even go there again, you drunken idiot.

"I am not an idiot."

"Of course not," Joel said. He carried her through the crooked room and laid her on the bed, all gentle and caring. Then, as she melted into the mattress, he untied her shoes.

"I feel like a gummy bear that's been left out in the sun."

Joel laughed. “You’re going to be fine, eventually.”

Her eyelids closed, and the day played back on them like a movie screen. Were they still in his truck?

“Well,” she said. She couldn’t help but be aggravated. “I would be a whole lot finer if you would please, for God’s sake, stop driving in circles.”

He laughed again. What was funny? His circular driving was making her nauseous.

He slipped off one of her shoes. Did the bed sink to the left, or was it the room-tilt problem? “What’s so funny?” she asked.

“Um, I was just thinking about the Fruity Fruit candy song. It made me laugh.”

“Me too!”

Maddy hummed the tune and broke into a giggle before it was done. Her smile faded into a frown. “Oh, God, I really am dizzy.” Maybe it was the tequila. How many shots had she downed? She couldn’t remember.

“Try opening your eyes.”

She did, and there he was, sitting beside her, all sweet and cute in the lamplight. Her dad would say Joel needed a haircut, but Maddy liked how it was a touch unkempt. It gave him a rebellious look, and it suited her mood. She scanned his strong build. Very sexy. Blend it all with the way he was taking care of her. It could make her swoon. Hahaha. Swoon. What a funny word. Swoooooon.

“Here,” Joel said. “You’re going to get a crick in your neck.” He straightened her head on the pillow.

“Thank you.” Maddy struggled to keep her eyes open. Her body was falling asleep before her mind was ready. Besides, that awful dizziness waited in the dark. She needed to stay awake until it was gone.

"You're a nice guy, Joel."

He grinned down at her. "I try."

"You know when I first met you, I thought you were a serial killer."

"Really?" Joel said. "I thought *you* were a serial killer."

She busted out laughing. This was funnier than the word swoon. "You did? Your first impression of me was I was a serial killer?"

"No," Joel said. "My first impression of you was…" He let out an airy chuckle.

Maddy laughed, too, though she didn't know why. "Tell me."

"I thought you were an angel."

"You thought I was an angel?"

"Sure, when I saw you standing there on the side of the road wearing a long white gown, a sunbeam making you kind of glow."

Joel thought I was an angel.

She drifted away on that cheery thought.

****

She still looked like an angel. Her face had a glow, and her wheat field hair spilled around the pillow like a halo. Did it feel as soft as it looked? His fingers brushed the silky ends before he drew back. She was drunk, and he wouldn't take advantage. Besides, if the two of them ever had time for touching, he wanted her awake and aware.

A time for touching? What was he thinking? She was engaged. Even if she wasn't, Maddy deserved better than him. All he'd ever managed to accomplish in his life, in his career, was to disappoint his family. Maddy had sacrificed her youth to care for her family. The woman was getting married, so her father would take his retirement and go on his dream trip. She really was an angel.

Her eyes had closed again, and he gazed down the length of her. Even under the covers, her perfect peaks and valleys were obvious. The woman had the heart of a saint but a body designed for sin. He doubted she was aware of how wonderful she was.

"I still think you're an angel," Joel said.

He'd spoken just above a whisper so as not to disturb her. Not that it was possible, given all the tequila she drank. He should have stopped her a couple shots in, but how could he? From what he'd learned, her whole life was lived at the directive of others. He refused to be another one.

He should get up off the bed and leave. Just one more minute.

How many people had he known in his life who would sacrifice so much for their family? Not many. Hell, last week, one of his friends griped about sacrificing a whole day to help his brother move.

Joel liked to think he was a charitable person. Was he? How far would he go with his time and his money? It was hard to say since he'd never had to sacrifice time, and money was never an issue for him.

With the share of the family business left to him by his grandparents, he didn't have to work if such was his pleasure. He would work, though. Lazing around on an income he hadn't earned wasn't his way. His parents had done a good job instilling his work ethic. Okay, so his recent excesses tell a different story, but that wasn't him. Not really.

He enjoyed the money, the nice things, and the good

times it bought. Accomplishments were what he needed to feel human, to feel like a man. It shamed him now, how he'd never given money much thought.

He worked for pay. He had a healthy income, aside from what he earned, thanks to the business his grandfather started and his allotted share in the company. His family was very charitable. He'd always considered himself a part of their donations. Maybe he should look into supporting some causes of his own. This little drunken angel was inspiring him.

"Wait," Maddy said. Not passed out after all. Though, she wasn't far from it. Her words were muddled, and her eyes were glossy slits. "Take the blanket from the closet. "And this."

She flung an arm over. Her fingers flexed but couldn't pick up the other pillow, as they were grasping at the air two inches above it. She frowned and then grunted in frustration.

Joel couldn't help but chuckle. "I'll get it," he said. He leaned across her to grab the extra pillow.

His face paused a few inches above hers. As he got hold of the pillow, Maddy lifted her head and kissed him on the lips. She then fell back and passed out cold.

Chapter 11

"Pasta salad!"

Almost finished with her shift, Joann stifled a yawn and stared at the lady from behind the hostess lectern.

Sunlight poured in through the front windows, giving a pleasant sense of warmth to the air-conditioned diner. From behind her, bubbled the sounds of the restaurant business. Silverware clinked on thick plates, and occasional laughter broke into the constant chatter, all of it cushioned by soft music floating from four ceiling speakers. Food smells permeated everything, mostly good. Sometimes the greasier smells roiled her stomach.

Joann stared at the woman before her. The creases on her face placed her somewhere in her seventies, thin, bordering on skinny. Hazel eyes, tense and lively against her dark-tanned skin, eyebrows plucked to remnants.

The woman could have stepped out of a 1950's sitcom. Pink sponge curlers covered her head like a wig. She wore a shiny, powder blue housecoat and clean, white sneakers. No makeup other than red lipstick on lips as thin as a butter knife. In her hands was an empty, party-sized storage bowl with a lid.

"Excuse me?" Joann said. She must have missed something. Too much on her mind lately, the lead-up to her best friend's wedding, then Maddy running away. Her mind was having trouble keeping it together. She tugged her white blouse over the waist of her jeans and focused on the woman.

Focus. It had eluded her all day. What little sleep she'd had the night before had been sporadic, worried she might sleep through Maddy's call. If her friend even called. She deserved Maddy's cold shoulder, and no amount of spin gave any real justification.

Maddy had every right to be mad at her. What kind of a person encourages a friend to enter a marriage she doesn't really want? Or worse, turns her back on a friend who is reaching out for support. A crappy friend, that's who. Just because her intentions were good didn't make her right. Maddy had all but pleaded for her backing. Joann had let her lack of confidence in Maddy blind her to Maddy's needs.

The woman in the housecoat and curlers stomped her foot. "Pasta salad! I said pasta salad! You have it here, don't you?"

"Um, yes, we do," Joann said. A strand of auburn hair had come loose from her ponytail. She tucked it behind her ear as she stared at the woman.

"Last night, my husband informed me we're having a party this afternoon for his golf buddies and their wives, the inconsiderate jackass. He'd known all day and forgot to mention it till bedtime. He's vying for the team leader position. If he doesn't get it this year, he says he'll quit the team."

Joann blinked at the woman. "I'm sorry to hear that."

"Not as sorry as I'll be if he doesn't get out of the house twice a week for golf. Since he retired, it's the only time I have to myself. You know, to do my beauty treatments, get my housework done, read without being interrupted because he can't find something in the refrigerator. It's a box! How many places can the salsa hide? This is a desperate situation here."

"I see."

"Now I have all these people coming over this afternoon, and I have to make a damn good impression, you know, so they'll want to come back. It's up to the team leader to host at certain markers, a winning streak, the opening of the season, the end of the season, etc. I've got everything else covered, but I don't have time to make a pasta salad." She held the bowl out to Joann. "I need pasta salad. This is an emergency."

"I'm sure we can accommodate you."

"Hey, do you sell whole pies?"

"We do."

"Great. I have a cake, but a pie selection would be good."

"I'll see what kind we have today."

The glass door swung open, and Maddy's grandmother, Sophie, blew in wearing a leopard-print top over black leggings and leopard-print ballet flats on her feet. She was not wearing her usual smile.

Her red hair was teased, sprayed, and swooped back from a face with no makeup except for red lipstick. It was the first time she'd seen Sophie without mascara, powder, and blush. Sophie didn't go to her mailbox without all her makeup, but today she'd only spent time on a quick swipe of red over her lips. She glanced at the woman in a housecoat, curlers, and lipstick. Must be a generational thing.

"I have to talk to you," Sophie said. Her voice had such an unfamiliar tone of urgency Joann's skin prickled. Sophie didn't get rattled. She was the one who did the rattling.

"Sophie. What are you doing here? Is Maddy all right?"

Sophie adjusted her giant, zebra-striped purse on her shoulder. "Maddy never came home last night. Have you heard from her?"

From what Rachel had told them, Maddy was on her way home. "No. I left a message on her cell, but she hasn't called or texted me back. Did she call the house again?"

"Not since Rachel and Sam bullied her."

"Pasta salad." the woman in the housecoat said. "And Pie."

"Yes, in a minute." To Sophie, Joann said, "But Maddy said she was on her way home."

"She never showed. That's all I know."

"Hey." the woman in curlers said. "I have an urgent situation here!"

Joann waved the attention of one of the waitresses. "Beth, would you help this lady, please?" Beth nodded and led the pasta salad lady to the counter in the back.

"I left a message on her phone yesterday," Sophie said. "I told her to call me if she needed anything and to call me when she got home. I fell asleep in front of the TV. When I woke up, I figured she got home late and tired and crawled into bed. I called the house after my shower this morning. Sam told me she was still gone. He's worried sick. I'm a little worried, too."

"Where do you think she could be?"

"I don't know. I was hoping you might have some idea. All I could think of was home, the Yarn Barn, my place, yours, Owen's, or Rachel's. I checked on all those this morning. Nothing."

Joann thought it through. It didn't take long. "I don't know. There aren't any bars where she'd go for a drink. Maddy almost never drinks anyway. She doesn't have any hangouts, or places she likes to wander. You know Maddy. Most of the time, she's either at home or at work."

Sophie tapped her purse with her red-painted fingernails. She wasn't even wearing any of her rings. "I thought she'd take off for a while, maybe be gone a few hours, then come back and tell everyone the wedding was off."

Joann cringed inside. She and Sophie had had a minor argument in the ladies' room yesterday, not long before Maddy disappeared. Sophie said Maddy didn't really want to get married. She said her granddaughter didn't have enough joy about the marriage.

Joann had the same feeling but still argued Maddy was just nervous and she should go through with the wedding. She couldn't stand the thought of poor, gullible, innocent Maddy out in the dating world. It could be so harsh.

When Maddy walked in on them, Sophie took her granddaughter's hands and, in her direct fashion, told Maddy she didn't have to go through with the wedding if she didn't want to. She even offered to drive the getaway car. Said she was going to wait out front for the next few minutes with her car keys in hand. Joann laughed as though it was a joke. Maddy did, too, but it was forced.

Once Joann and Maddy were alone, Joann gave her opinion. Her insensitive, crappy, insulting opinion.

Her intentions were good. Maddy was used to being insulated in her life. Not such a bad thing. Maddy had never had to deal with a lousy boyfriend or a rotten, cheating, scumbag husband like Joann had. Owen was a decent guy. A little stuck-up, on occasion, a bit bossy. But Maddy would have a good, easy life with him. No worries. No heartbreak. No waking up alone and in debt after her husband maxed out their credit cards on his girlfriend.

Nor would Maddy know true love.

True love. Did it even exist? Joann had loved her husband. Her husband had loved…some skank he met at work. Maddy was so removed from the real world a guy like Joann's ex could take advantage of her. She'd only meant to steer her friend in a safe direction. But that wasn't her call to make. God, she was as bad as Maddy's father and sister.

"What was I thinking, to stand out in front?" Sophie said. "I should have had the car ready and waiting out in back. It was too risky for her to escape out the front."

"I should have snuck her out to you."

Sophie stared at her with her sparse eyebrows raised. "You changed your mind?"

Joann struggled to keep from bursting into tears right there in the foyer of the restaurant. "After you left the ladies' room yesterday, Maddy turned to me. She was looking for support to help her call off the wedding, and I didn't give it. I told her she was just nervous. I told her she'd have a good life with Owen, that if she'd been out in the dating world, she'd know how awful some guys can be and how lucky she was to have him."

"Just because your ex-husband was a bum doesn't mean…"

"I know! I know!"

The truth ruptured her, and the tears flowed. Sophie

plunged elbow-deep into her bathtub-sized purse and found a tissue for her.

Joann dabbed at her eyes. “I’m a terrible friend.”

“You’re a good friend. You got sidelined by your own crap.”

“You didn’t. You’ve had *three* husbands.”

“I had three adventures.”

Despite her misery, Joann laughed. She couldn’t help it. Sophie was a treasure. The woman saw everything in life as an adventure, even bad marriages. Must be why she was happy most of the time. Maybe attitude was the secret to a long life.

Joann dabbed at her eyes. “Has anyone talked to Owen?”

The wrinkles between Sophie’s eyes deepened to a scowl so intense it sucked in her whole face. “That lying jackass.”

Joann froze. “What did Owen lie about?”

“I called his cell phone this morning right before I left the house, you know, to see if he’d heard from Maddy. He said no. Then he said he was home, and he was going to stay home in case she showed up at his place. He said he’d call the minute he found out anything.”

“You don’t believe him?”

Sophie jammed a fist on her narrow hip. “Something in his voice, I don’t know, I just had a feeling. So, I drove by his place first. It was only fifteen minutes after I got off the phone with him. His garage door was open, and his car was gone.”

Joann wiped the smeared mascara from under her eyes and tossed the tissue in the waste basket near the door. “Maybe he knows where Maddy is, and he left to go get her."

"Still means he lied to me. I don't trust him."

"I didn't trust him either, at first. But I got over it." Then Joann remembered what her mistrust had led her to do.

"What?" Sophie said. "You thought of something. I can see it on your face. What? What is it?"

"Yes. Well, um—"

Two women entered the restaurant. They were in their early twenties, stylish jeans, and concert T-shirt. One wore black, high-heeled boots, and the other one had on those popular slip-on sneakers. They were both laughing.

"I'll be right back," Joann said to Sophie. She slipped two menus from a shelf behind the hostess lectern and spoke to the women. "Just the two of you?"

"Yes," the one with the boots said. "Could we have a booth by the window?"

Joann stepped back into the dining area and scanned the booths by the window. "You're in luck. We have one open."

The young women followed Joann to the booth. She returned to the foyer to find Sophie pacing.

"What?" Sophie said. "Spill it, girl."

Joann lowered her voice. "I never told anyone. I'm a little embarrassed about what I did."

"Oh, please. Everybody's done stuff."

"I know, but…"

"Would you feel better if we traded secrets? Here," Sophie said. She leaned close to the side of Joann's face and spoke in her ear. "I once had a threesome with the Brooker Brothers."

Joann popped back. "The…you mean those brothers

who had a string of hit songs a million years ago?"

"It wasn't quite a million years ago."

"Sorry."

"And they were hot."

Joann laughed. Sophie grinned, not the least bit embarrassed. The threesome with the Brooker Brothers was more of a brag than a trade. Someone should write a book about this woman's life.

"So," Sophie said. "Come on now, tell me what you did."

"Okay, well, when it comes to men, I have a trust issue. I know it. I'm working on it. But when things were getting serious between Maddy and Owen, I wanted to make sure Owen wasn't cheating on her. So…" Joann swallowed hard.

"I'm not getting any younger here."

"I hid a tracker under the seat of Owen's car."

Sophie laughed and clapped her hands before giving Joann a big hug. "So, was he?"

"I tracked him for a few weeks, but he wasn't cheating, so I gave up on it. I meant to sneak the tracker out of his car. I kept missing the opportunity, and after a while, I forgot about it. I don't even know if the thing still works. Do you think he knows where Maddy is, and he's not telling us?"

"Maybe. She could have mentioned something to him about someplace she likes, gave him a clue without realizing it. When do you get off work?"

Joann lifted her wrist to see her watch. "Ten minutes."

The words were no sooner out of her mouth when Maria, the sweet young woman taking the next hostess shift, walked through the door. Fifteen minutes later,

Joann and Sophie were zipping down the road in Sophie's flaming red sports car, Joann's phone in her hand, following the signal still emitting from the tracker beneath the seat of Owen's car.

Once they hit the highway, Sophie slid in a CD. and pushed a button. "I'll Always Remember You" by the Brooker Brothers poured out of the speakers. Joann pressed her lips together to hold back the laughter. Her restraint didn't last long, and it didn't matter. Sophie was laughing, too.

Chapter 12

It's so cold. Why is this bed so cold? And so hard?

Maddy made a big effort to open her eyes, which were all tacky, like nail polish not quite dried. She managed to get them to a squint. What she could see of the world was out of focus and very, very white.

She blinked a few dry, uncomfortable times and forced her eyes open some more. It jostled the anvil pounding around in her head. She sucked in a breath. Had she eaten a bag of cotton balls?

Maddy blinked. What was she seeing? She couldn't tell. With some force, she got her eyes open a little more. She blinked again and gave her head a small shake. Big mistake. The anvil in her head dipped a fast twirl into her stomach and threatened to plunge up the sour glob churning around in there.

One slow breath, and then another. There. What…what *is* that? Oh no. She was facing a bolt-cover on the base of the toilet. Oh, God. She was curled up on her side on the bathroom floor.

She rotated until the back of her head was on the floor, and she was facing upward, staring at part of the ceiling and at the white underside of the sink.

Maddy worked her jaw a moment before raising her fingers to touch the odd sensation on her cheek. She glanced sideways before looking up again. What she was feeling was the daisy pattern of the linoleum floor imprinted on her face. But her bathroom floor didn't have a daisy pattern. What the hell?

Oh. A few memories peeked around the pain in her head.

She'd gotten drunk last night. And she spent the night in a motel. With a strange man. On what was supposed to be her wedding night after her marriage to Owen. Twenty-four hours ago, she was a normal person facing a normal life. Now she was hungover on the floor of a motel bathroom. How could so much change in such a short period of time? And how could she fix everything she messed up in her life?

She'd worry about everything later. She'd worry about it a lot. Right now, she needed to get off this floor. She shifted and tried lifting her head, but the pounding anvil made it weigh about two thousand pounds. A pathetic moan slogged through her dry lips.

How long had she been lying on this floor? Felt like days. Stiffness made her stretch, then the soreness made her stop. Those external discomforts paled in comparison to the retched death wish playing out in her head and stomach. Even her eyeballs had a headache.

She was half-covered with the blanket she last saw on the motel bed. She must have dragged it into the bathroom. Hopefully, she'd lain down on the floor in here after Joel had gone to sleep on the couch, and he didn't know where she'd spent the night.

Joel! Her last memory of the night returned and would have slammed her to the floor if she weren't already on it. She'd kissed him! She got drunk on tequila and kissed Joel. Oh! How could she? She was engaged! How could she behave that way? How could she do any of the things she had done since yesterday morning when her life was on track?

More important now, how could she get off this bathroom floor before Joel woke up and found her this way?

"Good morning. How are you feeling?"

Too late. It was Joel. He was standing up, looking down on her from over the toilet like Godzilla over a high rise.

"Oh, I'm fine," Maddy said. She did her best to sound casual as if they were old friends talking over lunch. Did he notice the scratchiness in her voice? "And how are you today?"

He looked fresh and well. The nerve.

"Oh, I'm all right," he told her. "I drove down the street this morning and got something for you to eat."

Breakfast. The image of anything food dropped from her pounding head to her sour stomach. All she wanted now was to get herself, and any scraps of dignity she had left, off the floor of the bathroom. She would consider eating sometime next week. Maybe.

"Would you like to get off the floor now?" Joel said. He didn't wait for an answer. He stepped around her and crouched down to help.

"Yes, thank you. I believe I would."

With a sympathetic smile, he helped her to a sitting position. She swayed a little and Joel placed a strong hand between her shoulder blades and steadied her. "I did try getting you back to your bed last night, but you didn't want to go there."

"I didn't?"

"No. You hugged the toilet until I agreed to two things."

Oh God. "What things?"

"One, let go of you. Which I did."

"And two?"

"You asked me to sing to you."

"I did?"

"Yes. You said you wanted a song or you wouldn't go to sleep. I was tired. All I could think of was the Happy Birthday song, so I sang it to you. You smiled and laid your head on the toilet seat."

Was she groaning out loud or just in her head?

"I tried again to carry you to the bed because you were using the toilet seat for a pillow, and I didn't want to leave you that way. I was afraid your head might roll in, and you'd drown. Terrible way to go."

The imagery. Someone kill me, now.

"You got pretty grouchy and told me to leave you there, or you'd bite me like a vampire."

She didn't need someone to kill her. She could just die of embarrassment right there on the spot.

"I wrapped a towel around my neck in case you were serious about the vampire thing. Then I lifted your head, put the lid down, and laid your head on the lid. I got the blanket from the bed and wrapped it around you."

"Thank you," she said. Quiet, as if to dampen the humiliation. Could it get any worse?

"Besides, I figured you'd um, need the facilities later."

A vague memory materialized in slow motion. Did Joel hear her throwing up in here last night? Oh no. Maybe he'd even seen her. Well, there was her answer to how much more embarrassing this can get.

So here she was, still sitting on the floor of a motel bathroom. It was the first of her long list of problems. Second, she still didn't know if she could stand up without his help. Her head and her legs were yelling accusations at each other. Everything in between was somewhat gelatinous. At this point, one more embarrassment shouldn't matter. But it did.

"I'm fine now." She would have smiled to support her statement, except the inside of her cheeks were stuck to her teeth.

"You're looking pretty pale," Joel said. He stared at her as if she was a new breed of bug. "Are you sure you're all right?"

No, she wasn't all right. Not even close, not in any way. Not physically or mentally, not inside or outside or any other side. She'd run away from her wedding, hitchhiked, got drunk on tequila in a motel room with a man she didn't know, and wanted so much to use a toilet seat for a pillow she threatened to bite a man like a vampire if he didn't let her. And sing her a song. 'All right' was a distant memory.

Since her dignity had already suffered the swirl and flush, Maddy told him the truth. Her brain wasn't functioning well enough to hide it anyway.

"My head is pounding. My tongue feels like it's too big for my mouth. And it's all fuzzy. And my brain feels kind of—" she waved her fingers in the direction of her head. "—Furry."

"What about your stomach?"

"Don't say stomach."

Joel chuckled and touched her cheek. "But you do have a lovely floral design on your face."

She'd tell him to shut up, but describing her pathetic state had drained her. Besides, she needed his stupid help to get off this stupid floor.

Joel slipped his arms under Maddy's, scooted her

out from beneath the sink, and lifted her as if she weighed no more than a pillow. Her head was so heavy it was hard to hold up, and her stomach was skipping and dipping like a carnival ride full of month-old kitchen scraps.

One glance in the mirror told her she looked as bad as she felt. Her red eyes gave her a demonic appearance. Her hair looked like an experiment gone awry, and she had to pick off little strips of toilet paper stuck to her chin. How did that happen?

"I never drank like that before," she said. "Really, I hardly ever drink."

"Actually," Joel said. "The phrase most people use on a morning like yours is, 'I'll never drink again.'"

"I agree with them." She did. Even her occasional glass of wine was out. And forget about ever having margaritas with Grandma Sophie again. The thought of it almost had her crumpling back to the floor.

"A long, hot shower will help you feel better," Joel said. He frowned at her and plucked off another strip of toilet paper from the back of her head. "Let the steam do its work."

Maddy considered a long, hot, steamy shower. It sounded wonderful. But so much effort.

"Take your time, Angel." Joel pointed to a bottle of water on the sink. "Drink some water. You're dehydrated." He left the bathroom and closed the door.

The first thing Maddy did was brush her teeth and then her entire mouth twice. It did make her feel better to get the nasty film out of there, but the task was exhausting. She sat on the closed toilet lid and took a little break.

God, she felt awful. This must be what it felt like to

be poisoned. All her internal organs were infected with the contamination of last night's stupidity. Her entire body was parched, from eyelashes to toenails. Oh, the water Joel left for her. She opened the bottle and drank it all. It helped a tiny bit.

Every movement riled the nausea. Her bones were as stiff as table legs. Even her muscles had the flexibility of a plastic doll. This must be what the Tin Man felt like when his oil can was empty.

With more than a small bit of effort, she stood up again, only to have her head try to pound her back down. She fought it, holding on to the edge of the sink. Her whole body was crispy and wavy at the same time. This was going to be a very long day.

Maddy stepped toward the shower to turn on the hot water, hoping the steam would give her enough energy to take off her clothes and get in. She shoved open the shower curtain. The bathtub was wet.

She looked around. A wet towel hung on the rack. Joel had showered with her lying there on the bathroom floor, with daisies being pressed into her face and toilet paper dangling from her head like the cheapest jewelry ever.

What if she'd woken up when he was standing there, naked and wet? Didn't he care? And why the hell was disappointment picking at her, making her hot?

Her long, miserable day had just got longer, and, impossible but true, even more embarrassing.

****

The siren blared seconds after the blue and red flashing lights assaulted the night along Route 66. Owen barely had time to get his fly zipped before the cop rounded the back of his car.

He was tall and broad, young but already thickening in the middle. His chin was up, his grin was snide, and he had a swagger. All methods of intimidation. Well, Owen wasn't one to be intimidated.

"Officer," Owen said. His tone was civil, not at all nervous. He wasn't a criminal. He straightened his bowtie and tuxedo jacket.

"Sir."

Good. Some respect.

"Did you know public urination is a misdemeanor?"

"A crime?" Oh, please. After sitting in that stink waiting for the crew to clean up the mess, he'd finally gotten off the highway and onto Route 66. He had to go, no one was around, so, what was the big deal? "Give me a break. I've been stuck in traffic for hours. I had to take a leak."

The officer glanced down the road to his right, and then to his left. There wasn't a headlight or taillight to be seen.

"Do you see traffic, sir?"

Wiseass. "No, I don't see any traffic. Not *now*."

"When did you see all this traffic?"

"Back there on the highway." He didn't have time for this. Maddy was still in the same place, and he was closing in on her. She could take off again at any moment. Maybe it'd be best to give this guy a quick explanation so he could get going.

"Okay," Owen said. "Here's what happened. There was this manure truck."

"A manure truck."

"Yes. And manure was everywhere."

"Must be why you reek. Were you walking around in this manure?"

"What? No, of course not."

"What else did you see, sir, besides traffic and manure?"

"Well, there were lights."

"Lights?"

"Yes. Big lights. You know, so everyone could see the manure."

"Sir, have you been drinking?"

"Drinking? Look, I'm in a hurry. But no, I have not been drinking."

"Let's just make sure."

Twenty minutes later, Owen passed every drunk test the cop gave him. More aggravation, more wasted time. All because his bladder had been full. Could nothing go his way today?

"There," Owen said. His loss of patience harshened his tone. "I told you I hadn't been drinking. Between you and that damn manure truck, I've lost precious hours when I should have been searching for my wife."

"Your wife is missing?"

"Yes. Well, she will be my wife once I find her and get her down the aisle. I have *got* to go. I passed all your tests. I'm sorry I pissed on the side of the road. It won't happen again. Goodbye." Owen swung around toward his car, more than ready to get the hell out of there.

"Sir."

Owen fumed but did his best to plaster a civil expression on his face when he rotated back toward the cop.

"Yes, Officer?"

"Just want to make sure I have this right. It's the middle of the night, and you're stalking a woman."

"Yes. No! You don't understand. She's already

mine. I mean, she will be."

"Once you get her down the aisle."

"Yes. Right. That's why I'm wearing this tuxedo."

"Okay. Let's go down to the station, and you can explain it all to me."

"You can't arrest me for stalking. I mean searching for my own wife, I mean fiancée."

"You're not under arrest. We're just going to have a little talk."

"No," Owen said. "I don't think so." Enough already! He was low on time, short of patience, but long on attitude.

"Sir—"

"I pay your salary. You know that, don't you? So, why don't you get in your fancy little car, drive away, go get some donuts, take a nap at your local speed trap, harass someone else? I don't give a shit. Bye-bye, Officer Asshole."

"Okay," the cop said. "Now you're under arrest."

Owen took two steps before he was face-down on the trunk of his car.

"For mouthing off? Talking back isn't a crime."

"Indecent exposure is."

"Indecent—"

The click of the handcuffs put an end to Owen's attitude.

****

Owen gave the officer at the desk one final glare before storming out of a police station the size of a convenience store. He'd lost a huge chunk of time because of some bullshit charge. Public urination and indecent exposure! Him!

Then they'd had to verify every damn thing he'd

said. Phone calls proved there had been a manure truck overturned on the highway tonight. The police officer called Pastor Murray, and yes, he was supposed to get married yesterday, but the wedding had been postponed. How was he going to explain *that* phone call to the pastor? He wouldn't. He'd find someone else to marry them.

Once they learned his fiancée had run away, Owen had been able to convince them Maddy had called and asked him to come and get her. This whole thing was a terrible misunderstanding.

They finally let him go with a hefty fine yet to be paid. Not to mention getting the charge off his record was going to cost him a small fortune.

Owen threw his tux jacket, vest, and bow tie in the back seat, flopped into the driver's seat, and slammed the door. Along the horizon, the sky stuck out an orange tongue. Morning was here, and all he'd gotten for a full night's effort was the reek of manure and an arrest record.

He squeezed his eyes shut and rubbed them with the heels of his hands. For a little while last night, he'd dozed off on the awful cot in his cell. It wasn't near enough, but sleep was going to have to wait.

They hadn't let him have his phone, so he had no way of knowing if Maddy was still where she stopped last night or if she'd moved on to somewhere else. She'd had plenty of time to get damn far away by now.

Owen lifted his phone to his face. Nothing. Of course, they wouldn't have the decency to charge it for him. He rummaged through his console, found his cord, and fired up his phone. He tapped the tracker app as soon as the phone lit and got his first break.

Maddy was still there.

****

Once Joel heard the shower running, he trotted down to the office to check them out of the room. He should probably thank Ted for the bottle of tequila, too. Opening the door to the office, he chuckled. Maddy might have some other words for Ted about the tequila.

A thin, elderly woman stood behind the counter. Must be Ted's wife. The Mrs., as Ted called her. She wore a pale green farmhouse dress, and her gray hair was in a bun on top of her head. A pair of glasses hung from a thin gold chain around her slender neck.

Joel got in line behind the only other person in the office, a blond-haired man with a dark suntan wearing black pants and a white dress shirt.

"I'm sorry, sir, but I can't do that," Ted's wife said to the man.

"Sure you can," the man said. He had a snarky tone, bordering on nasty. His dress clothes were wrinkled, and he smelled like manure. "Just look in your big book there and give me the room number."

"It's against policy to give out that information."

"It's your place. You make the policies. Just change it!"

"You don't understand, sir—"

"I don't have time for this," the man said. He leaned over the counter and snatched the sign-in book. Ted's Mrs. screamed, "No!" And grabbed the book so they were both holding onto it. She was no match for his strength, so Joel jumped in to help. He grabbed the book with one hand and the man's wrist with the other.

"Let go, you asshole," Joel said to the man. "What are you going to do? Beat up an old woman?"

The woman turned her head toward the back and yelled, "Ted! Ted!"

Five seconds later, Ted blasted through the curtain. He must have heard the commotion and already been on his way. "What the hell is going on out here?"

Before he finished the question, he reached his arms around his wife and added his hands to the grips on the book.

"Let go, old people," the smelly, blond-haired man said. "You don't want to mess with me today."

"That's it," Joel said. He head-butted the man hard enough to make him let go and step back.

It only stunned the guy for a moment, and then he took a swing at Joel.

Now, one might think spending a fair amount of time drinking in bars gives a man no advantages in life. Well, one would be wrong.

Due to his own foolishness, or maybe one of his friends', Joel had learned how to fight. He'd paid for the knowledge with some black eyes and a few bruised ribs. But those early mistakes had taught him the necessities of street fighting.

Joel ducked the guy's punch and popped up with one of his own. His fist landed, and so did the stinky blond man, flat on the floor, on his back. Ted marched around the counter, bent, and grabbed the guy by his collar.

"Get the door, kid," Ted said.

Joel obliged. Ted, showing an impressive degree of strength for an old guy, dragged the heap of stunned man out the door and dropped him in the parking lot. The man rolled over and maneuvered himself to his hands and knees. He stayed there, shaking his head like a wet dog.

"And don't come back, ever," Ted said. He then

lifted a foot, clad in a clunky, serviceable shoe, and shoved the guy over.

Chapter 13

Joel shifted the truck into third gear. Maddy slouched back against the seat and stared at the road through slitty eyes.

"How's the hangover?" Joel said.

"My death wish is easing a little. Your Hangover Helper reduced it to a low-grade misery."

Maddy dug through her purse and found her sunglasses. She didn't lift her face until they were protecting her eyes.

"Better?" he asked.

"How can the sun feel so bright with all this cloud cover?"

Joel leaned toward the steering wheel and glanced upward. The sky must be feeling benevolent today. Or it could be pity. A mass of white, wispy clouds filtered the worst of the sun's glare. "It'll get better. When you feel up to it, we'll stop and get something more substantial for you to eat."

"Have you eaten?"

"I had some chips and orange juice."

Maddy made a nauseous face at him, and he chuckled.

"What did you call your hangover cure again?" she asked. "Not that I ever plan to have another one of these horrid mornings, but my Grandma Sophie might be interested.

Joel grinned. “Your grandma?”

“She’s quite the character.”

“I call it C.A.G.E. It stands for Crackers, Aspirin, Ginger ale, Eye drops.

“How did you come up with that combo for a hangover remedy?”

“A lot of trial and error.”

Maddy’s burst of laughter died a quick death. Joel knew from experience the head-clanging it caused. He felt for her.

“A lot of trial and error, huh? How many hangovers have you had?”

Joel focused on the road as his mind fumbled for words. It’s not like he was a drunk or anything. He’d never had a problem with any kind of substance. But with each failure he’d suffered at work, his drinking *had* increased. Maybe he should examine that.

“I’m sorry,” Maddy said. “I didn’t mean to pry. It’s none of my business.”

Joel paused before the confession. “It’s all right. I’ve had a few hangovers.”

“I wasn’t judging you. Who am I to judge anyone? Not after the day I put in yesterday, for sure.”

Good thing Joel didn’t have a hangover. His own burst of laughter would have floored him. “You’ve been a busy girl.”

She laughed at herself, toned down this time. “I have.”

“For you, it was just one night,” Joel said. “Truth is, I’ve had many.”

Maddy gave a slow, scant shake of her head. “Don’t worry. I’m in no position to criticize.”

“Me either.”

"Thanks. I'm hoping that in exchange, you might be kind enough to forget seeing me at my worse."

He'd felt so sorry for her last night. She hadn't built up the tolerance to alcohol he had. Holding her hair back for her as her body rejected the tequila invasion and then wrapping her in a blanket was all the help she would allow. He couldn't have done much more for her anyway. He'd been there. He knew.

He had stayed with Maddy for a while, sitting beside her on the floor, petting her head like she was a sick dog. Every time he thought she was asleep, he tried carrying her to bed, only to have his hands slapped as she told him to leave her alone. The vampire threat she'd made was funny and a little scary. He'd slept with the towel around his neck.

"Consider it forgotten," he said.

"Thank you."

"You know," Joel said. "You didn't have to make the bed in the hotel."

"Habit. I can't sleep in a bed and not make it." She arched her spine in a stretch and then settled back into the passenger seat. For a few minutes, they were quiet. The truck hummed and rattled. The radio played something soft, the volume down low.

Maddy took a deep breath and let it out slowly. "I need to call Owen."

"I charged your phone this morning. I'll park and take a walk so you can have some privacy."

"Not yet. I want to give him the morning to calm down so I know he's really listening to me. Sometimes when I talk to him, it's like, like he's only listening with his eyes."

"How does someone listen with their eyes?"

She tucked her hair behind her ears. "He looks at me like he's listening, nods his head, occasionally says 'uh huh' or 'oh really,' but I get the feeling his mind is somewhere else. My father is the same way. Don't take this personally, but just once I'd like to talk to a man and feel like he's really hearing what I say. I mean, is it all men, or just the men in my life?"

"Not fair, Angel. It's like saying all women are bitches just because some are."

"Hm. I suppose."

****

Maybe Joel was right. In a way, he had proven it. Last night he was a good listener. Of course, she'd been too drunk to make any kind of accurate assessment. Given the poor clarity of her memory of the night, he could have been watching TV the whole time.

Joel plunged his hand into a brown paper bag on the floor between them. He handed her a bottle of water. "I drove to the little store this morning. That's where I got everything. Here, drink this. You're still dehydrated."

Maddy twisted off the top and took a drink. It was like watering a dry plant. She took another long swallow.

"Thanks," she said. She glanced over at him. The mark on his head was faded, but… "Hey, what happened to your knuckles? They're all red. Oh, God, did I hurt you last night?"

"No, no. Had nothing to do with you. When I was down in the office to check us out, some asshole was giving Ted's wife a hard time about something. He was trying to take their sign-in book. We tussled a little."

"You fought, like, a physical fight?"

"It was over quick. The guy had no skills. I'll tell you what, for an old dude, Ted's got some strength. He grabbed the guy by the collar and dragged him out to the parking lot all by himself."

"What happened to the man then?"

"The last time I saw him was when we drove out of the parking lot of the motel. He was sitting in his car with his face close to the rearview mirror, looking at what is sure to become a black eye."

"Wow."

"Oh, I almost forgot," Joel said. He dipped his hand into the paper sack again and handed her a small, colorful bag. "Here."

"Candy?"

"I guess you don't remember. Last night you were talking about how you used to love this particular candy."

She had zero memory of talking about candy. Maddy stared at the shiny little bag in her hand with smiling fruit floating around the name. "It's Fruity Fruit candy. I loved it when I was a kid."

"That's what you said."

"I can't believe you got Fruity Fruit candy for me."

Joel shrugged. "It wasn't any effort. I saw it in the store this morning. You'd just told me how much you used to like it. No big deal. Hey, don't get all weepy on me. It's just a little candy. It doesn't mean anything."

"You were listening."

Joel laughed. "This is the first time I ever saw a woman happy about being wrong."

He'd been listening. He heard her. About something so minor as a pack of candy, he heard, he remembered, and he acted. Joel was wrong. It was a big deal. It skewed what little she thought she knew about men. What else had she been wrong about?

Maddy blinked her eyes and shifted her gaze from Joel back to the pack of candy.

Could it be all she had to do was tell Owen what she wanted, and he, too, would be attentive and thoughtful? Maybe her sober speech was so indirect, so meandering and wimpy, he *couldn't* pay attention to what she was saying. Was it possible all the discontent she was blaming on Owen was her own fault? Maddy blinked slowly. Her head hurt too much for all this thinking.

Maddy slid a glance across the cab of the truck. Joel must have sensed her gaze because he turned her way and gave her one of his dimpled smiles before he faced the road again. She watched him a little more.

He was leaning back but not slouched. More casual, as though the drive was for pleasure and not a desperate day on the job. There was a natural ease about him she hadn't noticed when she thought he was a serial killer. Probably because, at the time, she thought he was a serial killer.

"What's so funny?" he asked.

"What?"

"You laughed."

"Oh. I was thinking about how we each thought the other might be a serial killer."

Joel laughed, rich and hearty. Again, so natural. Everything about him unpretentious. "Yeah. We were sitting here afraid of each other."

Maddy struggled to keep her laughter low. "Yeah. That's what I get for watching all those scary movies."

"You like scary movies?"

"I love them."

"Me too."

Maddy's eyes widened. "Really?"

"You bet. I just watched *Bring Me Your Dead* a few nights ago."

"I've seen it twice! The scene with the buzzsaw—"

"I groaned out loud!"

"Me too!"

Joel glanced over at her. "I never would have guessed you to be the kind of person who watches those things. I see you more as a light musical kind of woman."

"Oh, no. Give me something to make my blood pump, put me on the edge of my seat, make me jump."

Joel shook his head and gave her another one of those grins. "You are full of surprises, Angel."

"Well there's something no one has ever said to me before. Everyone sees me as my days."

"Your days?"

"Work, cook, clean, sleep, repeat. My life is…beige. I think that's why I like scary movies. They add color. Fear, suspense, it's all bright red. While I'm watching, I am, too."

Maddy stared down at the little bag of candy still cradled in the palm of her left hand. "Thanks for the candy."

"You're welcome. And if it means anything, I think you're pretty damn colorful."

She raised her head and stared at Joel for half a minute before she spoke. Joel didn't understand how dull she really was, the plainness of her life, of her. He'd seen her on the only colorful day she'd ever had.

Didn't mean it had to be her last colorful day. Maybe there's a little bit of Grandma Sophie in her after all.

"It means something," she said.

Maddy lifted the candy to her nose and breathed in the fruity scent. It carried with it old memories of a brief and beloved childhood and the fresh moment a man had retrieved it for her.

After lowering her left hand to her lap, Maddy rolled down the window and let her right hand hang out. She cupped the warm air rushing by, and it flowed like a waterfall along her arm and down her body. Her hair blew back from her face. She leaned her head back and stared at the passing landscape.

Route 66 was different during the day. More businesses were open, and the closed places looked less abandoned than nostalgic. They passed a grouping of a dozen or so teepees. A sign in front of the squat white building beside them read, *The Teepee Motel.* Maddy smiled and thought she'd like to stay there sometime. Today, the notion had a viable feel.

Ahead, shafts of sunlight streaked through breaks in the clouds and shone down like celestial tubes all the way to the ground.

Maddy rolled up the window and lowered her right hand over her left, covering her bag of candy as if to protect it. The truck rolled along at an easy speed. Low music from the radio soothed. She drifted off, wishing the trip would last forever.

Chapter 14

The sun fell fast, like it had a bad leak, calling a quick end to the day. Maddy removed her sunglasses, tucked them in their case, and dropped the case in her purse.

They'd been able to stay on Route 66, as it took them right into Flagstaff. After passing through some unexpected woodsy terrain, they rolled through a lovely downtown area. Shops with window displays, a variety of restaurants, a couple of bars, and a lot of red-brick buildings, some with arch-topped windows. Clean streets, along which grew some slender version of ash trees. Golden columbine splashed yellow here and there.

Joel followed the instructions from the GPS on his phone mounted on the dashboard. He made a couple of turns before steering them into a parking lot with fresh blacktop and newly painted white lines.

He drove to the end of the row of small to mid-sized stores, none of which bore corporate names. Some were quaint, with red or white brick. Others dressed in stucco in a variety of pastels. They blended together well, in an eclectic sort of way. Some outside décors like potted plants and wooden benches did a good job of tying them together.

The lighted sign of a candle shop called *Wicks* switched off as they passed. Someone in an olive oil store flipped the *open* sign in the glass door around to say *closed. Toys, Toys, Toys,* was the last and largest of the stores. Powder blue stucco with peach trim and statues of a teddy bear and a giraffe posed on either side of the front door.

Joel drove the truck around to the back and parked behind the toy store not far from two green dumpsters. He shut off the engine. The sudden silence like a death knell. Joel's face changed; his faded joviality replaced with apprehension. He had a lot riding on what happened in the next few minutes.

"I don't know how long I'll be in there," he said.

"Don't worry about me. I'm fine. Do you want to practice what you're going to say?"

"Thanks, but no. It's better if I don't sound rehearsed."

"Okay. Good luck, Joel."

She stared at him as he walked to the metal security door at the back of the toy store, feeling his anxiety. Joel knocked on the door. A moment later, it opened, and he disappeared inside.

Between her naps, Maddy had sipped on water and nibbled on crackers, bless Joel's thoughtful heart. They'd stopped to eat along the way, but all she'd been able to handle was a cup of soup. Even that was a challenge. A vague but notable taste of tequila still clung to her insides.

While her body was slow to heal, her mind had bounced back with amazing swiftness. The downside was the milky thoughts of her future. One of her problems—and the list kept growing—was what she *should* do did not jell with what she *wanted* to do. Mostly because what she wanted to do was too embarrassed to show itself.

Oh, people knew she sewed. She'd designed and sown clothes for her sister, Grandma Sophie, for Joann. But she'd never told anyone designing clothes was her dream career. It was too pie-in-the-sky, too out there, too…for other people.

One shop over from the toy store, a door opened. A trim woman around Maddy's age, wearing a blue pencil skirt, a white blouse, and some sensible flats, stepped out with a bag of trash. She carried the bag toward the toy store and heaved it into one of the dumpsters. As she walked away, the woman stopped at a scrap of paper on the ground. She scooped it up and tossed it into the dumpster.

She had to be a business owner. The way she was dressed, the way she cared about the tidiness surrounding her store, the pride in her shoulders, and the purposefulness of her crisp steps.

The woman marched back into the store, maybe to do some paperwork or straighten up a little before going home. Maddy chewed a thumbnail.

She could never be like that. The one time she'd taken her life into her own hands, she'd made a mess of things. She could have *told* Owen she didn't want to marry him instead of running off like a child and leaving him to handle the ordeal she'd left behind. Or, she could have married him and had a good life, as Joann had pointed out to her right before she'd bolted. But could she have pursued her dream of designing casual clothes?

No.

Women capable of pursuing careers were a different breed. No crossovers allowed. She didn't have the self-confidence and, frankly, doubted she had the talent to really make it in such a competitive business. So, what now?

Maddy scooted out of the truck. On the opposite side of the stores, where the blacktop ended just a few yards away, was a vacant stretch of land with patches of wild growth. She paced along the edge.

While she was still some distance from normal, her hangover had dwindled to a mild headache and a manageable amount of queasiness. Joel's hangover cure was a good one. One thing she knew for sure, if she ever saw a bottle of tequila again, she'd run the other way.

Maddy paused to stare across the undeveloped land, marred by the occasional cigarette butt or piece of broken plastic. She stretched in the last bit of warmth from the day, yawning fresh air into her brain, but all she found in the peace of her solitude was despair.

Her own business. She beat back the urge to get her design book out of her bag and stare at her work again. What would be the point? She was right about one thing. She didn't have the confidence of those crisp steps. Probably for good reason. The people closest to her knew it. Well, except for Grandma Sophie. But Grandma Sophie would support her if she said she wanted to sprout wings and fly to the moon to plant daisies. Sophie was a loving, sometimes delusional woman. Maddy knew her limits. It was all too depressing.

The back door to the toy store opened. She didn't have to see the grim expression on Joel's face to know what happened. He rolled out a flat cart stacked with carboard boxes. He guided the cart to the back of the truck, rolled up the door, and loaded the boxes.

Turning away from her own misery, she strolled over to the truck as he packed the last of his hope in the back.

Joel wiped his hands on his jeans as she approached. "The end."

"Can I see one?"

"One of the dolls? If you want to." The flaps were open on the last cardboard box he'd loaded. Must have been the ones on display. From that box, he removed a smaller, rectangular box. He tipped his head toward the others in the back of the truck. "She also has some set-ups for different jobs."

"Sold separately?"

"That's standard." He sat on the back of the truck and handed it to Maddy. "Here, Angel, happy birthday."

Thin cardboard of purple and pale green swirls decorated three sides. The front had a see-through covering showing the doll and two children, a boy and a girl. Maddy took the packaged doll and hopped up to sit on the back of the truck.

What she saw was a pleasant surprise. The doll looked better than she'd expected after hearing Joel describe her. She was about twelve inches tall, not terribly overweight, nor was she unattractive. Brunette, with a pleasant expression and a touch of makeup. She was actually a very realistic imitation of the average woman. Not a perfect body, not a perfect face, but lovely just the same. Except for the retched dress she wore.

The awful dress made her look like one of those perfect housewives of some 1950's sitcom. Huge white polka dots on a bright, pea-green dress, tight around the waist and flared out at the hips, stopping mid-calf.

This version of a woman would be more comfortable in obligatory servitude than going off to build her own career.

"Oh God," Maddy said aloud. Goose bumps popped

up on her arms, and the nausea was back. Still, she continued to stare at the doll. "She's me."

"What are you talking about?"

"She's what I've been, what I'll continue to be if I marry Owen."

Joel kept a steady gaze on her. "You do have a choice, you know."

Sure. She could continue working at the Yarn Barn for the next forty or so years. Maybe never connect with anyone because she was too picky. She'd die alone in some tiny apartment because by the time she realized all she said no to with Owen, her best years would be history. Or she could marry Owen and forever wonder what it would have been like if she'd had what it takes to pursue her dream. Some choice.

The ache in her head ramped up from more than last night's stupidity. She needed to think about something other than her own crappy life for a while. All this introspection was killing her.

Staring at the doll again, a doll with a lot of potential, she said, "I have one question."

"Ask away."

"Well, you gave her this normal appearance, made her a woman of today with a job, and kids, all so she would be realistic. Why did you dress her like a woman from forever ago?"

"What's wrong with her dress?"

"So they're all like this?" Maddy said. She held up the doll to emphasize her dismay.

"Well, no. Some of the dresses are bright pink with white polka dots."

Wow. Bright pink would be even worse than the green. Poor little doll.

Joel stared at her as if waiting for some sort of explanation. Maddy looked again at the wonderful doll in the horrible dress, a dress available in an even more horrible color.

"What? What's wrong with her dress?" he said.

Okay, tact and sensitivity were called for here. "It just seems, well…" Maddy stared at the dress again. She imagined it in bright pink. "Hideous. Truly, truly hideous." Wow, what happened to all her tact and sensitivity? Must be the hangover.

Joel straightened his spine. "My grandmother was a lovely woman, and this is how she dressed."

"Exactly. Put the doll in something from this decade. Something a woman like her would actually wear. Jeans, yoga pants, T-shirts, sneakers, maybe a comfortable sundress, even some office wear. But dear God, lose the giant polka dots. Wait here."

Maddy handed him the doll, hopped down, and trotted to the cab of the truck. Half a minute later, she sat next to him with her design book in hand. She thumbed through some pages until she found what she was looking for.

"Here, something like this," she said. She slid the book over to him and pointed to one of the designs. The pencil-drawn model wore a pair of jeans with a comfortably worn appearance, a maroon T-shirt with a row of tiny, peach-colored flowers around the scooped neck, and a pair of white sneakers.

Joel stared at the drawing. "When I designed the doll, I didn't give her clothing too much thought."

"No kidding."

He slanted her a look. But an instant later, he shifted his attention back to her book, turning the pages and studying her line of casual clothing designs.

"Joel, I know this sounds crazy, but…I have an idea." Excitement buzzed through her veins. Maybe this was it, the wormhole for possibilities and some form of self-confidence to make an appearance. Must be because she could picture it. She could *feel* it. This doll, her clothing designs. It would work.

"Maddy, I see where you're going with this, and—"

"Good. Now picture it. I could make any of these clothes in doll size. It would give her a whole new look, like really a woman of today. I'll bet she'd sell then. Come on. Let's do it. Let's do it today, right now."

He stared at her like she had monkeys crawling out of her ears. But she couldn't let go of it. Fabrics and colors shoved aside her headache to crowd her brain. Enthusiasm flourished so fast she couldn't keep up with it. The doll was a great idea. She just needed a realistic wardrobe.

"What do you think?" she asked.

****

He thought Maddy was sweet, beautiful, talented, and just as crazy as the moment he saw her standing on the side of the road in her wedding dress.

She swiveled to face him, folding her legs beneath her, and sitting back on her heels. Her wheat-field hair slid in loose waves over her shoulders as she shifted her gaze to the book he still held and then back. Her breathing had quickened, her eyes wide, alert, her face flushed with excitement. It was the most beautiful sight he'd ever seen.

He'd been on the cliff where she now perched, ready to fly, only to fall. Setting Maddy straight was going to kill him.

She believed what she was saying. There was a time when he would have, too. Not anymore. This last effort of his had damaged the business's reputation. They'd get it back, but not with anything he created. He couldn't let them down again. What's more, he couldn't stand the thought of Maddy suffering the inevitable failure.

"I…Yes, it would have been better to dress her like this instead of what I chose. But I don't think it would have made a difference in the sales."

She leaned forward a bit, a woman riled. "You don't know that."

"I do. I've been in this business my whole life. I know when it's time to cut your losses. Investing more in this doll would only dig a deeper hole."

"How about this, I'll make some new clothes for these dolls, at my expense—"

"I'm not going to let you pay for new clothes for her."

"I have some savings. It'll be my investment. I'll make her some more appropriate clothes, then we'll take her back here for another try. I'm sure if you show the new her to the owner of the store, he'll give it a little more time."

The last thing he wanted was to extend his failure. His neck tightened, as did his aggravation, at his failures, at his uncertain future, and at Maddy for dredging up hopes too far gone for life support.

"No," Joel said. His voice hardened while irritation at everything threatened a harshness she didn't deserve.

"You didn't give it any thought. If you'd just—"

"I said no, Maddy."

He'd made no effort to keep the anger from his voice, but he should have. The hurt on Maddy's face, the defeat, the death of her short-lived dream at his hands, was a knife through his heart. But it was better than letting her get her hopes up in the clouds. He'd dropped from up there. He wouldn't let her suffer such a fall. Better for her to suffer this small disappointment now than a crushing let-down later.

Maddy returned the doll to the cardboard box, and Joel leaped off the back of the truck.

"I'm sorry," he said. He offered her his hand, which she ignored, and got down on her own. He rolled down the door and locked it before facing her.

She stared up at him, clutching her book to her chest, one last glimmer of hope drilling into him from her emerald eyes. "Won't you at least think about it?"

His heart constricted. His conscience tapped on his shoulder, but he ignored it and kept his expression hard. Putting her through a failure would be so much worse. Better to cut it short now.

Unable to maintain eye contact, Joel said, "The doll is finished. It's time to go back." He then circled the truck to the driver's side.

****

Owen glared at the red light from his position four cars back. "Come on already."

He leaned over to have another look at his face in his rearview mirror. The swelling bruise at his left eye had gotten worse, turning into a half-plumb, limiting his vision in the eye. Nothing he could do about it now.

Shifting his attention, he lifted the right side of his upper lip and used his tongue to push on his eye tooth. When that freakishly strong old man had dropped him in the parking lot, his face hit the ground hard. The tooth wasn't loose, but he kept checking it anyway. He could have a delayed reaction. Maybe the awful swelling on the right side of his mouth was keeping the tooth in place.

He huffed and threw himself back against the seat. The stupid damn traffic light was still red. So, he stayed where he was, behind some big, bald, muscle-bound bruiser in a little red sports car. Owen doubted the man could even fit in there if the top wasn't down. The guy looked ridiculous in the tiny car, but whatever. No skin off his nose if the fool had no sense of proportional propriety. Probably compensating. All those steroids.

Owen swept a glance left and right. No traffic in either direction. He gave his steering wheel a few quick knocks. "Come on, light. Turn green already."

The dot on his tracker app showed Maddy was still stopped. For the second time today, he was so close he could walk to where she was stopped. If the light didn't change soon, he might park and do that. He huffed again and had a look around.

The town of Flagstaff looked like a decent enough place. The downtown area was lined with shops and restaurants. People strolled along the sidewalks on both sides, some carrying bags. Owen paid little attention to any of it. Again, he stared at the tracker app. Maddy was still there, wherever there was. The tracker gave a position, not the names of any places.

He smoothed back his hair and tidied his wrinkled, dirty, and probably smelly self as best he could. She didn't deserve the attention to his appearance, not after all she'd put him through. He did it anyway. He still had his dignity. Though, with every passing minute, Maddy was taking another bite out of it.

What had gotten into her? For the life of him, he couldn't figure. He was offering her a good life. She'd never have to worry about anything. All she'd have to do is take care of him, of their home. It's what she'd always done, so it's not like he was asking her to live so different than what she was used to, than what she already knew.

Simple. Maddy was simple. He should have considered the big picture from the start. The whole wedding thing, the planning, the organization, the stress, it was too much for her. She wasn't used to having so much on her plate. He should have taken things in hand himself. Well, it's a mistake he wouldn't make again.

The traffic light changed to green. *Finally!* Owen let his foot off the brake and rolled forward with the rest of the cars. He glanced at his phone to make sure Maddy hadn't taken off again. *Crap.* The red dot was moving. Where was she going now? *Hold on…* She was headed this way! All he had to do was pull over and wait and—

Boom!

Crap! Crap! Crap!

Owen stared at the little red sports coupe he'd just rear-ended. The driver-side door opened, and the big guy unfolded, drawing up to his full size. The man marched to the back of his car. His face reddened, and his muscles flexed outside the sleeveless gray T-shirt. His angry expression darkened to fury when he viewed the damage.

Owen threw his cell phone on the passenger seat. He grabbed his wallet as he got out of the car. Maddy was so close! As long as his car was drivable, he could throw money at this problem and make it go away.

The guy, who was the size of a porta-potty, swung around toward Owen. "You asshole! I've only had this car for two weeks!"

Owen gave a quick glance at the damage. The front of his own car was slightly crunched, but the stupid little ladybug of a car he hit had hardly any damage.

"It's just a scratch on your bumper," Owen said. He yanked a wad of cash from his wallet and handed it to the guy. "Look, I'm in a big hurry, and I really need to go. Here, this will more than cover that little nothing."

"We need to call the police."

"For this? Don't be ridiculous. Here," he said. "Take the money, get your car fixed, spend the rest on protein shakes, upgrading your gym membership, whatever you want."

The big guy gave him a squinting scowl. "We're not leaving here without a police report."

"Don't be a fool. You're coming out way ahead on this deal. I don't have time for this!"

Owen threw the money at the guy and spun around as the bills floated down. He took half a step before the bruiser had him by the collar. The bully used his other hand to call the police.

In an effort to escape, Owen shook his body, wet dog style, but the guy's grip might as well have been a steel clamp. The muscle man lifted him up until he had to stand on his toes to catch a breath. Owen dug his fingers between the collar of his shirt and his throat to keep from choking.

He gulped in some air and was about to expel it, along with some choice words, when he saw Maddy. She was in the passenger seat of a truck, looking out her window in the opposite direction of him.

"Maddy!"

Her name would have been a shout if he wasn't struggling to breathe. Instead, it was a croak. With a burst of fresh determination, Owen struggled in earnest, twisting his body in every direction, giving his best effort to escape. He was so close!

Owen managed to twist enough to give the muscle-head a good kick to the shin. It was a huge mistake. Instead of crumpling to the ground, or at least letting go, the bulging mass of wrath got even angrier. The guy's face reddened, and he actually bared his teeth and growled as if he were a feral beast.

Owen swallowed hard. *Crap.*

The last thing Owen saw was a giant fist rocketing toward his good eye.

The next thing he saw when he awoke who knows how long after, lying in the road like squashed gum, were Maddy's grandmother and best friend staring down at him.

Chapter 15

Maddy was hurt. For about five miles.

Then she was pissed. Pissed enough to use the word pissed, even if it was only in her mind.

He wouldn't even try. He wouldn't give her idea a minute's thought, not a single moment of consideration. Joel was stubborn and closed-minded, and…and, well, the last straw on this camel's back.

Now, one might argue that particular straw had fallen yesterday and was the impetus for her running out on her wedding. They'd be wrong. She hadn't been angry. She'd been freaked out, scared, even, but not angry. Not like now. Yesterday, her pulse hadn't pounded behind her eyes. Her jaw hadn't been tight. Her shoulders did not have the almost painful rigidity they did now.

It took a few miles of road rolling beneath the tires before the full picture of her life popped into focus, sudden and powerful. Like adjusting binoculars until the clarity was stunning.

Her dad worrying about her being on her own without a husband, as if she was less than all the other women who did just that, like she couldn't feed herself without guidance. Owen expecting her to spend the rest of her life being his good little girl. Now Joel, who wouldn't take even one minute to give her idea serious consideration. They all clipped her wings. Men. Wingclippers, that's what they were. She was tired of it. Damned tired.

She'd been denied a mother, her youth, college, experiences, and now, the chance to turn her dream into a reality. And that wasn't all. The way everyone thought about her shorn her of any sense of dignity.

So, what was she going to do about it?

What could she do?

Maybe it was too late. Had her time to fly passed with her twenties? Had it ever even been in her? Maybe some people were never meant to soar. Even Joann guided her toward marrying Owen. Maybe they all knew better than she did. The thought withered her because it might be true.

These were people who cared about her, who'd known her. They had no reason to steer her wrong. Okay, she hadn't known Joel very long, but he'd proven to be a decent sort. Her father, her sister, Owen, even Joann, all people who loved her, thought marrying Owen was best for her.

So why did it feel wrong?

A sudden, tornadic gust of wind and sand struck the passenger side of the truck with a million little ticks against the metal and glass. The dust devil spun around them for a few seconds and then blew along to swirl and dance across the desert. The gritty gust zipped over the land. It swished right, then left, before disappearing somewhere behind them. Maddy envied the wind.

She had the wild aspirations of a dreamer and the prospects of a delusional sad sack. She supposed it was true then; the first step to solving a problem is admitting there is a problem. Okay, well, there it was, laid out before her. It was time to face reality, and the reality was the opinion of people who cared about her weighed more than a foolish dream.

Warm air blew in from the partially opened driver's side window. The chill rocking Maddy came from the inside. She rifled through her purse for a few seconds, digging until she found her cell phone.

"I'll park and get out," Joel said. "Give you some privacy."

"Don't bother. It doesn't matter."

She caught his glance. "I'm calling Owen. I should have called him yesterday." It's what a decent, sane person would have done. "I'm going to ask him to forgive me for humiliating him on our wedding day, and ask him if he'll take me back. My dad thinks he still wants to marry me."

"You sure you want to marry him?"

Maddy glared at Joel. "It's really none of your business."

He gave her a curt nod before giving his attention back to the road.

Maddy tapped into her contacts, scrolled to Owen, and stared at the screen. There was his name, one tap away. What was she waiting for? *Just do it. Get it over with. Wow, some way to start a life.*

"You could pursue your aspirations elsewhere," Joel said. "It doesn't have to be with my doll."

She slanted a look his way. "My designs don't have what it takes to succeed. That's pretty much what you said. So, what would be the point in wasting my time, and everyone else's?"

"Your designs are great. You misunderstood me."

"I don't think so. You're saying my designs are okay for someone else but not good enough for you."

"All right, well, I can see how it sounded that way. But it's not what I meant. Not at all."

She held out her free hand, palm up, brow furrowed, attitude rising. "So what did you mean? Explain it to me. I'd really like to know. How am I supposed to take it when you say my designs are great, but I should try elsewhere?"

"I meant...Look, it doesn't matter. Do what you want. I don't care. It's none of my business."

"You're right. It's not any of your business," Maddy said.

She stared at the phone for half a minute or so before stabbing Owen's name with her finger. Maddy held the phone to her ear.

One ring. Two rings. Two more, then it sent her to voicemail. She drew in a breath. After disconnecting, she dropped her phone in her purse and stared at her hands folded in her lap. Was she going back to Owen because it's what everyone thought was best, or going back out of spite, angry at Joel's rejection of her idea? Or maybe a lack of options. God, she was a mess.

Maddy had no idea how much time had passed before she realized the truck wasn't moving, was sitting on the side of the road. An old pick-up sped past them, the music blaring so loud she could make out the classic rock tune.

She glanced at Joel. "What are you doing?"

****

What *was* he doing? If Maddy decided to abandon her dreams and get married to this Owen guy, it was her decision. It had nothing in the world to do with him. He had his own troubles. Plenty enough to keep him busy. Yet, seeing her ambitions crushed, crushed him a little.

He'd had the means and opportunity to get his product out there. He failed, but at least he'd had a chance. *He* was Maddy's chance. No. She could sell her idea to another toy company. Having designer clothes for a doll is brilliant, especially a line of clothing women actually wore. The idea could really catch. Maddy was spot on with her creative brainstorm.

While she'd stared at her folded hands, Joel stared at the road. Two more cars passed by them. Then another.

He'd thought his ideas were great, too. They'd all turned out to be disasters. Every one of them. He couldn't trust his judgment. The truth is, there was about a two percent chance of Maddy's idea succeeding, but hell, who knows, maybe she was right. Maybe it could work.

Or maybe there was another reason he was reconsidering. Maybe he wasn't ready to say goodbye.

She was nutty and sweet. Cute as can be. She got weepy over candy and had a dream to pursue. How could he not want to spend more time with her? Besides, if he was the one to shut down her hopes and dreams, it would continue to trouble him, maybe forever. He glanced over at her.

When Maddy tapped a number in her contacts and placed the phone to her ear, a panic washed over him. His relief when she hung up was so powerful it rocked him. So much so he had to pull over so he could sit and have a good think. Could he take the plunge again? No. Yes. Maybe…Maybe.

Joel tapped his fingers on the steering wheel.

So here he was, ready to jump into another project for the toy business. It would likely fail. They would both fall from the clouds. But the rush of possibility, the knowledge that even though the odds were against them, there was still a sliver of real potential, inflated his will.

So did Maddy.

The hope she'd had in her eyes stirred an old, familiar craving. Not since his doll's inception had he felt it, the dream-can-be-a-reality kind of hope. It put him in his favorite mindset, in the beautiful slice of potential wedged between the idea and the doubts. It was a place where everything was still possible.

"Let's do it," he said.

She twisted toward him. "My idea?"

"It's a good one. We'd be foolish to not try."

"You really mean it?"

"I really mean it, Angel."

Her smile bloomed slowly but became a sunburst. It glowed strong enough to light the darkness in his head and heat the rest of him to a beautiful torture.

"So?" Joel said. "What do you say?"

A yes was in her smile, but it wasn't a guarantee. His own hope for her 'yes' stunned him to the edge of his seat. He wanted it, too. Maybe even more than he had the first time he'd run the idea of the doll through the motions.

Say yes, Maddy. Say yes.

Her broadening smile lifted him before her words.

"I say yes."

****

Owen sat on the curb near his now-parked car, ticket in hand, as the muscle-bound brute cruised away in his ridiculous little sports car. The cop car followed. Never in his life had he had any interaction with the police. In a single day, he'd had two, and they'd both ended in a bad way for him.

He stared at the ticket. It was hard to read the details, as both his eyes were now swollen. The swelling in his mouth was a little better, but it revealed his tooth was indeed loose.

Stunned, shaken, sore, and puffed, he tipped his swollen face up to stare at Sophie and Joann.

Joann scrunched up her face. "Why do you stink so bad?"

"I don't stink!" Owen said.

Sophie jammed her fists against her skinny hips. "You're following Maddy, aren't you? How did you know where she was going?"

Owen never much cared for Maddy's grandmother. She was weird and brassy, dressed wild in a lot of animal prints and loud colors, rings on at least six fingers. She didn't like him either. He could tell. They'd always managed a frosty politeness for the sake of peace. Now, the frost was so thick they'd need a snowplow to clear it.

"Um." Normally he was quick with an answer, but he was too achy, tired, and swollen to think straight. "Uh." God, he sounded like an idiot. *Get it together, Owen.*

"You put a tracker in her purse, didn't you?" Joann said.

Maddy's best friend had always been an ally. That was over now. Joann glared down at him with the same angry expression as Maddy's grandmother.

"It's not in her purse. A man should never go into a lady's purse. It's an app I put on her phone. I tucked it into a folder with stuff she never uses."

Sophie gave him a swift kick to the thigh with her leopard print shoe. The woman had a surprising amount of strength in her scrawny little leg.

"Ow!"

"That's for tracking my granddaughter." Then she kicked him again in the exact same spot.

"Ow! What was that for?"

"Because I don't like you."

Owen was rubbing the side of his thigh when he was struck with the obvious question. "Hey, how did you find me?"

The two crazy bitches shared a look.

"You tracked me! How did you put a tracker on my phone? You don't know my code."

"I didn't put it on your phone," Joann said. "It's under the seat of your car."

"That…that's got to be illegal! How dare you?"

Sophie snarled at him. "Don't make me kick you again. My foot's getting sore."

Owen muttered under his breath so he wouldn't get another bruise. "Poor thing."

The old lady's right foot rose to her toes, knee bent and ready for another kick. "What did you say?"

"Nothing."

"Well," Joann said. "Where's Maddy?"

Owen pointed. "Headed down the road, the last I saw of her, in the passenger seat of a truck."

"What truck? Who was driving?" Sophie said.

Owen stared up at her through his puffy squint. "How the hell would I know? Some guy."

"Well, come on," Sophie said. "Get in my back seat, turn on your app, and tell me where to go."

"I'm not going with you. And I'm tossing your tracker out of my car before I leave."

"See, Joann, I told you." To him, Sophie said, "I

knew you'd be an ass about it. Well, you're not going anywhere without this." She dug around in her giant, zebra-striped purse, and her hand flew out with…something mechanical-looking."

"What the hell is that?" he asked.

Sophie shot utter disdain at him. "It's a distributor cap. What kind of man are you?"

"I'm so impressed," Joann said to Maddy's grandmother.

"I learned how to do it a long time ago when I first started tending bar. It's an easy way to keep drunks from driving. They'd just think their car broke down, and I'd call a taxi for them. I always put it back so they could get their car the next day."

Owen stared up at Maddy's grandmother. Of all the nerve. "You took my…Put it back right now. I demand it."

Sophie shook her head. "If he keeps this up, I'm going to have to buy some of those hard, pointy-toed cowboy boots."

As he quivered at the thought of getting kicked with hard, pointy-toed cowboy boots, the two women each grabbed one of his arms. His struggle was lame. Due to his various injuries, lack of sleep, and many hours since he'd had a decent meal, dizziness had him leaning into them more than fighting to get away. For all the same reasons, he couldn't whip up a good verbal argument.

By the time he'd strung a few words together, the two women had him stuffed him into the tiny back seat of Sophie's car.

Chapter 16

Joel got off the route and steered them into the first town they found. The main street was six blocks long, with five cross streets and not a lot of traffic. Most of the shops were still open.

Joel slowed the truck, and the two of them scanned the stores. Maddy leaned forward at the cross streets, searching for what they wanted. At the end of the road, Joel rounded the block and cruised the cross streets while Maddy kept a sharp eye.

A few people meandered about, saying hello to others. Everyone appeared to know everyone else. Small-town life. Halfway down the second cross street, Maddy bolted upright.

"There!" she said. She pointed to a yellow building with a big, black sign lettered in white.

Joel parked in front of the pawnshop. Twenty minutes later, they left with what Maddy said was a decent sewing machine. One step closer to their goal and one notch higher on her excitement meter. Next, they found a fabric store, and the real fun began. All of it Joel got from watching Maddy.

The woman had a radiance to her, almost feverish, as she talked about doll-sized purses, accessories, and comfort clothes.

Comfort clothes. She's a plastic doll. Comfort didn't matter. But it did. At least, the appearance of it did.

Maddy was right, and her positivity had her revved.

Sometimes she wouldn't even finish a description of an idea before another one took hold of her. She knew what she was doing. This was her thing. For the first time since he'd picked her up, she moved and spoke with utter confidence. So much so it roused his own optimism from its grave. Some of his old self, too.

As they wandered the aisles, Joel played a little. He found a stuffed lion in a display and shoved it toward her from between two rolls of fabric, roared, and made her laugh. She got him back two aisles over when she popped out and shouted 'Boo', making him jump. For a few minutes, they hid from and dodged each other, playing like children. They'd laughed loud enough to draw the attention of others.

Maddy pressed her lips together and almost ironed out her smile. "Okay, no more goofing around. We've got work to do," she said. Within seconds, the work absorbed her. Then it had her in complete possession. Nothing escaped her attention. Everything she passed, everything she touched, was under consideration.

Maddy's eyes glowed. Her face was flushed. She was on fire. A blazing rocket headed for the stars. His doubts struggled to keep a foothold.

He helped pick out fabric as best he could, but it was all guesswork on his part. Most of the time, he stood by the cart, mesmerized as Maddy's delicate fingers tested fabrics, compared colors and textures. Her creative mind worked, forming outfits to save his creation from the garbage bin.

Joel stood beside a button display. A long table against a wall held several upright boards with buttons tacked to them. Beneath each button was a cup full of corresponding buttons. For a few minutes, he pretended to look at the display. The effort lost its bones, and before long, his attention focused where it wanted—to Maddy.

She made picks from a huge choice of threads. A crease formed between her brows, along with an expression as serious as if she was figuring out nuclear codes. Maddy held one of the spools up and inspected it against the fluorescent ceiling lights. Her tongue peeked out from between her lips, slow, and just for a moment. Joel leaned back and almost upended the button display.

A rush of lust shot through him, powerful, alien. Oh, he'd been drawn to plenty of women in the past, even had a few short-term girlfriends. He'd need a calculator to count the one-night stands. All of them were attractive in their own special way. He enjoyed women and did his best to see they enjoyed their time with him.

But this…this was unlike anything he'd ever experienced. This was desire with some depth to it, one threatening to grow roots, and he wasn't sure how he felt about that.

He enjoyed his single life. It was the only thing about his life he *did* enjoy anymore. Never had he misled a woman into believing there'd be more with him. Sometimes he'd see guys use such a tactic, playing with a woman's feelings to get what they wanted. It sickened him. He'd gotten good at figuring which women were just out for some fun and which ones were marriage-minded, and he left the latter alone. It was a rule he didn't break.

Now here he was, sucked into a woman who was literally dressed for a wedding when he met her. The dress alone should have served as a physical deterrent. But it didn't. He wanted her enough to feel possessive, something else he'd never experienced before.

Doesn't matter. She's engaged to someone else.

But not married.

Another rule of his; he didn't play around with married women. It was a line he never crossed. Ever. He didn't have a lot of rules in his life, but he was firm on the ones he had. Now, Maddy was graying everything. She'd run away from her wedding, so was she still engaged? Even she couldn't say for certain. Still, to make a move on her now would be to take advantage of a vulnerable woman. He would never do such a thing.

So, Joel stayed next to the button display, savoring the view of her, fantasizing about more.

Every so often, Maddy would glance his way. When their eyes met, she always smiled. A real smile. Not flirtatious or seductive, not drunk, just pure joy for what they were doing. Her smile was so big it crinkled her eyes and burrowed into his chest. If he wasn't careful, he might fall for her. The hell with his rules. He'd have to watch it and keep a safe distance.

Joel managed to drag his attention away from her and stare at the buttons. He lasted all of five seconds. Maddy was a magnet, and he couldn't pry himself away. He should have tried harder.

Something in the clearance bin drew Maddy's attention. She bent over, reaching for whatever it was, teasing him without meaning to. Honest to God, he made an effort to turn away, to at least not stare at her fabulous little bottom like some pervert. But he was just a man, and the pose bewitched him.

All the blood rushed from his head, releasing any control he'd had over his thoughts. Erotic images he shouldn't have about a woman pledged to someone else swamped his brain.

The fit of her jeans was too good to be legal, the way they stretched over her rounded rump. When she lifted up on her toes to lean farther into the clearance bin, his body reacted to her in ways far, far inappropriate for a fabric store.

What the hell was wrong with him? Looking away from Maddy was impossible. If he was going to get his thoughts under control, he'd have to physically get away from her. He spun around, stepping at the same time. Joel crashed loud and chaotic into the button display.

The table lurched, the boards tumbled, buttons flew into the air like the chips of an angry gambler.

****

Maddy had never, ever, had so much fun. Playing around, making each other jump like characters in one of those scary movies they both loved so much, had her laughing from her belly. She laughed again now, thinking about that silly stuffed lion popping out from between bolts of fabric and Joel roaring.

The laughing, the silliness, the goofing around, were all things her little sister enjoyed while Maddy was doing her best to keep their home life normal. It was as if Joel was giving her back a bit of her missed youth. For that alone, she would forever appreciate him.

The clearance bin caught her attention. After a debate at the pawnshop over who would pay for the sewing machine, they'd agreed to split the cost of everything. She had some savings. This was her investment, too. So, she kept an eye out for bargains. Penny-watching was nothing new.

She'd just gotten a grip on a four-pack of odd-colored thread from the clearance bin when a crash snagged her attention.

Maybe laughter wasn't the best response for the moment, but she couldn't help it. The sight of Joel sitting on the floor getting rained on by buttons was hilarious. When the downpour finished, he stared up at her, somewhat stunned and a little embarrassed, with at least half a dozen buttons on his head.

Chuckling, she knelt beside him and picked buttons out of his hair. "What happened?"

"Oh, um, I tripped."

"Are you hurt?"

"No. I'm all right."

****

It wasn't quite true. His body already ached for her. Now, with her this close, his other senses took over what was left of him. He caught a soft scent. Perfume? No. Her. Just her. Flecks of gold accented the green of her eyes. Her touch, limited as it was, had every sense buzzing. Her lips…God, her lips, inches away, full, a tiny smile, tempting his weakened will.

****

Maddy picked out the last button, careful not to tug out any of his hair. It was an effort to hold back a chuckle with him sitting dazed on the floor with a head full of buttons. Then, she met his gaze, and her smile faded. Her whole body got soft and melty.

He didn't look embarrassed over the incident anymore. He didn't look like there'd been an incident at all. His eyelids lowered a fraction. His expression intensified as if they were alone, maybe sitting on a blanket before a fireplace drinking champagne, about to…

He was thinking about kissing her. It was obvious.

It was unnerving. It was…exciting.

Before another thought made its way into Maddy's head, Joel leaned forward, and his lips touched hers. Light and sweet, no more than a whisper of a touch. The effect, however, was a ramming bull.

Heat flared, and passion and boldness collided, vitalizing Maddy like a supernatural force. The buttons she'd been holding clattered to the floor. She grabbed hold of his shoulders and kissed him with a raging might.

Joel wrapped an arm around her waist, squeezed her closer. His other hand cradled her head. His fingers massaged the base of her skull, wringing a moan from her throat. She had no idea the spot was so sensitive, so erotic. Maddy lost her breath and fell on top of him. This is what passion is supposed to feel like, an overwhelming, all-powerful, mindless, driving desire. She wanted more.

****

The want surging through Joel made every thought but Maddy skip the tracks. He tightened his arm around her, hugging her as close to his body as he could, but it wasn't near to close enough, or naked enough. If he didn't get more of her and soon, he might die of frustration.

His hand reached up the back of her shirt. Skin, silky and warm, heating further beneath his touch. She gasped, moaned, her entire body responding to his impassioned strokes. He was on fire for her.

"Maddy," he said against her lips. "I—"

"Excuse me."

The woman's voice was harsh, ticked-off, scolding. They deserved it.

****

Maddy jerked back and straightened her shirt as best she could with her trembling hands. What the hell were they doing, making out on the floor of the fabric store? Her co-workers at the Yarn Barn would be horrified.

****

In their scramble to get up off the floor, they knocked into the other table. Joel caught the second button board before it, too, took a tumble. The woman, somewhere in her fifties, crossed her arms and scowled at them through her tortoiseshell glasses with the beaded chain. A severe bun sucked up all her dark hair. Red lipstick and slashes of blush on her fair skin accentuated her puckered expression.

"I'll get all these buttons in the right cups," Joel said.

He was halfway to the floor when the woman's words snipped him straight.

"Just. Go."

Joel followed Maddy as she pushed their cart to the front of the store in what could easily be called a walk of shame. It was obvious from the looks they were getting, the woman who stopped them wasn't the only one who'd seen them behaving like a couple of bonobo apes.

Two other employees gave them disapproving glares. The few customers in the store parted at their approach, backing away as if they were radioactive. Word of this disgrace would surely make its way to the next fabric expo. The gossip in the velvet section would be brutal.

****

After the most embarrassing checkout of her life, Maddy helped Joel load their purchases into the back of the truck. Still not having said a word, they climbed into the cab, sitting in silence as they stared out the windshield.

"I'm sorry," Joel said.

"No," Maddy said. "I am."

"It was my doing."

"I threw myself at you."

"I started it by kissing you. Then I got hold of you and wouldn't let go. That's on me."

Maddy scooted around sideways and, for the first time since they parted lips, faced Joel. "I didn't want you to let go."

He stared at her, head tilted just a fraction, gaze focused. What was he thinking? That an attraction they'd both been feeling had burst through? Or that she was a woman with an uncontrollable sex drive, and he was convenient. Which was worse?

"Look," she said. "Let's just forget about it, okay? Like it never happened. Yes, that's what we'll do. It never happened."

Joel stiffened. "It happened."

"No, it didn't."

Joel frowned at her. "Yes, it did. And don't even try telling me you didn't like what we were doing. I may have started it, but you were on me like a bear on honey."

Maddy gasped and hooked her fingers together so she wouldn't slap him for pointing out her bad behavior. Then she let go and waved her hands in front of her forehead like she was swishing away bees.

"What are you doing?" Joel asked.

"Washing it away like I used to do for my little sister when we were kids, and one of us said or did something we wanted to take back. There." She dropped her hands in her lap. "It never happened."

His laughter had her hooking her fingers together

again and glaring at his arrogance. It didn't matter if he was right about her liking what they'd done. It was vulgar of him to point out her eager participation. What happened to his manners, his sense of decency? Ten minutes ago, she was ready to rip off his clothes. Now she'd like to rip off his head.

Joel's laughter faded, and his tone had a note of seriousness. "You can scrub all you want but you can't erase the past. It happened."

Maddy shook her head. "Did not. Never did. Never would."

Joel jammed in the key and started the truck, but he didn't put it in gear. He just sat there, staring out the window with a stiff jaw. Maddy flipped herself to face forward and did the same. *Arrogant ass.* She was tempted to get out of the truck and walk away. He wouldn't be the first man she left this week.

No. This was business. Well, it would be from now on, period. No more kissing. No more touching. No more thinking about kissing and touching.

"Do you need any more?" he asked.

A slow turn of her head had Maddy facing him again. "Excuse me?"

Joel ticked up his little smile, the one that made his dimple prominent. "Any more stuff to make the clothes?"

Oh, right. The clothes. Business, Maddy. Stick to business. Okay, did she have everything she needed to get to work? She ran a mental inventory. Thank goodness she'd gotten everything she needed before, well, before nothing happened on the floor of the fabric store.

"No. I don't think so," she said. Then it hit her. "Oh..."

"What?"

"I can't go home to make the clothing," she said. "There's a mess waiting for me there, and I'm not ready to deal with it."

"Oh, right," Joel said. "We can't go to my place either. Someone from my family might show up, and I'd rather they not see anything until it's ready."

Maddy chewed her lip for a second. "I could call my Grandma Sophie. She'd let us use her apartment."

"Someone else from your family might show up there."

"Hmm. Yeah, they might." Plus, you never could tell what Grandma Sophie might have going on at her place, anything from cookie party to a seance. "Any ideas?"

As Joel stared out the window, a slow smile lifted his face, accentuating his dimple again. Damn him for being so attractive. She didn't lift her hands, but Maddy did another mental scrub. That exciting, exhilarating incident on the floor of the fabric store didn't happen. She sighed at the memory, then scrubbed again.

Back to business. "You thought of a place?"

Joel's grin widened. "Maybe the Presidential Suite at the Last Chance Motel is available."

The last time they'd checked into the Last Chance Motel, she'd had lingering concerns about him being a serial killer. Now she had to worry about her own hands and keeping them to herself.

Oh, but that rush of lust was exquisite.

Scrub, scrub.

What was wrong with her? She'd never been sexually aggressive. Until a few minutes ago, sex wasn't even something she thought about much. Sex with Owen was pleasant. His skills were…efficient. But he'd never driven her to madness, not like she'd just experienced.

Maddy did another mental scrub.

This was a business venture. Nothing more. What happened in the fabric store was a release of built-up tension. She'd had a stressful day, followed by a drunken night, followed by a monster of a hangover. Yes. That was the reason for her temporary loss of sense and dignity. It was over now. Business. This was business. *Scrub the rest from your mind, girl.*

"The Last Chance Motel is perfect," she said. "Come on, let's go. I'm anxious to get started."

Joel shifted into first gear, and the truck rumbled down the road, heading back to Route 66 and the Last Chance Motel. Maddy kept her eyes straight ahead, except for once when she glanced sideways for a peek at Joel. A sexy, cute partner in a variety of dreams.

Scrub. Scrub.

****

"This is illegal, what you're doing. It's torture."

Both Sophie and Joann rolled their eyes. Okay, well, Owen could only see Sophie in the rearview mirror from his place in the tiny back seat of her sports car, but he'd bet hard cash Joann did it, too.

"I'm starving!" he said. It was true but secondary. If they stopped somewhere to eat, he might be able to figure out how to get away from them and get to Maddy first. "And roll up your windows. I'm getting dust blown in my face."

"We're not rolling up our windows," Sophie said. She spoke loud enough for him to hear her over the air whooshing through the car. "You stink too bad to leave them up."

"I don't stink!"

"Look at your app," Joann said. "Is Maddy still stopped?"

Owen shifted what he had of his vision to his phone and raised it closer to his face. Both eyes were swollen to slits making it hard to see much of anything. His whole face hurt. His stomach growled, his head ached, and yes, he stunk. It was bad enough he had to sit in this cramped backseat and smell himself. He wasn't going to admit it to these two car-wrecking kidnappers.

Joann twisted around and reached for his phone. "Here, let me look."

"No! It's my phone, my fiancée. I'll look." He did, shifting the phone so he could see the whole screen with his limited vision. "She's still in the same spot, some little town not too much farther. Come on, just something quick. I haven't eaten much of anything in two days. I'm getting light-headed. I'm afraid I'll pass out it I don't get something in my stomach."

"All right. I guess we could all use something to eat," Sophie said.

Joann nodded. "I wouldn't mind a break from the stench."

"I don't stink!"

"Just fast food," Sophie said.

Owen flopped back against the seat. "Fine!"

"We'll leave the car doors open when we go in," Joann said. "Let the car air out."

"I don't stink!"

"Owen," Sophie said. "You are way past stink and well into…what's the word I'm looking for?"

"Reek?" Joann said. "Odorous? Rotting?"

"No, but those are good."

"Foul. Rank."

"He fits all those, but none of them are the word I had in mind," Sophie said. "Something like deathly, decay, decomposing…"

Owen's head fell back against the seat. "Oh, for God's sake."

Sophie snapped her fingers. "Putrid! That's the word."

Owen sank farther into the cramped space. He needed a shower, food, and sleep. Maybe he could doze off for a few minutes and take a break from this nightmare. In an effort to get more comfortable, he shifted so he could lay sideways, his head resting against the small window. He took a deep breath to calm himself and would have lost his lunch if he'd had anything in his stomach. God, he really was putrid.

His first bit of luck had him drifting off to sleep. He woke up to the car jerking and the shout of Sophie's angry voice yelling, "Shit!"

Chapter 17

Ted greeted them with a big, welcoming smile. The presidential suite at the Last Chance Motel was available. To thank Joel for his help with the crazy, stinky guy who'd tried taking their sign-in book, Ted rented it to them for the same price as a regular room again.

While Maddy set up her workstation at the small kitchen table, Joel carried up a dozen dolls. She kept one with her and had him set up the rest on the coffee table where the night before she'd learned to shoot tequila. The memory bounced her between a laugh and a cringe.

Maddy found the measuring tape in one of the fabric store bags and used it on the doll, writing down every number and checking them with a second measurement. Using those numbers, she copied ideas from her design book onto the pattern paper. Once that was done, she pinned the patterns to the fabric. Then she cut.

Joel got some Chinese food for them. She barely stopped to eat. Except for an occasional bathroom break and a stretch, Maddy stayed at her station at the table in the kitchenette. She was a woman focused. The used sewing machine they'd gotten at the pawnshop hummed throughout the evening, the night, and into the early morning hours.

She pinned, cut, sewed, and dressed the dolls in a variety of outfits. Why should they all be dressed exactly the same? Women aren't. Maddy had clothed six of them in varying styles of blue jeans, some paired with different color T-shirts, others had blouses. She made two with little yoga pants, two with shorts, and two with sundresses. By the time she'd clothed the twelve dolls, the sun peeked around the edges of the motel drapes.

Maddy stood and stretched some of the stiffness from her body. Her neck ached, her fingers hurt, and her entire spine throbbed in complaint. She'd never felt so great.

Exhausted and exhilarated, she circled the coffee table, on which stood twelve dolls in their new clothes. The light from over the kitchen table and the one next to the couch shone enough for her to see them well. She couldn't help but smile. Pride reduced her physical pains to minor annoyances. Pride. Her own.

This wasn't the same as the pride she felt when she'd thrown Rachel's birthday parties or put someone's favorite meal on the table. It wasn't the same as keeping the house clean and running. This kind of pride was all for her, and it made her buoyant.

She glanced at Joel sound asleep on the couch. After she'd shown him how he'd helped with the pinning and cutting. He then worked by her side until two or three in the morning. Every so often, she would glance up from her work to see him looking at her as if he was the one full of gratitude instead of the other way around.

She stood across the coffee table from the couch, massaging her neck and watching Joel sleep in the overflow of the kitchen light.

He was stretched out on his back. Too tall for the length of the couch, his socked feet were propped up on the armrest. One of his muscled arms dangled off the side. She had to smile at the little pieces of tissue still stuck on two of his fingers that had long ago stopped bleeding from the pinpricks he'd given himself.

His other arm draped across his forehead in drama queen fashion. No denying he was adorable. Maddy moved in a little closer, taking advantage of the free view.

One of his socks had a small hole in the big toe of his right foot. Such a thing shouldn't be cute, but it was. His shirt had risen up a bit, exposing abs toned to a V and disappearing into the waistband of his jeans. *All right, girl. Better look away now.*

She let her eyes wander upward, her gaze traveling over the breadth of his chest, the contours lined in the snug fit of his black T-shirt. What would it be like to lay her hands on his chest, to feel his heart beating, to make it race? She should drag herself away before boldness had her groping him again. Okay, so she hadn't scrubbed away the memory. How could she when it had been so mind-blowing to be kissed? By him.

In his slumber, Joel's lips parted a little, and she could see the even edges of his upper teeth and the slightly uneven edges of his lower teeth. The sight of him lying there, all masculine and vulnerable at the same time, tugged at her heart. And heated her body. She knelt beside the couch.

Her face was inches from his. Would he wake up if she kissed him? Would she want him to wake up to finish what they started on the floor of the fabric store? Would he set her afire again, or had it just been a crazy moment, never to be repeated?

Staring at the sleeping man, Joel's treatment of her over the past twenty-four hours played back in her head.

At home, on the rare occasions she hadn't felt well, she always got an "Oh, poor thing." It was often followed by something like, "What's for dinner?" Her dad and sister cared about her, loved her, yet they never thought of her as having needs. She was the one who doled out the care, not someone who needed it. But she was human. Sometimes she needed care, too.

Yesterday, Joel took care of her when she was drunk out of her mind and then again during her awful hangover. He'd gone out to get his special remedy for her. He tended to her needs as if it was the natural thing to do. It was so indulgent, someone taking care of her. Then again, shouldn't it be that way with the people in your world? What would it be like to have a man like Joel as a part of her life?

Be fair. Owen has plenty of good qualities.

Owen. Her fiancé. Or was he? She couldn't blame him if he didn't want her anymore. Not only had she jilted him, but she'd done it at the last minute, leaving him to deal with the fallout. Owen probably hated her. In his shoes, she would.

Her dad thought the marriage-to-be was still salvageable. Might just be wishful thinking on his part. Maybe the better question, the question her Grandma Sophie had asked not long before Maddy had run away, was did she really want him?

Okay, Owen was a little distant and a tad bit self-centered. He was also stable. He was sensible, predictable. Even if she didn't always like it, she knew what to expect from him. Every day. Shower at seven thirty a.m. Breakfast of toast, a grapefruit, and dark-roast coffee every morning at exactly eight a.m. His shirts ironed with specific creases in the sleeves, hung on the hanger with the top button buttoned, and facing left in the closet. And so on and so on.

For the rest of the day.

For the rest of her life.

Joann had mentioned the lack of stability in her ex-husband as an ongoing problem. Owen's reliability was one of the reasons her friend was so adamant she married him. Joann's ex couldn't hold a job for more than a couple of months. Joann never knew when her husband was coming home or when the next paycheck might come in from his share of the marriage.

Not as bad as his cheating, but a tough life just the same.

Joann had told her how her ex was great in bed. Out of the sheets, well, he wasn't much of a husband. Maddy wouldn't have any of those problems with Owen. Maybe the price for stability was fire and passion, was desire so strong you lose yourself and become indecent on the floor of a fabric store.

Passion didn't pay the bills. Steady and reliable paid the bills. Steady and reliable was life in the real world, and Owen would be a good partner in that respect. If she made use of her good sense, she'd learn from Joann's mistake.

Maddy stared at Joel. Her problem was she'd never gotten to go out and sow her wild oats like other people did before they settled down. Since she was twelve years old, she'd been too busy with grown-up tasks. She needed that pause. Maybe Joel was supposed to be her thrill of youth before she got married. Her wild oat.

It was an intriguing thought.

It was a ridiculous thought.

She was tired, and Joel was sexy. The combination

had her thinking all scrambled. A night without sleep, following a night zonked out on a bathroom floor, was taking its toll.

Maddy shook her head, got up, and drifted to the window. She nudged the drape aside, yawning at the early morning. Sunrise cast deep orange light across the near to empty parking lot. A senior couple crossed the lot, the man dragging a suitcase on wheels. The woman at his side rolled a smaller bag. They loaded their things into the trunk of one of the few cars out there and left on their early start.

Maddy's wonderful night was near the end.

The new day dropped new worries. What if her ideas were a flop? What if she only made Joel's situation worse? And of course, what was she going to do about Owen and her maybe marriage? In the fading high of her productivity, Maddy couldn't even say for sure what she wanted.

She let the drape fall and turned away from the outside world toward the dolls in their new clothes.

As she'd finished each doll, she had placed it on the coffee table in front of the couch so when Joel opened his eyes, he would see the finished product. They looked like his children, waiting for their creator to wake up and play the game one more time.' It's kind of what they were.

In a way, they were her children, too.

Maddy leaned back against the wall. After a minute or so, she lifted her purse from the wooden chair by the window and set it on the floor before sitting. A glimpse of something colorful in her purse caught her eye. It was the package of Fruity Fruit candy Joel had given her.

Maddy picked up the small bag and clutched it to

her chest like a precious jewel before tearing off the end. The nostalgic, fruity aroma made her smile. She picked out one of the little round candies, a purple one, grape, and popped it into her mouth.

****

In Joel's nightmare, an army of demons chased him down the road as he sped away in his truck. There were dozens of them, and the space between him and the demons was shrinking fast.

Joel mashed the gas pedal to the floor and plowed through night and mist. But instead of picking up speed, the truck slowed. He stomped the pedal again. The truck continued to lose speed. Soon the demons would be on him, devouring him like eager zombies out for fresh flesh. His only consolation was his Angel wasn't there to suffer his horrible fate.

The truck rolled to a stop. The engine died. He twisted the key and got nothing but a useless click. Snarls and growls grew louder as the demons closed in on him.

Joel stared at his side mirrors. A few yards away, the demons emerged from the mist. Between the night and the fog, all he could make out were shapes; large, hunched, long arms, horns like buffalo, lurching his way. Joel closed his eyes. He waited. He waited some more. He knew they were there, but they'd gone quiet. With a slowness born of utter terror, he opened his eyes.

****

A terrified scream had Maddy choking on her grape-flavored candy.

Joel let out another shriek.

He thrashed and bolted upright, leaping from the sofa like he'd been electrocuted.

He crouched a little. His head snapped around the

room, gaping at everything. When he saw his fingers, the ones with bits of tissue still stuck to them, he yelled out again. He plucked at the tissues and flicked them away. Then his eyes shot to the dolls.

Joel stared at the coffee table full of dolls, all of them facing the couch where he'd been sleeping. When he'd opened his eyes in the murky morning light, it must have looked to him like he was under attack by a miniature army marching straight out of a horror movie.

"Oh Joel, I'm sorry. I didn't mean to scare you. I thought it'd be a nice surprise for you to wake up and see the dolls." Maddy switched on the light beside the couch, hoping to chase away the fright she'd given him.

"It's okay, I'm fine," he said. "Not scared. Not scared at all."

His words had some breath to them, but he collected himself pretty fast. He cleared his throat, straightened, and gave her a smile, sweet, sexy, and a little embarrassed.

"Bad dream?"

He nodded and laughed at himself. "A little bit."

"It happens to me sometimes. Probably because we both like to watch scary movies."

Joel rounded the coffee table, flopped down on the couch, and looked at her. "You'd think that'd be a deterrent. I don't know why I still watch them."

"Rachel, my sister, once asked me why I liked those movies so much."

"Did you have an answer?"

Maddy sat on the other end of the couch. "I had to think about it for a minute before I had an answer. I told her how I love the rush of adrenaline, how my heart speeds up while I wait to see what happens next."

"I like that, too. It's a real charge."

"Right. You get all the excitement and none of the danger."

"Scary," Joel said. "But safe."

Scary but safe. Maddy dove a layer deeper. Maybe she'd outgrown safe, more than a decade later than most people did. Okay, she was a late bloomer. Very late. But twenty-eight wasn't ancient. She was still capable of changing directions. With a tilt of her head, Maddy stared at the dolls on the coffee table, illuminated well enough by the kitchen light.

****

Joel leaned forward, head down, elbows on his knees. Wow, how embarrassing, screaming like a little girl. It's a good thing none of his friends were here. He'd never live it down. When he'd opened his eyes, fearing an army, and then seeing one right in front of him, well, who wouldn't have had a fright? It really was like something out of a horror movie.

Joel turned his attention to the dolls standing in a staggered display on the coffee table.

With his nightmare in the past, he could now give them a good viewing. He stared at the army of dolls and how they were dressed. He knelt before the coffee table, his gaze roving from one to the next, awed at the difference Maddy's clothing designs had on the doll's appearance.

"Maddy, I can't believe this is the same doll."

The concept of the doll was supposed to be her selling point. Her wardrobe, what little thought he'd given it, was inconsequential. He'd been wrong. So wrong.

The jeans and T-shirts were the best, like something

straight from the mall, but the other clothing items were great, too. The stretchy pants, the sun dresses, all stuff you see women wearing every day. Paired with the realistic body shape of his design, they looked like actual women with a wardrobe any child's mother would own.

This could work. This toy could sell.

How could he have been so blind? And why hadn't anyone else caught the clothing issue? Maddy had barely gotten the doll in her hands before she saw what was wrong. It should have been obvious, especially to those like himself who'd spent years in the toy business. Maybe that was the problem. Everyone, including him, had treated the doll as a business.

While the company had focused on polls and production, his Angel looked at the doll through the eyes of a woman living in the real world. It reminded him of when he was a kid. His grandfather never relied on statistics or opinions to greenlight a toy. He let his grandchildren, and sometimes their friends, play with them, and he paid attention. Using this method, his grandfather built a successful business.

"These are amazing," Joel said.

"You really think so?"

He gave Maddy his biggest smile. She deserved it. "Better than amazing. They're perfect! They're amazingly perfect! You were right. Her clothing changes everything."

Maddy shot to her feet, waved her fists in the air in a silent cheer, and grinned while she did a little hip-wiggling circle dance. Damn, she was adorable. And sexy as hell. Too sexy. The way she made him forget everything else in existence was scarier than any cabin-in-the-woods horror movie scenario he'd ever watched.

He'd never been one of those puppy-in-love kind of guys. Didn't want to be one. They always seemed sort of spellbound, existing in another realm where their lives were split and entangled with another. He never understood why a man would give up all the choices in women for one. Maybe because he hadn't met the right woman.

While Maddy danced another circle, the scene in the fabric store ran through his mind.

He hadn't planned to kiss her. The move hadn't even been deliberate. Sitting on the floor with her inches away picking buttons out of his hair, all he could see were her lips, and all he could do was kiss them. It was like he was on remote control. He'd half expected a slap to the face. What he hadn't expected was her explosive reaction.

Her enthusiastic response tore him away from his brain. For a moment there, he actually forgot they were in a public place. He hadn't been that worked up in years. Maybe not ever.

Joel intensified his gaze on Maddy as she continued to dance. The circular swing of her hips had his hands aching to clutch them, to dance with her, to hold her close and kiss away her troubles, to rekindle the fire she'd shown him yesterday and put the sunrise to shame with their blaze.

He'd only gotten a small taste of her, but damn, she was delicious. Since the moment their lips separated yesterday, the desire to kiss her again kept up a continuous nudge. He wanted what he knew was there. What he doubted others saw. Beneath her good girl exterior beat the heart of a wild woman.

Someone else's wild woman.

Or was she? Maddy had run away from her

wedding, and she didn't act like a woman anxious to get back to what she left behind. Just the opposite. She was more like a butterfly spreading her wings for the first time, colorful, expanding, ready to fly and show her assets to the world.

Maddy danced another circle, and Joel smiled through the discomfort her moves caused his body. What was wrong with him?

Put your mind somewhere else.

She had something in her hand, waving it around as her hips swirled in another enticing undulation.

"What are you holding?" he asked.

"Oh, it's the Fruity Fruit candy you got for me."

Maddy stopped dancing, and he couldn't say if he was disappointed or grateful. She held out her arm, tilting the little package toward him. He'd never been big on sweets, but this was a special occasion. A little candy was in order. After he took a piece from the bag, she took one, too.

"Cheers," he said.

Maddy laughed and tapped her candy against his. "Cheers."

After popping the little treat in his mouth, Joel sat on the floor with his back against the couch and picked up each doll, giving a closer study to the details of their outfits. Maddy sat on the couch, two or three inches to his left.

Joel glanced over his shoulder. "I'm sorry I fell asleep and left you with all the work."

"You were a big help with the cutting. There really wasn't anything else you could do. Besides, I enjoyed it."

Joel rested a forearm on his bent knee and twisted to

better see her. "You really did?"

"It was the best night of my life!"

She beamed so bright it warmed his skin. Her joy, her excitement, rolled off the couch in a waterfall. It infused him. Everything she said, everything she did, made her more tempting until it was an effort to think straight.

"I've been drawing these fashions for years, and last night I got to bring them to life," Maddy said. Her tired eyes widened beneath raised brows, and her hands waved through the air, expressing herself. "Okay, the clothes are smaller than how I'd pictured them, but still, they're my designs."

Joel faced the table and set the doll with the rest, but he didn't see them anymore. He saw Maddy hitchhiking in a wedding dress, then silly drunk for the first time in her life, then working at the little kitchen table making clothes for his dolls. He saw a woman create her dream, giving fresh hope to his.

He twisted enough to look up at her. She was staring at him. Her smile was still there, but it was different, softer, thoughtful. A decision settled in her eyes.

****

Maddy made the decision without having to think about it.

She leaned forward, her arm grazing Joel's. It wasn't an accident. It was her wrapping her hands around the steering wheel, taking her chance. For once in her life, she was doing what she wanted, and she wanted Joel. Her only concern was if Joel felt the same. It was a short-lived concern.

They held still for half a minute or so, gazing at each other in a pure, carnal exchange, until Joel unfolded his tall body and stood. He offered her his hand. Maddy didn't break eye contact as she slipped her fingers into his palm and rose to stand before him.

Joel dragged the backs of his fingers along her cheek, down her throat, her collar bone, before sliding his hand beneath her T-shirt to caress the bare skin of her shoulder. The reverberation of his touch quaked through her body.

Maddy slam-closed the inches between them, all but throwing herself against him, grabbing onto his head for a zealous kiss. The man made her lose her mind. Not great in the fabric store. But here, in the privacy of the presidential suite of the Last Chance Motel, she could toss rationale and accountability out the window and let her body have its way.

"Easy," Joel said. He whispered the words against her lips, then teased her by drizzling soft kisses across her face to whisper in her ear. "We have hours."

"Hours?"

****

He smiled against her cheek in mid-kiss. Somehow the woman was making his body both solid and compliant. "Extra hours once I call for late checkout."

Her response began with a sigh as he cupped her bottom and crushed their bodies together, leaving them both panting. "Hmmm. Late checkout."

Joel chuckled through his suffering. While he liked to take his time with a woman, he'd never spent more than a couple of hours in bed with one. He couldn't do everything he wanted to do with Maddy in a matter of hours. He'd need days. Weeks. Maybe a long, long vacation.

She rocked against him. Or maybe he was the one

rocking her. Neither could say. They could only revel and writhe in the power of their desire for each other.

Joel drew in a heavy, ragged breath as his hand molded to Maddy's perfect breast. They groaned in tandem. "Screw late checkout," Joel said. "I'm paying for another day."

Emboldened by wild want, Maddy slid her hand down the hard planes of his chest, to his stomach. Farther, farther, and did some cupping of her own.

Joel sucked in a breath. "A week," he said. "Let's make it a week. Does this place rent by the month?"

Maddy's laugh was breathy and unsteady. How much time would it take to make up for all the life that had marched past her house while she was inside cooking and cleaning her youth away? Way more than a month, for sure. But she'd take this. She'd take and keep every bit of it for as long as it would last.

Maddy treated herself to another feel of him. Joel was impressive, in every way. Her entire body dampened.

Joel massaged her back in slow, intense movements, inching his way up her spine. She did her best to play along with the easing-in pace he set, but she was ready to scoot this show along. All the urges and impulses she'd long ignored hit her like a sudden fever. She wanted everything. Now.

She let go of Joel to slip off her T-shirt. For the first time in her life, Maddy wished she was wearing a pretty bra, something with frilly lace or some peek-a-boo transparency. Then again, her simple, white cotton bra had Joel's full attention.

Joel stared at her breasts, hidden from him with a bra that strove for nothing. The simplicity made it more erotic. He *had* to see her. He took a half-step back, keeping his hands on her hips and his eyes on her breasts. "Take it off."

The order might have annoyed Maddy if she hadn't wanted so much to get out of her bra, to give him more access to her skin, to have his hands on every part of her without any clothing in the way. Between the heat of his gaze and the heat of her body, she was surprised the fabric hadn't incinerated.

Seconds later, she tossed her bra in the air.

"Jesus," Joel said. Or maybe he just thought it. He couldn't tell. Hell, he could hardly breathe, much less think. Her breasts were magnificent. Even better than he imagined, which never happened. Full, high, tipped with proof of how turned on she was. The sight fired up his hunger a thousand more degrees. He paused to gain some control for fear of devouring her in a single bite.

Maddy's growing need ousted her usual embarrassment about showing her body. Good. To hell with embarrassment. To hell with shyness. To hell with the reserve of her life.

"Touch me," she said.

Joel had never been more pleased to follow an order. He touched, he kissed, he drove her to sweet whimpers. He backed off for a second or two, and only because she was choking him in her effort to yank off his T-shirt. Something tore.

She giggled. "Oops. Sorry."

"You don't sound sorry."

"I'm not."

"Oh, you naughty girl. I'm going to make you pay for that."

Maddy giggled again, breathy, half out of her mind

with lust. "Please do."

She squealed when he lifted her. As he carried her into the bedroom, Maddy twisted into him, clinging to him, kissing him, reveling in the feel of her bare breasts roughed by the hairs on the solid plane of his chest.

Joel lay her on the bed, pausing to admire her half-naked, breathing hard, for him. He plucked off her shoes, her socks, and unbuttoned her jeans, tugging on them until she lay there in nothing but her plain, white panties. Sexy as hell. five seconds later, the panties were gone, too.

Maddy tugged at his jeans, not seeming to care if she tore off the button. It was his turn to be undressed. Her turn to touch. But he wouldn't let her. Instead, Joel clasped her wrists and secured them against the mattress. He bit off her protest with another dazing kiss.

Joel left his jeans on for the moment, afraid he'd rush through the foreplay if he took them off now. First, he would touch every part of her, kiss her, taste her, learn what she liked, what lit her fire. He would drive her so crazy with need, having him would be all she could think about.

Oh, how she loved being lost in lust! It was exquisite and maddening. His hands trailed a sensual glide over her skin, across areas she never even knew were so sensitive, teasing places that were. His hands were strong and warm, intuitive and relentless. Wasn't she going to do something with her hands? Yes, she, ah! Maddy sucked in air and then some more.

Joel reveled in having his hands everywhere, from the soft skin behind her earlobes to the lean muscle of her calves. He kissed. He stroked. He cajoled more of those gratifying whimpers from her sweet lips, drawing out their foreplay as long as he could.

Maddy wanted this, but more, more of this first. Her thoughts made less sense than when she drank the tequila. Fine. It didn't matter. No need to think. For now, she could exist just to feel.

Joel couldn't wait another minute, not another second. If he didn't have Maddy now his entire body would explode. He rolled off the bed, taking his hands off her long enough to get rid of the rest of his clothes. As soon as he tossed down his jeans, he snatched them up again. He slipped the condom from his wallet and was ready to go in seconds.

And then they were one. Joel's easy pace lived a short life. Maddy wouldn't let their sex be controlled anyway. Her need expanded, infusing his, blowing away everything but sensation. Maddy cried out her fervor, hovering on the edge. Joel gave her more. Then she gave him more, until they both shattered.

Later, when she dozed in his arms, Joel toyed with the soft ends of her hair. Yesterday she was considering going back to her fiancé. Ex-fiancé. If this Owen character thought there was any chance in the world he could marry Maddy now, he was wrong, in a big way.

Chapter 18

"I can't believe you let your little brother go to pick up those dolls," Katherine Tyler said. She brushed a wayward ash from the thigh of her navy blue pant leg. A beige blouse ruffled down the neckline and into the jacket matching the pants.

Katherine paced across the sable carpet in her high-heeled shoes, past her daughter to her white, lacquered, Grulu desk. The top was smooth and cool beneath the drag of her fingertips. She took one last puff of her cigarette before crushing it out in her crystal ashtray. Smoking was her only vice. It was a bad one. It drove her loved ones to scowl and to nag, but she'd quit quitting a long time ago and accepted her single weakness.

Katherine rounded her desk. It was massive, but not too large for the generous space of her office. She opened a drawer and took out her pack. She tapped out another cigarette. After scooping her brass lighter from the same drawer and firing it up, she drew a sharp intake before huffing a cone of smoke toward the ceiling. Her daughter, Mariel, twisted her face away from the spreading haze. Mariel's shoulder-length, walnut hair brushed the cap sleeves of her teal dress.

Last Christmas, Mariel had given her one of those ashtrays with an inside fan to suck up smoke. The big, brown contraption was ugly and noisy and in complete contrast with her orchestrated décor of black and white contemporary with a few accent splashes of red. She'd tossed the ashtray straight into her donation bag.

Mariel sat straight on one of the two white, tufted regent chairs in front of her mother's desk. "The dolls had to be picked up by someone, Mom. Besides, Joel is a grown man. He doesn't need my permission."

"Wrong," Katherine said. She pointed a finger at Mariel, red nail polish gleaming. "He *does* need your permission. You are his superior."

"I still can't believe you did that to us."

"Made you Joel's boss? What choice did your father and I have? It wouldn't have been fair to keep a promotion from you because your brother couldn't get his act in order. And we certainly couldn't advance Joel. Such a blatant act of nepotism would come back to bite all of us, and you know it."

"You could have promoted me in another department. You didn't have to humiliate him."

"Your brother humiliates himself. We gave him a decent office, accounting responsibilities, and a clear path to elevate his status with this company. Instead of dedicating himself to what's been offered, he spends his time in Development, or in the warehouse. Joel actually prefers manual labor over his comfortable position with this business."

"You want him to be an executive, sitting behind a desk all day. He's tactile. He's creative. Development is where he wants to be, and not overseeing the creations of others. Joel has had some great ideas. You'd see that if you'd quit trying so hard to browbeat him."

"I never browbeat," Katherine said.

"You do. Well, you try, but it doesn't faze Joel any

more than when you scarce glance at his ideas or when you'd sunk so low as to make me his superior."

Katherine arched a brow halfway to the short cut of her auburn hairline. "We'd hoped promoting you over Joel would inspire him. And I suppose you're forgetting these dolls of his were greenlighted by your father. Your brother had his chance."

Mariel shook her head. "You didn't assign a team to the project like you do for the other creators. No brainstorming meetings, no troubleshooting, no collaboration with anyone. Even though he was pretty much on his own with his creation, Joel did a damn fine job."

"Need I remind you the dolls didn't sell?"

Mariel pushed up from her seat and crossed her arms. "Oh, like every other creator in this building never had a fail. And it's not like you supported it with any kind of marketing. You put the doll in *one* small store for *one* month. No promo. No advertising. Not exactly full support there, Mom."

Katherine leaned her slim hip against her desk and took another drag off her cigarette. After a moment, she strolled around, sat in her comfortable office chair, and rolled close to her desk.

Mariel released a quiet sigh and lowered herself to her seat. "Like you, I'm a businessperson. I see this company through pragmatic eyes and make decisions based on sound assessments. Unlike you, I make an effort to temper my business decisions with some heart."

Katherine flicked an ash into the crystal tray. "That's harsh."

"Maybe, but it's true." Her daughter softened her tone. Her way of swinging back to civility. Katherine never saw the point. Once a discussion got heated, it was best to turn the fire up all the way and see who emerges from the ashes. Maybe Mariel's comment wasn't as harsh as it was accurate.

"Mom, Joel takes after Grandpa, and the way Dad used to be before he got absorbed in the business aspects."

"Your father still makes an occasional appearance at creative meetings."

"Occasional? Dad never misses one."

Katherine stared at her daughter for a moment. "He doesn't?"

"I think he'd like to spend all his time in Development."

Katherine shook her head and couldn't help a tiny smile for her husband.

"Dad enjoys the creative aspect of the business. Joel does, too. You act like that's a bad thing, like it's beneath what the executives do. It's not. If it weren't for creativity, this business wouldn't exist."

"Your dad really goes to all those creative meetings?"

"I can't believe you didn't know."

She shook her head and grinned some more. "I guess some part of him will always be a little boy."

"Considering the business we're in, that's a good thing. You should see Dad when he's in there. He lights up like Christmas morning. Joel, Dad, and Grandpa before them, they're geared for the creative aspect of the business. We're not. Doesn't make them wrong, or us wrong. Just different."

She gave Mariel a two-finger point, the cigarette forcing a V. "Without us, those toys would never see the light of day."

"I see us all as equally important. I see Joel clearer than you do."

"And?"

"He's a grown man. He's got his pride and whatever dignity you've seen fit to leave him. It's why…"

Katherine tapped an ash. "Go on."

"I'm worried he might leave the business."

"What!" Katherine crushed out her cigarette with half a dozen quick taps in the ashtray. "Joel can't leave. This is a family business."

Mariel said nothing. A tactic she'd learned from her mother. How very grating.

Katherine folded her hands in front of her. "Have you mentioned this to your father?"

"No, because I don't know it for a fact, and I don't want to break Dad's heart. In his mind, Joel will do the same thing he did, work in the business end and slip into the Development meetings."

"I can't believe I didn't know your father attends every meeting."

"Neither can I."

Katherine forced her jaw to loosen so she could respond. "You really think I'm so awful. Let me tell you something. Without me, this place would have fallen apart a long time ago."

"You're the glue. I'm not being sarcastic. Your head for business has gotten us through the lean times and kept us running, kept us growing."

"Damn right."

"But a business needs more than glue. You know, Mom, if you look at this from a practical aspect, you're not making the best use of Joel."

"What are you talking about?"

"You and I both know the only way to remain competitive is to put out new and unique products on a regular basis. For that, we need strong, inventive minds."

"We have a great team of creators."

"We do. We could use one more. Mom, Joel is one of the best creative minds we've ever had. You would see that if you'd give him the same respect you give people who aren't your son."

Katherine leaned back against the tufted fabric of her chair. There was nothing she hated more than being wrong. She stared at her daughter through the lingering cloud of cigarette smoke. Had Mariel gained some more weight? Last Christmas, the Christmas of the electric ashtray, she'd given her daughter a gym membership. It was on the tip of her tongue to ask Mariel if she was using it. No. One child at a time mad at her was enough.

She opened her desk drawer and then closed it again. Two cigarettes in a row could be chalked up to stress. Three was chain smoking. She was *not* a chain smoker.

They continued to stare at each other a little longer. Neither looked away. It left Katherine somewhere between proud and annoyed. She tapped her fingertips on the arms of her chair three times before opening the drawer again. As she fired up her cigarette—surely a full minute had passed, therefore, it wasn't chain-smoking—she thought about her motives. Is it really so wrong to want your children to reach their full potential? Of course not. Mariel was just being obstinate. Too much time with her brother.

Katherine glanced at the small, crystal clock on her desk. A quiver rolled through her stomach. "Joel has been gone too long."

"I wouldn't worry. We know he called yesterday and left a message with your secretary saying he was running late. You know how Joel is. He's very social. He probably made some friends or met up with some old ones and decided to stay an extra day or so somewhere along the road."

"Hm. One party after another."

"Mom—"

Katherine answered her daughter with a palm up and out. "I have work to do. You know, being the glue." When Mariel remained in her chair, she said, "And so do you, young lady."

After her daughter had closed the door behind her, Katherine flicked her cigarette over the ashtray. Her attention swept a distant glance over the stack of invoices on her desk waiting to be reviewed.

Joel had always been a reasonably good son. Respectful, considerate. He partied more than he should. He'd never had a committed relationship. Unless one considered a few weeks committed, which she did not. Well, there is that one girl, Roz. But she's all wrong for Joel.

Katherine always believed time would correct Joel's lacking. In a few months, he was turning thirty. Maybe the milestone birthday would jar him to maturity.

Outside, a sudden gust of wind kicked up, rattling her office window, and pelting it with tiny bits of dirt and debris. Just a dust devil.

The ash on her cigarette had grown long. It was a careful balancing act getting it to the ashtray. Well, this family matter had taken up enough of her time. The company wasn't going to run itself.

Katherine hit three keys on her computer before

stopping to buzz her secretary.

"Yes?" Natalie said.

"Have you heard from Joel yet today?"

"No. Haven't heard anything since yesterday."

"Let me know if you do."

"I will," Natalie said.

Her secretary showed no agitation with having been asked the same question, for the fourth time that day.

****

One of the mechanics passed Owen and crinkled his nose while slanting a quick glimpse. Owen scowled at the man. You'd think over the thick odors of grease, gasoline, and whatever else reeked in this filthy little waiting room, his stink would have been unnoticeable.

Owen ate a pretzel from the little bag he held. When the salty snack burned the cuts in his mouth, he hurried a sip from his cool can of orange soda.

At the other end of the row of gray, plastic seats, Sophie and Joann huddled together in a private conversation. They had no reason to leave him out of the discussion. He had a right to be in on the planning. They were acting like they were the law and he was a captured criminal.

They should have gone in his car. It was more reliable than Sophie's *classic* sports car by about a hundred times. Classic. Old piece of junk is a more accurate description. Better yet, he should have ditched those two right away and continued on his mission solo. The problem was he hadn't been thinking clearly at the time. Who could blame him? He'd been tired, hungry, and moments off a fresh beating.

Owen popped another salty pretzel into his mouth. *Ouch!* He sucked in some more orange soda.

Two days ago, he was about to walk down the aisle and marry a woman who was made to be his wife: old-fashioned, docile, wonderfully domestic, zero outside interests. Then Maddy lost her mind and ran away.

Since then, he'd been punched out twice, dragged out of a motel lobby, arrested, ticketed, followed, and kidnapped. Now he was stuck in some grimy garage with his abductors, eating junk food, which he never, ever ate. How had his life taken such a turn? One minute everything was cruising along just fine. The next, he was in hell with, oh, damn, he smelled awful!

Owen ate another pretzel, winced, and had another sip of soda. He sent a hard glare toward Sophie and Joann. They didn't notice. He continued to glare at them anyway.

Of all the nerve, tracking him! Okay, okay, so he'd been tracking Maddy, but that was different. He was about to bind himself for life to this woman, and he had a responsibility to himself to settle any doubts. Besides, as soon as he confirmed her whereabouts were always in line with what she'd told him, he'd stopped.

Another mechanic pushed through the door and entered the room. The man had a long, brown beard, a shade darker than the hair poking out around his cap. He wore dark blue pants and a matching button-down shirt with stitching over the left breast pocket, telling everyone his name was Randy. He was the same man they'd talked to when the tow truck hauled in Sophie's car.

"The good news is," Randy said to Sophie.

The three of them stood. Owen set his can of orange soda on the little table but held onto his bag of pretzels.

"Your transmission is fixable," he said. "But your

torque converter needs to be replaced."

"And the bad news is you don't have the part," Sophie said. To Joann she said, "These places never have the part."

"We have the part," Randy said. "The cost, including parts and labor, is $1,500. We have to remove the transmission, so it'll take several hours, and we close at six. We'll start on it today and finish it in the morning."

"Not acceptable," Owen said. He tipped his head back and looked down his nose at the man as if he weren't wearing the same wrinkled clothes he'd had on for two days and reeking of BO and manure. Not to mention looking like he'd lost several boxing matches in a row. God, his entire face ached. "We have to have the car today. I'll pay extra to have it done right now."

"Sir, my guys have already worked a long day. Your car will be finished as soon as possible."

Owen screwed his sore face. "That piece of crap is not mine."

Sophie swung to him, hands on her skinny hips. "What did you call my car?"

Uh oh. The old woman had fire in her eyes. Who knew she'd get so worked up about an old piece of junk? "I just meant…um…"

"Yeah, that's what I thought," Sophie said.

He couldn't think straight. Between his aching face and his rancid odor, all he could manage was stuffing another pretzel in his mouth. *Ouch! Damn salt!* Where did he set his orange soda?

"What are we supposed to do until then?" Joann asked. "We're nowhere near our homes."

The man nodded toward the front of the business.

They all swung their heads, but there weren't any windows in the waiting room. "There's a motel across the street called Best Sleep. It's a decent place, reasonable rates. A couple restaurants in the area deliver food there."

Owen stared at the wall as if he could see through it. A motel. A shower. He could wash, get some sleep, and find Maddy in the morning. Maybe even figure out a way to ditch these two crazy bitches. Things were looking up, finally. He grinned at the wall and slid another pretzel in his mouth. *Ouch! Damn it!*

Chapter 19

Maddy snuggled her back against Joel's spooning front, deeper in their cocoon, immersing herself in every sensation. Firm muscle against her shoulder blades, his hand resting on her bare hip, the front of his thighs warm against the back of hers, other parts of him she wouldn't forget if she lived five hundred years.

Due to the motel's blackout drapes, the room was dark even though it was day. She had no idea what time of day it was. Every second blended into a precious minute, into a prized hour. Or hours. Maddy couldn't say. For the first time since she was twelve years old, she wasn't tied to a clock.

A couple hours ago, Joel called the front desk from the phone in the living room area. She didn't know if he'd asked for a late checkout or if he did indeed pay for another day. She should probably ask.

Mmmm. A whole day in between the sheets with Joel.

What was it about this guy that turned her loose? She'd always been kind of inhibited, embarrassed even about intimacy. With Joel, she'd become a wild woman. She took and gave at her pleasure. From the way he couldn't get enough of her, couldn't stop praising her body, her actions, Maddy could safely assume Joel enjoyed a good amount of pleasure himself.

A crazy fantasy played through her head. One where

the two of them stayed right there forever. They'd have sex, eat food from the nearby diner, and then have more sex. Sounded like happily ever after. Especially since the time she'd spent with Joel showed her how sensational life could be, at least in bed, with a man dedicated to making good use of his talents.

Okay, not realistic, but a pleasing fantasy. Maddy released a sigh, a quiet one. She would hold on to this escape a little longer, and if Joel woke up, he might say it was time to leave. Not yet, but soon, she would have to figure out a new direction. All she knew now was no matter what happened with the dolls, with Joel, all, nothing, or something in between, she was moving on to a new phase. She'd figure out a way to get her dad to move on, too.

Her old life didn't fit anymore.

Though a part of her mourned it, the stability, the comfort of the routines, the excitement of her future outweighed the negative. Okay, mostly. A blank page could lead to wonders or disasters. But at least they would be her wonders or disasters. What they would be, she didn't know and wouldn't take time out of her pleasure to think about right now. She would Scarlett O'Hara this and worry about it tomorrow.

Maddy almost laughed out loud at the attitude. She never put off a worry until tomorrow. Worries made a pesky companion of themselves, clinging to her, shaping her every move, her every decision. Maybe they would again tomorrow, but not today. For the first time in her life, she was claiming selfish time.

"What are you smiling about?" Joel asked.

Maddy peeked over her shoulder to find Joel grinning down at her. She wiggled around to face him and kissed his chin. "I was just thinking."

"About what?"

How could she explain it to him? How could she tell him what she hadn't given a thorough sort-through herself? Then he was tracing her earlobe with a fingertip, and it didn't matter. Her thoughts melted to slush.

"Tell me what's on your mind," Joel said. His voice was low and husky, a massaging rumble throughout her body. He skimmed a single finger down her neck, and traced her collarbone.

Was something on her mind? Did she have a mind? Instead of going lower, as she'd hoped, he dragged his finger up and tilted her chin until she faced him.

"Do you have any regrets?" he said.

"Hmm? Regrets? About this?"

He nodded.

"No. Not a single one."

"Good." He sighed then and closed his eyes for a few seconds before holding her in his gaze again. "Because there's something I need to tell you."

"Sounds ominous." His beautiful smile had disappeared, amplifying the whomp of a serious turn. Maddy's stomach tightened.

Joel pressed a slow kiss to her forehead, his lips pausing in what had the feel of an apology.

"Maddy, promise you'll let me explain."

She studied his face in the dim light of the room, and her stomach twisted a little tighter. A frown marred his handsome face. It squeezed out all the fun. "…Okay."

"When I—" Joel said. A pounding at the door of their suite cut off his sentence.

"Maybe it's the maid," Maddy said. "Are we supposed to be out by now?"

"No. I paid for another day."

Maddy smiled. The whole day. And night. Her smile faded at more pounding.

"What the hell?" Joel said. Then he muttered. "Oh no."

He flung away the covers, jumped out of bed, yanked on his jeans and nothing else, and headed for the door.

Maddy hopped out of bed, slipped on her underwear, snatched Joel's shirt from the floor, and shrugged into it. The hem was halfway down her thighs. Appropriate enough. She walked into the living room area just as Joel was swinging away from the peephole.

His words were little more than a mumble, but they were clear, as was his irritation. "I don't believe this."

"Believe what?" Maddy said. She crossed the room. "Who's at the door?"

"Joel!" A woman's voice shouted from outside. "I know you're in there. Open this damn door, or I'll break it down!"

Maddy stopped, then took a step back when the pounding changed to what had to be a full-body slam. Boom! Boom!

"Shit," Joel said. Then to Maddy, "I'm sorry."

He unlocked the door and opened it. A rectangle of morning sun blasted into the dim room, chasing away all the coziness.

A woman, back against the railing, hunched, head down, shoulder ready, rushed the door. She stopped several steps in, three feet in front of Maddy. The two women stared at each other with confusion and irritation from Maddy, and pure fury on the stranger's part.

She was in her late twenties, attractive, and a collar

away from full goth. Black hair a few inches past her shoulders hung lank around her pale, powdered face. She wore dark eye shadow, red lipstick, tight black pants, and a black long-sleeved shirt, with black, silver-studded boots. A small stud sparkled in her nose, and she had at least five black rings in each ear.

The woman's head ticked back for a quick glance at Joel before facing Maddy again. "Who the hell are you?"

"Mad…" Not Maddy. She was mad. Yes. Yes, she was mad at this woman's intrusion. Mad, and done pretending she wasn't when she was. And she was done taking crap from people, too, including this psycho bitch who ruined her selfish day.

"How did you find me?" Joel said.

The woman twisted her head toward him. "You told me you were taking Route 66. You're driving a big blue truck with rainbows and teddy bears on it, which you left in the front of the parking lot right out by the road. Finding you wasn't much of a challenge. And as far as figuring out which room you were in, well, this place is dead. All the other rooms are empty with the curtains open. This is the only room where the curtains were closed."

Joel said nothing but shook his tipped-down head with a slow blink.

Maddy jammed her hands on her hips in an effort to imitate the woman's defiance. Something in the shoulders and chin placement she wasn't getting right. Okay, she'd have to practice attitude. She'd start with borrowing the woman's question. "Who the hell are *you*?"

"I'm Roz, Joel's fiancée. Or did he forget to mention me before you two checked into a motel room?"

Maddy's shock darted from Roz to Joel. "Is this what you were about to tell me? You're engaged?"

"You said you'd let me explain," Joel said.

"Yes," Roz said. "He *is* engaged. To *me*."

The woman raised her left hand, fingers up and wiggling. On her ring finger was a thin, silver band with a red stone. "I wanted a ruby instead of a diamond, so this is what he got for me."

"Roz," Joel said. The tension in his jaw shaved a detectable edge to his words. "Let me talk to her for a minute."

Roz glared at him. "Don't you dare insult me by saying you checked into a motel room to talk. How long have you been seeing this one?"

"This one?" Maddy said. The twist in her stomach tightened.

The woman smirked at Maddy. "What, did you think you were special?"

Maddy stared at Joel. "This is a thing with you, picking up women when your fiancée isn't around? Charm them into bed? Oh my God, I'm such a fool. All I did was jump from one disaster to another."

"Hold on, Maddy," Joel said. He took a step toward her, pain on his face. He stopped when she took an equal step back.

Maddy's hands slid from her hips and her arms hung limp at her sides. Her spine, however, grew like the Grinch's heart. "You used me to cheat on your fiancée."

Joel stiffened. "Is that really the card you want to play?"

"I never lied to you about anything. You knew my situation from the start. Besides, I'm not engaged anymore."

"The hell you're not."

All three of their heads swung to the new voice coming from the open doorway.

Another shock had Maddy gaping. "Owen?"

He strode through the door and hugged her. Maddy recoiled. Not from shock, but from the smell.

"Owen, my God, what happened to you? What happened to your face? And why do you smell like…like…"

"Manure," Owen said. "It's manure. Yeah, yeah. I know I smell. I was able to take a shower at the motel, but I didn't have any clean clothes with me, so I had to put these on again. Maddy, you wouldn't believe what I've been through. You've caused a lot of trouble, young lady."

Did he really just call her young lady?

Owen squinted around the room. At least, Maddy thought it was a squint. It was hard to tell with all the swelling. "What's with all the dolls? What the hell are you up to in here?"

Owen stepped back and stared at her, had a quick glance around the room before focusing on her again. "All you're wearing is a man's T-shirt. Maddy, what are you doing in a motel room with these two?"

Her first thought was to tell him she was wearing underwear, but that seemed a weak defense.

"Hey," Owen said. He'd swung his attention to Joel and stretched his neck toward him. "You're the guy who hit me."

Maddy swiveled toward Joel. "You hit him?"

"Remember I told you about the guy giving Ted and his wife a hard time down in the lobby? This was the guy. But I only hit him once."

"The other guy hit me the second time."

"What other guy?" Maddy said. Before Owen could answer, she said, "You were here yesterday?"

"I…Hey, don't turn this around. What are *you* doing in here in this motel room with these two characters?"

"Nothing with me," Roz said. "I got here a minute before you. To find my fiancé boinking your fiancée."

Owen's head veered her way. "Maddy?"

The hurt in his eyes hurt her right back. Owen was arrogant and a little bossy, but he didn't deserve being screwed over, twice now. "I'm sorry, Owen. Once I decided I didn't want the life laid out before me, I guess I got a little crazy."

Owen swallowed hard. His fingers twitched. His lips pressed together, and he gave his head a few sharp nods.

"We'll talk about this later," Owen said. "We can reschedule the wedding for tomorrow morning. Hmm, but I don't know if we can get the hall. I know what we'll do. When we get back in town, we'll go straight to the courthouse and get married. We can have some sort of reception at a later date. Don't worry. I'll get it figured out for us. Go get your things, Maddy."

Maddy stayed where she was, gaping at him. Dad said Owen was still talking about marrying her even after she ran off, but he'd just caught her in a motel room with another man. "You still want to marry me?"

"Of course we're still getting married," Owen said. His eyes were as wide as the bruising would allow, a little wild, almost jiggly. Maybe she'd driven the poor man crazy. "Come on, I have a car waiting downstairs. I'll work out the details of the story on the way home and tell you what we're going to say to everyone."

"My granddaughter can speak for herself."

Everyone swung to the new voice in the doorway.

"Grandma?" Maddy said.

"I'm here, too," Joann said. She stepped into the room behind Sophie.

The two women passed Roz and Owen to hug her from both sides.

"I thought I lost you two," Owen said.

Joann swung on him. "We saw you get into the ride share this morning."

"Yeah," Sophie said. She punched her fists on her hips. Now *she* managed attitude well. "Did you really think you could ditch us? We were on you like that nasty stink. Good thing my car was ready."

Owen's lips moved, but he sputtered a moment before he could speak. "You two are unbelievable." Then he mumbled, "Stupid ride share couldn't pick me up any sooner." He swung an arm and pointed to Sophie and Joann. To Maddy, he said, "They kidnapped me!"

"He's being dramatic," Joann said. "We were so worried about you, Maddy. We needed his help to find you."

"How *did* you guys find me?" Maddy said to the three. "When I left, *I* didn't even know where I was going."

"Well," Joann said. "Your grandma and I suspected Owen might know something, so we drove to his house, but he was gone. So, we chased after him."

Owen's eyes got bigger. He nodded and pointed to Joann. "Yeah, this one put a tracker under the seat of my car. Can you believe it?"

To Joann, Maddy said, "You did? You put a tracker in Owen's car?"

"It was when you first got engaged. I was just

making sure he wasn't cheating on you," Joann said.

Maddy was a little stumped. On the one hand, it was kind of loving how her friend cared so much about her she'd track Owen. At the same time, it was a terrible invasion of privacy.

"Tell her the rest, Owen," Sophie said. Her grandma's scowl had Maddy dreading *the rest*.

Owen stepped over and wrapped his hand around Maddy's upper arm. "We'll talk later, Maddy. Let's get your stuff and get out of here."

He tugged her toward the bedroom, toward the future that was her past. Maddy jerked free of his grip. "Tell me now."

Owen shook his hands in front of him. "It's been months since I've used it. Forget about it."

"Used what?" Maddy said. "What are you talking about?"

"The son of a bitch put a tracker app on your phone," Sophie said.

Owen's eyes got wilder, sliding into crazed beneath the bruising on his face. "Oh, you two should talk." Then he veered back to Maddy. "And who is this guy anyway? How did you end up here with him?"

"It's none of your business," Sophie said to Owen.

"The hell it's not my business!"

Then the room bulged with arguments and accusations as everybody shouted at once. Except for Joel and Maddy. She locked eyes with him. He stood back from the noisy fray, silent, his expression unreadable.

Anger escalated into shouts. Maddy crossed her arms and then shot them out. "Shut up! Everyone! Just. Shut. Up."

Everyone did. Owen and Joann stared at her as if she'd morphed into a dragon. Maddy never told people to shut up or even raised her voice. Grandma Sophie grinned at her with such pride Maddy almost smiled.

"Grandma, Joann," Maddy said. "Let's go." She walked out the door as she was, wearing nothing but her panties and Joel's T-shirt.

Chapter 20

"Damn her!" Sam Haydon paced beside the kitchen table where Sophie and Joann sat with their hands wrapped around hot cups of coffee. "I don't know what's gotten into her."

He really didn't. Maddy had always been a good girl, never gave him a lick of trouble. Her little sister, Rachel, now she was a handful. His youngest was emotional and needy. Maybe it was his own fault. He'd been indulgent with her because she'd been so young when their mother died. Maddy had been young, too, but much more mature. She was a natural at taking over her mother's role.

Even when she was a tiny little thing, Maddy was adult-like, helping her mother around the house. She never sassed him or complained about anything. Maddy had always been his little mouse. What in the hell happened to her?

Drugs? No, not Maddy. The girl barely drank. She wouldn't do drugs. Some kind of female thing? Could be. It was times like this he missed his late wife the most. Raising two daughters on his own had given him many challenges. Sophie, his mother-in-law, was a help. Though at times she was a hindrance, with her wild ways. Maybe Maddy had become susceptible.

Sophie and Joann had come in with Maddy almost an hour ago. His daughter had said hello as she passed him and marched straight up to her room without any explanation for her behavior. All she'd had on was a big T-shirt. She wasn't even wearing shoes.

He'd asked the women where his daughter had been. Joann said nothing. Sophie told him she'd been with a man. His mother-in-law had said it with a prideful grin like it was something good. Sometimes the woman drove him to the far side of sanity. Lord, he missed his wife.

Sam, tired of pacing, sat at the kitchen table across from Sophie, Joann to his left, his untouched coffee in front of him. The second hand of the kitchen clock ticked a few clicks. "Who's this man she was with?"

"Don't know," Sophie said. "Maddy didn't want to talk about him."

"Well, what did she talk about?"

Sophie and Joann glanced at each other. He wasn't going to get the full story from either of them. Women. Sticking together. Keeping each other's secrets.

"Mostly, she slept," Joann said. "She did say she plans to design clothes."

"She…what?"

"Maddy is going to follow her dream to design clothes," Sophie said. "Maybe even start her own line. She has a flair for it." At his silence, she added, "You've seen her make clothes for Rachel. She's very good."

Sam shook his head. "Making some clothes for her sister is a long way from a career. Maybe Owen can talk some sense into her."

"She doesn't want to marry Owen," Sophie said. "She made that clear when she ran away from the wedding."

There had to be more to it than her just getting cold feet. Sam rubbed the stubble on his face. He hadn't shaved in a couple of days. All his routines were scrambled. "How can she not want to marry Owen? He's perfect for her. He's got a good job, he a decent guy, he's…got a good job."

"Maddy has a job, too," Sophie said.

"Selling thread at the Yarn Barn? Why doesn't she want to settle down, have some kids, be normal?"

"Sam," Sophie said. "Step out of the dark ages. Women having careers is perfectly normal."

"You know what I mean. I know my daughter. She's not the kind of woman to have a career. She's very domestic. She's good at that kind of stuff. It's what Owen loves about her."

"She could be a career woman," Joann said. "Maybe she already would have been if she'd felt she had the support."

Sophie slid her hand across the table and laid it on top of Joann's. *More secret woman talk. How do they do that, look at each other and know?*

"I don't like it," Sam said. Not these wordless conversations of women, not Maddy running out on her wedding with some crazy idea of a career—and who was the man she was with?—and he was tired of dealing with these women all by himself.

"Sam," Sophie said. "Look at the big picture. Maddy has always been a homebody because it's what the family needed her to be. The girl has essentially lived as a mother and housewife since she was twelve years old."

"You're exaggerating," Sam said. Though, maybe it wasn't such a stretch. Okay, the girl did a lot around the house, but it's not like she was chained up there. She was free to do things. "I've given her a good life."

"She's given *you* a good life," Sophie said. "She's

kept this place running since she was a kid. How many meals has she cooked for you over the years, Sam? How many times has she ironed your shirts or mended clothes for you? How many dresses has she made for Rachel to wear for one occasion or another while Maddy stayed home with little time for her own social life?"

Sam stared at his cup of coffee, his stomach sinking, twitching an ache in his shoulders.

"How many Saturday nights did she stay here and cater to you and your poker buddies," Sophie said. "Or to tend to things around the house she hadn't gotten to during her work week? Nights when other girls her age were going on dates or to parties, being young and growing up gradually?"

Sam raised his chin. "It's not like Maddy was a prisoner here. I didn't tell her to do those things. She just did them."

Sophie pointed a finger at him. "Exactly. When my daughter died, Maddy stepped right into her shoes. She didn't have to be told or even asked. She did those things because they needed to be done. Sam, Maddy *needs* some of the life she never got to have. She deserves it."

The sting of her words stifled his. How had he never considered any of that? And damn Sophie for throwing it in his face. He sipped his cooling coffee. Maddy had always seemed happy with her life. At the very least, content. Had his daughter really been denied her youth?

All these years he had viewed his home through the eyes of a caretaker. He earned the money for the bills. He mowed the lawn. He made repairs. It shook him to think he had been the one being cared for.

"Sam," Joann said. "Maddy needs to spread her wings, see what she can do."

He flipped his attention to Joann. "You're the one who said she just had wedding day jitters when she started acting funny. I was standing right there when you told her everything would be great once she got married."

Joann's head dipped for a few ticks of the kitchen clock before she met his gaze. "I was wrong. Just like you, Sam. I didn't believe in her."

Sophie said, "Maddy is squeezing some life out of her life, finally. Let her be, Sam."

Sam took his cup to the sink and dumped out the rest of his cold coffee. Dirty dishes piled well over the lip of the sink. No one had washed a dish since the last time Maddy had done it, the morning of her wedding. She'd cooked everyone a big breakfast and cleaned the kitchen to a shine before going upstairs to get ready. Now, crumbs dotted the counter among dull smudges of something someone needed to clean before it drew ants.

Rachel and her four-year-old twin daughters had come three days ago to stay for the wedding. He'd assumed she'd been helping Maddy around the house with all the extra work. Clearly, no one had done any kind of housekeeping for a couple of days. Had Rachel ever helped out around here?

Sam turned away from the unkempt condition of the kitchen and leaned against the counter, wincing when his hand rested on something sticky, which he then had to wipe off on a filthy dishtowel.

This morning, the coffee wasn't made and waiting for him, so he looked in the pantry and found it on the sparse side of normal. That never happened. From where he stood, he could see into the laundry room. An overflowing basket of laundry sat on top of the dryer. A pile of towels was on the floor in front of the washer. Good Lord, the girl was gone for two days, and the place fell apart. The condition of the house supported what Sophie was saying.

It's not like he wasn't aware Maddy kept the house running. But she made it seem so effortless, like it was nothing. His wife had been the same way, going around, tending to things, keeping everyone happy and right. Had his wife been dissatisfied? No. Linda used to sing while she did things around here. She smiled a lot, too. Maddy never sang. She didn't even smile much.

Maybe he could have handled things better, divided the workload between his two girls. But he'd been grieving the loss of his wife. Rachel was so emotional, and Maddy, well, the girl stepped up and did what needed to be done. She'd made it seem so natural. Things just stuck that way. She was a good girl, a grown-up now.

Sam rubbed his hand down his face. "Maddy is almost thirty years old. Her time for rebelling has passed. I'm sorry if she missed out on some things, but she can't go back and be a kid again. And the fact is, Maddy made a commitment to the only man who has ever been seriously interested in her. Without Owen, what kind of a future will she have?"

Sophie gave him a hard look. "On behalf of women everywhere, I take offense at what you're saying."

"Me too," Joann said.

"Take anything you want from it. I know my daughter. She's used to things a certain way. I think it was the stress of the last few weeks. It caught up with her. She'll be right now." Then, having had the last word, Sam Hayden walked out of the kitchen and into the living room.

Sophie's voice was low, but it caught up with him just outside the kitchen. Probably deliberate. He stopped and considered going back in to argue with the woman. No. Arguing with Sophie was like wrestling a riled cat. He might come out on top in the end, but she'd claw the hell out of him first. It was a wonder such a brazen mouthy woman had raised a sweet girl like his Linda.

Sam headed for the stairs and heard it again. No doubt about it. Sophie called him a jackass.

Halfway up the stairs, the sound of the front door opening, followed by two screaming little girls and their mother hollering after them, tensed his shoulders. He loved his youngest daughter, Rachel. He loved her four-year-old twin daughters. But Lord, they tested his patience, and he had little to spare today.

Sam continued up the stairs on his way to Maddy's room.

Chapter 21

It wasn't fair.

Before she got married, her sister Rachel had gone out on numerous dates. She had activities. She'd gone clubbing. Maddy wasn't even sure what clubbing entailed. Just that Rachel would get dressed up and be all smiles and excitement, waiting for her friends to come pick her up. Rachel would sleep late the next day, her dress on the washer for Maddy to launder.

Well, Maddy hadn't gone clubbing, but damn it, she was going to sleep in this morning—for the first time in her life. While she was at it, she'd indulge in some serious sulking.

Her back was to her bedroom window, where white, lacey curtains did a super crappy job of keeping out the morning sun. It never mattered before, as she was an early riser. She always had to be up early. Things to be done and all that. Not today.

Rachel was an expert at ordering out. They wouldn't starve. Someone would figure out how to work the washing machine when they ran out of clean underwear. She was on sabbatical, sick leave, vacation, whatever you want to call it. Her family had been on their own for the last couple of days. They could handle one more.

Maddy curled deeper into her covers and buried her face in the pillow. As the house awoke, dozing became a challenge.

Water turned on and off in the bathroom next to her bedroom. Doors with squeaky hinges opened and then slammed shut with inconsiderate force. Four equally sized feet ran up and down the stairs as her four-year-old twin nieces took part in a race without a finish line.

These noises mingled with Rachel's frustrated voice hollering at her daughters to brush their teeth, get dressed, and demanding the return of her new shoes. Rachel was answered with two obstinate little voices claiming, "We did, we will, and we don't have them."

Finally, her sister and nieces toddled downstairs and stayed there. The front door opened and closed, and the house was quiet for about half an hour. Maybe they went for a walk, waiting for her to get up and do her thing, no doubt.

Maddy fought back her normalcy, the part nudging her from her bed, telling her to throw in a load of laundry and get breakfast started. She was done. Checked out. Joel was engaged. Owen still believed they were engaged. Life sucked.

Joel had used her for a good time on the side. Lying, cheating bastard. Was she any better? Yes. Unlike him, she'd been honest from the start. Plus, she'd called off her marriage before she even met Joel. A fact Owen wasn't accepting. He'd left about a dozen messages on her freshly cleared voicemail since she'd walked out of the motel room at the Last Chance and had her half convinced they were still getting married.

Owen. Her other headache. Jilting him, causing him such an embarrassment, weighed on her. No one should have to suffer such a thing. But she wasn't going to marry him to make up for it. Why would he want to marry her anyway, after what she'd done? And what the hell, tracking her?

Owen was a stalker. Joel was a liar and a cheat. Well, screw them both. She was going to rest, sleep, and maybe read some books right here. Not just for the day, either. For the rest of her life.

At the knock on her door, she dragged the covers over her head.

More knocking, firmer this time. “Maddy, I know you’re in there.”

Great. Her little sister, Rachel. The only person she wanted to see less was her father. She’d hurried past him when she walked into the house last night. He’d been too stunned to say anything. Who could blame him? After running away in her wedding dress, she’d returned two days later wearing nothing but a man’s T-shirt.

Once upstairs, she showered, got into one of her boring nightgowns and crawled into bed.

After another knock, the door jiggled.

“Maddy,” Rachel said. “Unlock this door right now. What’s the matter with you? You never lock your door.”

She also never ran out on a wedding, hitchhiked, or had sex in motels with men she hardly knew. But hey, let’s focus on a locked door.

“I’ll tell Dad,” Rachel said.

Really? She was going to tattle?

“He was on his way up here,” Rachel said. “I convinced him to let me talk to you first. But if you’d rather talk to him…”

Maddy flung the covers off her body.

“Fine!” She marched over to the door, unlocked it, and climbed back into her bed, where she yanked her beige comforter up to her chin and stared at the ceiling. The ceiling was white, like her walls, like her vanilla life.

A blank canvas waiting for some color.

Rachel stepped in and closed the door behind her. She wore navy blue pants with pink pumps and a pink blouse with white buttons. Her auburn hair was straightened to perfection, and her makeup could have been done by a professional. Maddy ran her fingers through her hair. They stuck in the tangles.

Her little sister scanned the room, dragged a white, ladder-back chair from the corner, and placed it next to the bed.

"Planning to stay a while?" Maddy said. The annoyance in her voice was real. Why couldn't the world leave her alone? All she wanted was her bed and some solitude. Maybe some cookies.

Rachel sat in the chair and crossed her legs, ever graceful. "You can talk to me, or you can talk to Dad."

"Fine," Maddy said. She sat up and fluffed a pillow against the headboard, then flopped back against it. "We'll talk. Lovely weather we're having lately, isn't it?"

"Funny. Come on, Maddy. What happened? You've always been so…dependable."

"Oh, you noticed."

"Of course I noticed. You're my sister. I know you."

"You can't know me," Maddy said. "I'm just getting to know myself."

"You're not making any sense."

Maddy stared at her sister, annoyed but grateful it wasn't her father sitting there. She wasn't ready to face him.

She hadn't said a lot on the ride home. Grandma Sophie and Joann didn't push much. She deflected their few questions with noncommittal answers. Grandma caught her in the rearview mirror a couple of times, grinned, and winked. After telling them she planned to design clothes, she laid her head back and slept most of the way.

Maybe it would have helped to talk to them. She'd been too tired, too stunned, and too muddled to talk to anyone. Now she was awake, and her sister was here.

Rachel had been spoiled and pampered her whole life, first by their dad, then by her husband. But her sister wasn't an awful person. Inconsiderate sometimes, a little whiney. Not cruel, though. They'd had some good talks over the years. Maybe she could offer some insight.

"I thought I was one kind of person, but I wasn't. I tried being another kind of person, but I wasn't her either."

"Because you already are who you are," Rachel said. "You're very good at what you do. Stop fighting against it."

"What I've been isn't who I want to be."

"You're almost thirty years old. It's a little late in life to be playing *What do I want to be when I grow up?*"

"I'm not ninety. Lots of people find their calling later in life."

"You have a calling?"

"I could have a calling."

"So, what is it?"

Maddy smoothed the comforter over her lap. "I want a career. I want to live somewhere other than this house. I want to make a living designing clothes."

"Designing clothes? I mean, you've made some really nice things for me, and your T-shirts are always cute, but that's way different from making a living at it. Besides, you'd need some kind of business knowledge and a history of working in the industry. No, I can't see it."

"I could learn business, take a class, maybe get a mentor. I'm a different person than I was when I left a couple days ago."

Rachel laughed. "No, you're not. You took a little leave. Time to get back to reality."

Maddy sat up straight and crossed her legs. "I did more than take a walk while I was gone. I designed a line of clothes for dolls. I made some, too."

The perfect arch of Rachel's dark brows rose halfway up her forehead. "You…get out. You were only gone for two days. And…dolls?"

"Dolls need clothes, too. I was thinking I could design clothes for them. Start a trend, you know? A whole fashion line for dolls of all different sizes. I could have a website for shopping, you know, start a brand."

"Hmm. Kind of interesting. My girls would enjoy shopping for doll clothes online."

"I did something else, too. I hitchhiked."

"You did not!"

"Yes, I did." Maddy chuckled at her sister's shock. This was kind of fun. "That's how I met Joel."

"Who's Joel?"

"He picked me up on Route 66. We checked into a cheesy motel, and I got drunk on tequila."

Rachel sucked in her breath. "You *didn't*. No way. I don't believe you."

"Well, believe it, because I did. And you know what else? I had sex with Joel."

"You had *sex* with him!"

"Stop yelling. The whole house will hear."

Rachel sat back and stared at her as if seeing her for

the first time. "Wow. I was worried you might still be a virgin."

"Worried?"

"Even a homebody like you should have some experiences."

"I've had experiences."

"Besides Owen?"

Maddy sighed.

"So, did you, um, enjoy yourself?"

Maddy couldn't help but grin. Joel was a liar and a cheat, but he knew how to ring her bell, repeatedly. "It was great."

"Wow, Meek Maddy having good sex with a man she just met. Didn't see that coming."

Meek Maddy. She always hated the nickname Rachel had come up with a few years ago. What she hated more was it fit. At least it used to fit. Time to blow her old image to bits. Hehehe.

"It was way better than great," Maddy said. She leaned forward, widened her eyes, and raised her voice. "It was mind-blowing, rock my world, rattle the headboard till it busts the wall, lose your mind and don't want to find it kind of sex!" Kaboom!

"Stop yelling. The whole house is going to hear."

"I just said the same thing to you."

"Well, I'm saying it back. I have children in this house. My daughters don't need to hear what you've been…doing."

"The same thing their mother did in her heyday."

"Shh! I didn't…I never…I never hitchhiked."

"You steamed up a few car windows."

"Shh. And you don't know that."

"Are you denying it?"

Rachel looked off to the side. “I was young. You do things when you’re young.”

“I didn’t. Unless you count cooking and cleaning. The wildest I ever got was the time I added more jalapenos to my homemade salsa.”

“Delicious, by the way. Why didn’t you ever make it again?”

“Dad said it was too hot.”

Rachel uncrossed her legs and then crossed them the other way. “We’ve gotten way off topic.”

Maddy’s words were a mumble. “Okay with me.”

“Oh, no. You don’t get to do that. You can’t throw everyone’s life into turmoil and then change the subject.”

“Fine. Look, Rachel, I’ve supported you through endless endeavors over the years. Like when you told everyone you were going to be a writer and I bought you a new pen and a notebook. I didn’t give you a hard time, even though you never wrote a single word. How about when you were learning to play the violin, which was a nightmare to listen to, I still encouraged you to practice. Going back further, I even supported you when you said you were a princess and insisted I call you Lady Rachel.”

“I was just a kid.”

“Mom was sick for a long time before she died. I have almost no memory of ever having been *just a kid.*”

Rachel paused before answering. “I know.”

Was there a note of guilt in her sister’s voice? For once in her life, Maddy was going to take advantage. Selfish? Self-serving? Maybe. Okay, yes. The scale had been tipped one way for so long it was natural for there to be a bit of teetering before she found balance.

Maddy directed a steady gaze toward her sister. “I covered for you when you snuck in past your curfew.

Remember the time you had a terrible hangover? I told Dad you had the stomach flu. You left for college while I stayed here and took care of Dad, the house, and my job at the Yarn Barn. Don't you think it's time I claim a life for myself? Rachel, I've never asked for your support before. I could really use it now."

"I just want what's best for you. I figured with Owen—"

"Why does everyone think I need someone to take care of me when I've been the one taking care of everyone?"

"I don't know. It's like, like inside these walls, you're the most capable person I've ever known. But out there in the world, you'd have to deal with a lot of reality. I don't know if you could handle it."

Her sister and her best friend sounded the same. Did everyone think she was an inept wimp? Joann *did* apologize yesterday. Was she sorry for being wrong or sorry because the truth was hurtful?

Maddy quirked an eyebrow. "Well, that's not insulting at all."

"I didn't mean…I just meant…It doesn't scare you at all, turning away from a comfortable life, jumping into the unknown?"

"It scares the hell out of me. Didn't it scare you when you moved three states away to go to college?"

"Sure. I was a nervous wreck for weeks before I left. The first few days there, I was overwhelmed with all the…the different."

"And then?"

"Then…I had one hell of a good time."

Maddy let it steep.

Her sister huffed and slouched back in her chair.

"Fine. Design clothes. I just hope you don't regret this later when Owen finds someone else. A guy like him isn't going to wait forever."

Owen marrying someone else. It was weird, after having been together for two years, but not upsetting. If she really loved him, wouldn't she be upset or at least a little jealous? Maybe this was the universe's weird way of setting things right for her, letting her know she was on the right path.

The big question now—what was her next step?

****

Joel woke up like a lightning bolt.

He had no idea what time he got home yesterday. After driving for hours, his head racing with a thousand different thoughts, he trudged through the door of his spacious, two-bedroom condominium and headed straight for his bedroom, undressing and dropping his clothes along the way.

He sat on the edge of his bed and set his phone on the charger, checking once more to make sure the ringer was off. The number three showed for his messages. He picked up the phone again to listen.

The first message was from his sister, Mariel, checking in on him. The next was from some woman he apparently met one night at the Shark Club, one of his nighttime hangouts. She wanted to get together for drinks and fun. He had no memory of her whatsoever.

The last message was from Bunny, a woman with impressive flexibility he'd spent a night with about a week ago. She said she like really had a really good time and like really wanted to see him again and like really, really hoped he felt the same. Like, really.

After erasing all the messages, Joel fell into a deep

sleep. He awoke well before the sun with a mission he couldn't fully define.

He sprang out of bed and walked through his condo with absolute dismay. When had his place gone to such utter hell?

When he'd first moved in, he'd kept the place clean and reasonably organized. He did the laundry on a regular basis. He kept the kitchen nice, ran the vacuum every now and then, and did some occasional dusting. It was as if his failing career grabbed at everything else in his life on the way down. He wandered through the rooms. The sight of his home left him nauseated.

Dirty clothes dotted the floor in every room. Items of clothing lay where he removed them. When had he started walking around while undressing? Dirty dishes, fast-food bags, empty beer bottles, opened and unopened mail, and various other debris, littered every flat surface in his home. He could write a message in the dust on the dark wood of his coffee table, and there was an unpleasant odor he couldn't pinpoint.

He gathered up the fast-food bags first. Whoa, there was the odor! He didn't dare peek inside the bag. He crumpled it up with the others and threw them away. From there, he became a man on a mission, picking up, scrubbing, sweeping, and organizing as if his future depended on it.

There was something kind of symbolic about cleaning up his place in real time. Like straightening out his life began with straightening out his living conditions. If that was true, he was off to a roaring start.

Joel washed every item of clothing on the floor, even the clothes in the clean pile, as some of them had been lying there for a while. He found a couple of items, like his Rain concert T-shirt he thought he'd lost, actually in the hamper. Everything was laundered and then hung up or folded and put away.

As he placed his folded T-shirts in a drawer, Joel made a plan to buy a few new dress shirts, maybe a tie, and some pants not made of blue denim. He would do some shopping later. First, the filth.

He threw away all of the expired and unidentifiable food from his refrigerator, gagging at something fuzzy sitting unwrapped on a plate. Could be a muffin. Could be a mouse. He gave the fridge a super scrubbing. If there was a prize for the cleanest refrigerator in the building, he was sure to win.

Along with some new clothes, he would buy some new food, real food, something to be cooked. He'd pick up a cookbook, too, so he could learn how to make something that didn't come with instructions on the box.

He mopped, dusted, and scrubbed each room in the apartment using every cleaning product his sister had given him. His kitchen sparkled, his bathroom shined, and he even used all of the attachments on his vacuum cleaner. Though, for the life of him Joel couldn't figure out what the little round brush attachment could be for. He used it anyway, sweeping it around the bottom of his oven and watching it suck up burnt black remnants of crust from countless reheated pizzas.

By the time Joel had finished making his bed with clean bedding, his silly parrot clock showed *7:45 a.m.* across its belly. He double tapped the parrot's head before the alarm started. After a shower in his immaculate bathroom, he ate a few crackers with peanut butter. He would do some serious grocery shopping later. Maybe buy some oatmeal instead of breakfast pastries.

For the first time in a long time, maybe for the first time ever, Joel was one of the first to arrive at work.

Wearing a short-sleeved dress shirt and clean jeans, carrying a cardboard box, he took the elevator to the fourth floor of the four-story building. He passed his own office before carrying his box farther down the hall. The black carpet with color swirls muffled his steps as he passed his father's closed door.

It would be hours before his dad was in his office. His father started every day down in the warehouse, then to the second floor to production. After that, he'd go up to the third floor, where he would attend the morning creative meeting. An hour or so before lunch, his dad would take the elevator to the fourth floor, the floor with all the offices.

Joel continued down the hall, glancing at the walls lined with wooden plaques with engraved brass plates commemorating their charitable endeavors and community services, alongside photos of award ceremonies and framed newspaper clippings.

He carried the box through the door bearing his mother's name. Neither his mother nor her secretary would be in yet, and he didn't have to check to know his mother's door would be locked. So, he took the keys and the doll, all dressed in her new clothes, from the box and set them on her secretary's desk. Natalie would give the doll to his mother when she arrived.

On the way home, he stopped and bought a new alarm clock.

Chapter 22

The landline rang while Maddy was walking from the bathroom to her bedroom. She tightened the belt on her terry robe, fingered back her wet hair, and headed for the little table at the end of the hall where sat their upstairs phone. The sound of all the voices coming from downstairs stopped her. Someone else could answer it today.

Not until she was dressed in some clean jeans, sneakers, and a powder blue T-shirt she'd made with tiny, colorful butterflies trimming the hem, did Maddy go downstairs. She took each step in slow motion, listening as she descended.

Voices from the kitchen told her it was full in there. Of course it was. Everyone was waiting for her to come in and cook, like she did every day, even on her wedding day.

The temptation to bolt rushed over her again. No, she couldn't keep running from situations she didn't want. It's what Meek Maddy did. From now on, she would be Self-Confident Maddy. Okay, didn't have the same ring. How about Proud Maddy. No, that wasn't right either. Glorious Maddy. No, that was just silly. Oh, Oh, Mad Maddy! Yes. From now on, she would be Mad Maddy.

Mad Maddy sounded wild and a little bit scary. Perfect. She smoothed her smile and entered the kitchen.

At the table facing her way sat her twin nieces, Jennifer and Jessica, in their princess pajamas. Four years old with their mother's beauty, dark ponytails swaying as they shot looks to each other and then to her, staring with laser beam eyes. They each pointed at her with one finger while scraping the other across the top in a *shame on you* motion.

Onward.

Her next step into the kitchen shut down every voice and had all heads swinging her way. Grandma Sophie and Rachel stood near the coffee maker. It was running, so someone had gotten it going. Her money was on Grandma. Just the smell of the coffee bolstered Maddy. She'd have a cup, soon. Maybe she'd sit out in the backyard under the umbrella tree and drink it.

Today, Grandma was a zebra. Zebra-striped leggings encased her thin legs. The outfit was topped with a red, blousy shirt with a zebra lightning bolt running diagonal across the front. Several rings of colorful bracelets dangled on her wrist. A black bow clipped her red hair on the side. Standing next to Rachel and her demure attire, they were a picture of opposites.

Her father sat at the kitchen table dressed in a short-sleeved plaid shirt and jeans. Across from him sat her fiancé. Her ex-fiancé.

Owen stood. He was clean, his neat blond hair combed and sprayed. He wore navy dress pants and a white button-down shirt with no tie. He looked nice, except for the bruises on his face. The swelling had gone down. The color, though, was darker. Coupled with the hopefulness in his eyes, the sight of him hurt her heart. Owen had offered her a good life, and she'd accepted. He hadn't misrepresented himself. She had.

"Owen, I'm sorry. For everything. I wouldn't blame you if you hated me."

Without a word, he stepped in front of her, placed his hands on her shoulders and his tired, bruised eyes locked onto hers. Owen spoke with a kindness she didn't expect or deserve. "Are you all right?"

Maddy's throat tightened, choking her words. All she could do was nod. Owen took her in his arms and squeezed.

"Madeline." Her father used her full first name. A sure sign she was in big trouble.

Maddy stepped back. "Owen, I have to talk to you alone."

"You owe all of us an explanation," her dad said.

She glanced at her father. His face was tight. His eyes had a hard glint. He was angry. A little worried but mostly angry. Her dad could wait. Maddy shifted her attention back to Owen. The man deserved a full apology and an explanation. Yes, he'd tracked her. A low move, for sure. But what she'd done was much worse. "Owen—"

"We'll put it behind us," Owen said.

Maddy shook her head. "You don't understand."

Her father got up from the table, his aggravation with her simmering over. "Of course he doesn't understand. I don't understand. Nobody understands."

"Sam," Grandma Sophie said. "Let's take a walk."

"The hell I will! I want to know why. Why did you take off like that? Why would you do such a terrible thing? And why, when you tell me you're on your way home, does it take you two damn days to get here! Where the hell did you go, to the moon?"

Grandma Sophie must not have told him where they

found her or the company she kept at the motel. She met her grandma's eyes and got a quick wink to confirm, bless her wild heart. Maddy didn't know how her grandma had managed it, but she was grateful. She gave the woman a discreet nod before turning back to her father.

"Dad, please. I need to talk to Owen."

"Sam," Sophie said. Her voice had more insistence this time, and her grandma took her father's arm. "Let them talk."

Owen squeezed her shoulders again, drawing her attention. "Maddy, we're just going to forget about all this, okay? You got scared, got a little crazy for a while. I sure didn't help. It was obvious you had concerns, and I looked the other way. I'm sorry for that."

Owen apologizing? No, he's the one who deserves the apology.

"Owen," she said.

He pressed his finger against her lips. "Not another word. Let's have a fresh start. I've already spoken to someone who can perform the ceremony. We can be married as soon as I make the arrangements." He then removed his finger and kissed her.

"Owen," she said again. When he leaned back, Maddy stared at his bruised face. The poor guy had been through a horrible couple of days because of her. "I never meant to—"

"It's all right, Maddy. Like I said, we can put this behind us." Then Owen glanced over his shoulder toward her father. "Sam, walk out to my car with me, will you?"

Her father looked at Owen, then to Maddy. He wasn't one to keep his thoughts to himself, but he wanted this marriage to happen as much as Owen. He strode out the kitchen door without a word. Owen kissed Maddy once on the lips, and she cursed herself for thinking about Joel and how his kisses were so passionate you could float away on them. Owen's kisses were handshakes with lips.

"I love you," Owen said. "I'm going to make you happy."

He loved her. He was still ready to pledge his life to her, even after everything she'd done. Yet, here she stood, thinking about Joel's kisses. She was truly horrible. Maybe she was wrong, too.

Maybe this is how it's supposed to be. Not the part about her being horrible, but the part where she'd dismissed comfort and stability as being less important than passion, fun, and lust. Maybe what she'd had with Joel had been like a Fourth of July sparkler, bright and exciting, yet fizzling to a quick death. A flash too bright to last.

Maybe Joel was her wild time, meant to make her appreciate the solidity of marriage and give her a fond memory for her old age.

Owen was a slow burn, an ashy coal without shine or sparkle, but would stay warm throughout her life.

Five minutes later, Maddy was sitting at the kitchen table having coffee with her Grandma Sophie. Rachel had taken the twins upstairs to get them dressed. Whatever Owen had said to her father had taken less than fifteen minutes and worked like magic. The front door opened and closed, along with the sound of a car driving away, then her dad's footsteps going upstairs.

The spell wouldn't last. No way her father was going to let all this slide. In the meantime, there was

Grandma. Maddy needed to talk, and Grandma Sophie was a great listener. All those years of tending bar took the shock out of anything you could tell her and gave her a unique perspective. So, Maddy told her everything.

"Designer clothes for dolls." Sophie beamed and clapped her hands together. Her bracelets clinked and slid up her arm. "That's genius!"

Maddy smiled. She should have talked to her grandma about her dream of designing clothes a long time ago.

"Oh, I wish I'd noticed the dolls when I was there. I'll bet they're all fabulous."

"I'm proud of them."

"As you should be. It's a great idea."

"About the other stuff…Grandma, are you disappointed in me?"

"Disappointed? Are you kidding? I'm thrilled!"

Maddy laughed. Of course Grandma was thrilled. This was a woman who taught her the best way to stuff a bra. Still, it had been a worry in the back of her mind.

"How long have I been telling you to go out and have some fun?" Grandma said.

"A long time." She'd always brushed off her grandma's nudge to fun. There were things to be done, then she was tired from doing it all.

"Shots of tequila, huh? Heheee! It's high time you grabbed a hand full of life." Sophie lowered her voice. "You used a condom, didn't you? I taught you about protection."

Maddy's face heated. With Grandma, no subject was taboo. Still, Maddy got embarrassed sometimes. "Yes, Grandma."

"Good girl. Ah, I miss the days before you always

had to be so careful. Really put a damper on promiscuity. Honey, don't you dare feel ashamed. You can't go through life holding in your urges. You've been living like a nun. It was only a matter of time before you exploded. Granted, your timing could have been better, but I'm overjoyed you've finally gone out and had a taste of life. About damn time."

This drew a burst of laughter from Maddy. "You really think it's a good thing I slept with another man?"

Sophie had a sip of her coffee. "Let me tell you something, sweetie. When I first started tending bar, I worked at this place called The Mayfair. On Saturday nights, they had live bands, and the place really got to jumping. Anyhow, there was this woman, Molly. Molly developed quite a thing for this new guy who started coming around. His name was Ray. He was a real looker, and Molly wasn't the only one who noticed. One night Ray asked Molly to dance with him. It was a slow dance, and he was quite the romantic. He really swept her off her feet."

Sophie had another sip of coffee.

"After that," Sophie said. "Every Saturday night, Molly came in and sat at a table all by herself. She turned down every guy who asked her to dance because she was waiting for Ray to ask her again. He never did, and she didn't have the courage to ask him. Watching her sit there every Saturday night all by herself, I decided something."

"What, Grandma?"

"I decided I would rather live it up on the dance floor for fifty years than live for a hundred and fifty years sitting at a table watching the party, waiting for anyone in particular to ask me to dance. Listen to me now. You have to seek out the good parts of life wherever you can. The bad parts won't hesitate to find you. Yes, Maddy. I'm tickled pink. From the spark in your eyes when you talk about Joel, I suspect you had yourself a real good time."

"For God's sake, Maddy!" Rachel strode into the kitchen. Her phone was in her hand, and she waved it around as she spoke. "Must you announce it to everyone? Have you no self-respect whatsoever? Am I going to read about this in tomorrow's paper? Maybe see it on a billboard along the highway? *Maddy Hayden Checks into a Motel with a Man She Hardly Knows.*"

"Actually," Sophie said. "We're thinking about calling the local news channel and getting it on TV, or maybe one of those internet thingies. Besides, I picked her up at the motel. I already knew."

Rachel let out a long, exaggerated breath and slid into a chair next to Maddy and across from Sophie. She set her phone on the table. "Grandma, even you have to see how reckless she's been. I mean, come on." Rachel faced Maddy, speaking before Sophie had a chance. "I just got off the phone with Owen. I'm glad you've decided to go through with the wedding."

Maddy sucked in a breath. She never agreed to that. Or did she? Her mind raced through the conversation. He'd cut her off when she was saying something. Had he misunderstood? Did she, in some part of her practical thinking, want to get married to Owen, want what was comfortable, what she knew? Maddy blinked a couple of times. She needed to think.

"She's not going to marry him," Sophie said.

Rachel gave their grandma a look. "She has to marry him. This might be her last chance for love."

"Nonsense," Sophie said. "Besides, any woman who's done what Maddy has obviously doesn't want to get married."

Rachel was worked up now. Her hands swung with every word. "Any man who would take her back after what she's done is worth holding on to."

Then the two women were talking over each other, Rachel pushing for marriage, Grandma Sophie pushing the other way. They both meant well, but damn! She was a grown woman, capable of making her own decisions. Okay, running away minutes before her wedding could have been thought through a little better. But if she hadn't run away, she wouldn't have gotten her first real adventure, mind-blowing sex, or a line on a new career.

At the rise of their voices, the height of their argument, Maddy had enough. "Stop it! Both of you, stop it! I'll decide what I'm going to do. Me. And what I've decided is…I've decided I'm…going to take a walk."

Two minutes later, she was marching down her street. She passed the modest, working-class homes she'd known her whole life. Squares of neat-trimmed yards with mature sycamores and Indian laurels shaded sections of the sidewalk. Mr. Hernandez washed his car in the driveway. Mrs. Jankowski looked up from weeding her bed of lilacs and waved.

Several blocks down, Maddy rounded a corner to wander a street of small stores and restaurants. A coffee shop had two bistro tables set up outside. An elderly man sat at one, sipping from a mug.

She walked by a deli, a bookshop, a store selling sports clothing, and another coffee shop. Maddy kept going until her steps slowed, and she searched for a bench to sit down and take a break. She spotted something better than a bench.

Maddy chuckled at her change. Why not? Her hangover was a memory, and she was still making up for lost time. She'd limit herself to one and keep it soft.

So that's how she ended up sitting on a barstool drinking a beer at ten o'clock in the morning.

****

Natalie arrived at her secretarial office fronting Mrs. Tyler's office at exactly eight thirty-five a.m. She wasn't due at the toy company until nine. On a normal day she would get there at ten to nine, ten minutes before her boss. Try as she might, she just never mastered being a morning person. Yet, being seated and settled when Mrs. Tyler walked through the door made a good impression. Making a good impression was something she *had* mastered.

But this morning, her seventeen-year-old niece, Samantha, who had come to visit, had to be at the airport crazy early to catch her plane back to Colorado. After consuming two cups of overpriced coffee and a bear claw pastry in the airport cafe, Natalie had no choice but to show up for work early, a full twenty-five minutes before Mrs. Tyler would arrive.

Before she walked behind her tidy desk, before she put her oversized purse containing all her stuff, including her romance novel and her lunch into her desk drawer, Natalie saw the doll.

It stood on the desk facing her comfy ergonomic chair, the one Mrs. Tyler gave her on her last birthday. Natalie rounded her desk while reaching into her candy bowl for an early morning nibble. Three candy-covered chocolates were in her mouth before she spotted the block of wood with the keys next to the doll. They were the keys to the old truck, number three, the one Joel had taken.

Natalie picked up the doll and plopped down in her chair. “Poor little doll. Such a shame nobody wanted you.” She placed the doll with her purse in the deep bottom drawer of her desk. Then she picked it up again.

The doll looked different. She couldn’t put her finger on it, but it had a more appealing appearance than what she remembered. Maybe it was her hope and disappointment colliding. She’d had real optimism for this concept. Joel had a good mind for the creative side of the toy company, even when he was a kid. He just hadn’t landed on the right concept of his own yet. She couldn’t help but worry about Joel’s future. She heard things, saw things.

Joel was far too fond of going out with his friends. Sometimes he showed up for work late. Sometimes with a hangover. But he was a good guy, and he had an inventive side that could pay off for the company if he’d straighten up some. Even with his wild lifestyle, Joel managed some creative ideas. They were flops before they made it to production, but they were creative.

This doll, though, was different. It had real potential. Things have changed, and it was time to move on from anorexia-inspiring dolls. Well, maybe not. The doll hadn’t sold, and she’d overheard Mr. and Mrs. Tyler talking. This was Joel’s last chance to develop a product. The poor guy would be stuck in his office now. He hated office work.

Natalie set the doll in the drawer and closed it before munching a couple more candies. Then she scribbled a note for herself on the little pad beside her business phone. *Thank Joel for the doll.* She fired up her computer and got to work.

Mrs. Tyler strode through the door at exactly nine o'clock. Today she wore a coal gray business skirt and matching jacket with a pristine white blouse underneath. She had a trim waist, and her short, blonde hair was sprayed into compliance.

"Good morning, Mrs. Tyler."

"Good morning, Natalie. Have you seen Joel this morning?"

"No, but he left these on my desk." Natalie handed her the truck keys attached to the wooden block.

Mrs. Tyler took the keys and stared at them. "Two days late."

"Would you like me to take those downstairs for you?"

"No. I'm going down there in a little while, anyway. I'll take them. Thank you."

Then her boss unlocked her door and stepped into her office. She closed the door with a solemn click.

****

Joel sat at his kitchen table, with his laptop open in front of him. He'd spent the better part of two hours searching what kind of positions were out there. Gathering his options.

His momentum toward betterment took hit after hit as he scoured the listings. What was he qualified to do? He'd worked at the toy factory since he was a little kid. Having worked in virtually every department over the years, he'd logged on with a decent attitude. He had a variety of experiences on his resume. However, none of his qualifications aligned with what was available.

He picked up his phone to see the time. *1:45*. Well

after lunch, and he still hadn't heard from either of his parents about the doll he'd left for his mother. A very bad sign. If she'd loved the doll's new look, she would have called right away. Mom was always quick to respond with good news. Bad news took more thought. The writing was on the wall, and his vision was twenty-twenty.

Joel checked to make sure he'd turned the ringer back on before setting down his phone. He leaned back, stroking his shaved jaw for a moment, before changing paths. It was time to go to some businesses in person. He stood and grabbed his phone just as it rang.

He glanced at the screen. His mother. He considered not answering, knowing it wasn't going to be good news. To do so would not be the action of the man he was striving to be now.

"Hi, Mom."

"First things first," she said. "Are you all right?"

She didn't sound angry. Nor did she sound pleased. "I'm fine. I've been waiting to hear what you have to say. Natalie gave it to you, didn't she?"

What was that sound? Keys. His mom must be holding the keys to the truck he'd left next to the doll. He recognized the light clunk of them against the wooden block they used for a key chain. Did she have the doll in front of her?

"Yes, she gave it to me. Frankly, Joel, It's a little late."

Because she hadn't called first thing this morning, he already knew it wasn't going to be good news. Still, hope dies hard when you've put your heart into a project.

"I'm sure you did your best," his mother said. So giving you the benefit of the doubt, why don't we just agree to drop the matter? Okay?"

Joel blinked his eyes. She was acting as though she was doing him a favor by not even discussing the doll's new look. Saving him from another humiliation.

"Did you hear me?" she said. "We'll just let this go."

Odd, but his first thought wasn't for himself. Maddy had worked so hard on the new clothes. She'd stayed up all night perfecting his creation. He had a whole fantasy going about how he would tell her the clothes she'd made had gotten a green light. Then he could explain everything to her, his…situation with Roz.

Maddy. He hadn't stopped thinking about her since she'd walked out of the hotel room. Her laugh, her sweet voice, her devotion to family, her talent and passion for a career, the work she put in to make his creation better. The way the mere thought of her body sent him to another world.

A quick online search told him where he could find the Yarn Barn. There was only one. Without good news about the doll, however, he'd lost his last chance to connect with her. Besides, he didn't even know if she'd gone back to work there, and even if she did, showing up at her work was too close to what Owen had done.

He understood the man's drive to keep her. Who wouldn't put themselves out all kinds of ways for Maddy? Still, tracking her had been low and creepy. Stalking her at her workplace would be just as bad. The thought was a desperate grab.

Joel glanced around his apartment. It was neat and clean. Aside from the toys he'd helped develop, now in the hall closet, it was the home of an adult. Almost.

Something in his head tightened. Pieces clicked together. He stood taller. His career, his life, had gone stagnant. He'd been reevaluating, maybe for a while now. Today was a day of action.

"No."

"No what?" his mother said.

He glanced around again. With the cleaning of his apartment, he'd likewise dusted off his pride, scrubbed his dignity, and laundered some fresh ambition. "I'm leaving the company."

"Joel, you can't leave," she said. Firm, but with a slight, underlying tremble. "You're a part of this company."

"Not an important part. I have to go now." Not wanting to end the conversation in what his mother would see as a complete ruin, before he hung up, he said, "I love you, Mom. I'll call you later in the week."

Okay. What next?

Going to the competition was out of the question. He would never backstab his family. Marketing the doll on his own was his only option. It would be harder not to have an entire toy factory at his disposal. But it wasn't impossible. Others had done it. He had lots of contacts, he had money in his savings, and he had renewed determination.

Joel spent the better part of the next hour on the phone, advancing his life.

****

Maddy entered the house through the front and closed the door, slow and quiet, sneaking in like a teen after curfew.

If she leaned to the right a little and peeked around the stairs, she could see into the kitchen. In her partial view was her father sitting at the table and Rachel buzzing back and forth. Grandma Sophie and her father's conversation was drowned out by the twin's argument over who was the best princess.

After the single beer she drank, Maddy was tempted to flop down on the couch. She could do it. They didn't know she was here. No. No more avoidance. While the beer made her a little sleepy, it also bolstered her backbone. Or maybe that had started already, and the beer just made it easier to spot. Or harder to ignore. *Whatever. Face the family. Get it over with. On to yonder kitchen.*

"Maddy," Sophie said. Grandma got up from her seat across the table from her father. Her dad raised his head to stare at her, his irritated expression tempered with uncertainty.

"I know, breakfast is very late," she said. Maybe if she fed him, she could get his anger toned down a little more.

Her sister boasted from over at the stove. "Don't worry about breakfast. I'm cooking."

Alarm shot up Maddy's spine. Rachel didn't cook. In her sister's house, breakfast was cereal, lunch was sandwiches, and dinner was ordered. Twice, back when Rachel still lived with them, she'd tried cooking a meal. Most of what she'd made was unidentifiable. There was semi-raw pasta in one of them. The slops and splatters and burned-on messes she'd left took Maddy forever to scrub clean.

Maddy swung her head toward the stove where her sister stood, stirring a steaming pot. No, not steaming. Smoking.

Rachel threw a smug grin over her shoulder toward Maddy. "I'm making oatmeal."

After three cautious but hurried steps, Maddy

gasped at the blue and orange flame of the gas burner. Her sister had the knob turned all the way to high. Fire slapped up the side of the smoking pot and was doing its best to engulf it. Maddy's hand darted out, aiming for the knob to lower the flame. Rachel slapped her hand away.

"I've got this under control," Rachel said.

"You've got the fire way too high."

"It's fine. It's—" Rachel didn't get to finish her sentence because the smoke alarm screeched like a pissed-off chimp.

Rachel and the twins covered their ears and screamed at a pitch high enough to rival the alarm. Her dad slapped his hands over his ears and hollered at them to "Shut that damn thing off right now!" At least, that's what Maddy thought he was saying. It was hard to tell over all the shrieking.

Grandma Sophie leaped from her seat and yanked the door all the way open, swinging it back and forth in an effort to air out the room. Dad jumped up and grabbed his toolbox from the utility closet, set it on the table, and dug through it. Right behind him, Maddy snatched the broom from the narrow closet and swept at the air around the alarm. The stupid thing continued to screech, so she flipped the broom around and pounded the stick end into the plastic several times. It died a crunchy death.

The twins and her sister stopped screaming, and the kitchen rang silent. Her dad stopped rummaging through his toolbox. Everyone breathed hard as if the ungodly noise took physical effort to survive.

Rachel was the first to speak, her words marching from her red lips in the full regalia of her anger. "Great. Now you've ruined breakfast!"

Maddy glared at her sister. "It was already ruined."

"Everything was fine until you turned the knob all the way to high." Rachel slid the pot to a cold burner.

Maddy rotated her body in slow motion, her neck as hot as the burned oatmeal. She stopped when she faced her sister. Her fist clenched around the broom handle. "The flame was already turned up all the way, *Rachel*. I was turning it down."

"All I know is everything was fine until you walked over here. Maddy…Maddy, put down that broom."

She'd put it down, all right. Down Rachel's throat.

Rachel grabbed the big, silver spoon from the pot and held it in front of her like a cross to a vampire. Oatmeal dropped to the floor in clumps. "Maddy, don't make me use this."

"What are you going to do, Rachel, lower my cholesterol?"

"Girls!" their father said. "Enough!" At any other time, it would have sounded like a shout. Not today. With her ears still ringing from the smoke alarm, her dad's voice had a bit of distance to it. "Put down those weapons before somebody gets hurt."

"Your father is right," Grandma Sophie said. She was still swinging the door, airing out the smoke. "Beating each other with kitchen items won't solve anything."

Her father stood and headed for the pantry, taking his cup of coffee with him. He turned back with a box of chocolate chip cookies. "Jessica, Jennifer, let's go watch some cartoons." The twins shouted with joy and skipped behind their grandpa into the living room.

Rachel tossed the spoon into the pot. It stuck straight up without so much as a waver. The center of the oatmeal must be solidifying. Maddy lowered the broom, but she kept a good grip on it.

"Grandma," Maddy said. "Your purse is ringing."

Her grandma hurried to the counter to her big, zebra-striped purse. The old-fashion telephone ring got louder when she slid her cell out of the side pocket. "Thanks. I thought the ringing was coming from inside my ears. Hello? Oh! Hold on." To her granddaughters, she said, "I'm going outside to take this."

Grandma Sophie left through the back door, closing it behind her.

Maddy and Rachel bent over and stared into the pot like they were staring at a semi-dangerous science experiment. The oatmeal clotted gray/brown around the spoon in the center of the pot and was burned hard and dark around the edges.

"Well, I'm not cleaning this mess," Rachel said.

Maddy glared at her sister. "You made the mess. You can clean it."

Her sister stared back. The times Rachel had made a disastrous effort in the kitchen before, Maddy sent her on her way while she cleaned it all. Not today. Not anymore. She headed for the doorway, intending to go up to her room where she'd take a nap, maybe for the rest of the day.

"Maddy, you can't leave now! I don't even know *how* to clean this."

"I don't care if you lick it clean."

Then, for the first time in her life, Maddy walked out on a dirty kitchen.

Chapter 23

"It's good having you back," Lois said. "We missed you."

Maddy smiled up at her boss from her seat at a worktable where she was unpacking colorful spools of thread and organizing them into trays. Organizing threads and thinking about Joel.

Thinking about Joel wasn't what she wanted, but her mind wouldn't stop, hadn't stopped since she'd walked out on him. The worst thoughts were the ones making her body a traitor to her good sense. Well, worst and best. When that man touched her, it was like no man ever had before, not really. He was like lightning wrapped in Jersey fabric, intense and cozy at the same time. Joel wasn't going to fade from her thoughts any time soon. Damn him.

If it was just great sex, maybe she could smother the memory with new ones. Although, she'd have to up her sexual history list to a number far above two. It didn't matter anyway. She missed the rest of him, too.

Joel had helped her realize her dream or rather the pursuit of it. It was yet another fantasy of hers he'd infused with life. The man was a sexy mechanism for such things. Like the way he made laughter a regular part of the day and how he made her feel so free even when she was on the run. Bottom line, Joel made her happy.

It was all a lie. He's engaged to be married to

someone else.

So was I. This debate ran on a loop in her head.

It was different with her. As she'd told him, she was upfront about her situation from the start. She was wearing a wedding dress when he picked her up on the side of the road, duh. Besides, she was running away from her wedding. He was just taking a vacation from his obligations. Big difference. Big. Huge. The lying, two-timing, cheating ball of slime.

The worst thing was she missed the lying, two-timing, cheating ball of slime. Damn him. Damn her, too, for hopscotching from one bad situation to another. Maybe she was cursed.

She shooed Joel out of her head and gave her attention to her boss.

Lois was about twenty years older than her. A strong-built woman with fluffy, auburn hair touching her shoulders. Every day she wore blue eye shadow and pink lipstick. She was as good a boss as you could ask for, always in charge but understanding of the realities of life. Lois was the one who'd hired her to work at the Yarn Barn, twelve years ago when she'd still been in high school. It was only a couple hours after school back then. After graduation, Maddy started working full time.

It was supposed to be a temporary job. After Rachel finished college, Maddy would have her chance for higher education. Finances wouldn't allow both of them to be in school at the same time. Maddy never got to the point of application.

Rachel got engaged right after she graduated, and Maddy's turn was pushed back. She designed and sewed her sister's wedding dress and all six of the bridesmaid dresses. Her turn was pushed back again when Dad had to have both knees replaced.

Then the twins were born after a difficult pregnancy, and Rachel needed help. Maddy drove the hour to her sister's house at least three days a week with a car full of meals and clean laundry. With each passing event, Maddy's future converted to her past and became her present.

"It's good to be back," Maddy said to Lois.

In a way, it was. She'd been back at work for a few days. She was comfortable here, surrounded by the familiar, the people, the work. But her adventure had cleared away a haze, and she'd glimpsed possibilities. An actual career rather than a pipe dream. A want and desire not so far-fetched as it once seemed.

Every evening after she cleaned up the dinner mess, Maddy sat in her room, or outside if it was nice, designing clothes for dolls. Her plan was to have a good variety of designs for different-sized dolls before she made her approach to companies.

She even had a name for her business; Mad Maddy's Designs. She'd get a logo, something wild and free. Right now, she was concentrating on building her collection.

A customer set two bolts of green velvet on the counter, along with her handbasket of notions. Lois left to ring up the sale. Maddy glanced at the clock on the wall and sighed. Two more hours left on her shift. The downside to making such grand plans was her daily routines had become humdrum. It all got in the way of her designing.

The next day, her day off, Maddy rang out the dishrag after cleaning up from lunch and took her design book and pencils out to the small but well-tended backyard. Dad had gone upstairs, maybe to take a nap. Rachel and the girls had gone home days ago. Though life was more peaceful and easier, she missed having all her family around. Well, in part.

Oh, that reminded her. She needed to buy a new pot. Rachel's way of cleaning the one she'd used to cook oatmeal was to throw it in the trash. Maddy learned about the pot last night when she was looking for it. Dad told her he'd seen it in the garbage can outside.

She strolled across the yard beneath a sky full of fluffy white clouds. They acted as a mild filter to the sun, giving the yard light without being too bright. Maddy settled into her lawn chair beneath the thick, clustered leaves of the umbrella tree.

Warm, fresh air engulfed her. Blue hydrangeas along the back wooden fence bloomed full and lovely against the whitewash. The scent of her two dwarf lemon trees blended well with the pink lilacs along the back of the house. Two tortoiseshell butterflies danced by, then fluttered over the fence and into the neighbor's yard.

Maddy opened her book to where she'd left off yesterday, drawing a pair of denim shorts with little daisies along both outside seams, and then picked up a white pencil to color in the tiny petals. She'd been at it for about half an hour before the commotion began.

Voices, a man's laughter, then, was that the twins?

She put her pencil back in the box and set her book on the chair. Halfway across the yard, a crowd rounded the house from the driveway. Rachel, wearing her yellow maid-of-honor dress, with her dressed-up husband, followed by the twins in their flower girl dresses. Rachel was ripping a thin plastic covering from something voluminous and white. A silver shopping bag hung from her arm.

Joann, wearing her bridesmaid dress, and Grandma Sophie, wearing the same pink dress she'd worn to the wedding, followed. Worry pinched both their faces. Her dad walked out of the house then, also dressed up for an occasion.

The hairs on Maddy's neck stood at attention. "What's going on?"

Owen stepped up and took both her hands in his, gazing into her eyes. The smile he gave her was a touch off sane. "It's a surprise wedding."

Maddy steadied herself against what was either alarm or dread. She refused to accept panic. "A surprise wedding?"

"It's a thing," Owen said. He nodded as if to confirm his own statement. "Really. Look it up online. Women love it."

Women love surprise weddings? She found that hard to believe. A woman wants to be ready for such a thing. Hair, makeup, a dress. She had an image in her mind of her wedding dress tumbling down the road and would have laughed if not for sensing a cage dangling over her head.

The twins laughed and twirled across the lawn, making the skirts of their little yellow dresses float. Maddy looked around and met eyes with Grandma Sophie. She stood next to Joann.

Sophie quick-stepped over in her low-heeled shoes, her big, zebra-striped purse on her shoulder. She locked onto Maddy's left arm and turned her away from Owen. "You don't have to do this."

Then Joann was there. "She's right. Oh, Maddy, I've picked up my phone a hundred times to call you the last few days. I just couldn't figure out the best way to say everything. I wanted to tell you on the ride home the other day, but you slept most of the time, and, well, I didn't think the opportunity was right."

"What do you mean?"

"Maddy," Joann said. Her face tightened with anguish, and she shook her head. "I'm so sorry I ignored your concerns before. I thought I was saying the right things, but I was wrong to try and convince you it was best to marry Owen. Unless this is what you really want."

Maddy glanced at Owen, who was talking to a heavyset man with slicked-back blond hair, a ruddy face, and a bright smile. She'd never seen him before.

To Joann, she said, "I know you were just looking out for me."

Joann shook her head again. "It wasn't my decision to make. I'm so sorry, Maddy. Can you ever forgive me?"

"You said those things out of love. Besides, I think the way I lived my life, I didn't give anyone reason to believe I wanted to be something more than what I've always been. That's on me."

Maddy hugged her friend, then stood back and glanced around. Grandma and Joann were telling her she didn't have to get married. Yet, here was a surprise wedding. Had they been planning it with Owen since they got back? "How long has this surprise wedding been in the works?"

"None of us knew anything about it until Owen called us all early this morning," Joann said. "He told everyone it was a surprise because you wanted to get married but didn't want the hassle of all the planning and such. Is that true?"

"I haven't spoken to Owen in days," Maddy said. She figured he'd come to his senses and moved on with his life. What kind of man would still want her after what she'd done?

The kind of man who would stick with her through all the good and bad life threw at them.

Had she been too harsh about Owen? Had panic clouded her vision?

You've made your decision on this. Come on, girl. Get it together.

Then Owen had her right arm, tugging her around to face him. "I know I've been distant these past few days, but I've been busy planning this surprise. Look," he said. Everyone looked to where he gestured, toward the driveway. Two women were each hauling a red wagon filled with white vases of colorful tulips.

Owen beamed at her. "Tulips are your favorite, right?"

Rachel tipped her head and said, "Aw. How sweet!" Her sister then swung on her husband. "Do you know my favorite flower?"

Brad, her brother-in-law, stood beside Rachel, handsome in a pale-gray suit and crimson tie, his maple hair trimmed short and neat. He had a moment of obvious worry before he said, "Pansies?"

"Roses. It's red roses." Rachel lifted her chin and swiveled her head away, muttering. "Pansies." That was going to cost Brad.

Maddy stared at the two wagons, now crossing the yard. A man in a gray T-shirt and jeans followed the wagons with a flatbed wagon of his own holding varying sizes of pedestal tables.

"Yes. Tulips," Maddy said. Owen remembered her

favorite flower. That meant something, didn't it?

"See," Owen said. His smile took over his face. "Do I know my Maddy or what?"

He looked so happy. So…pleased about pleasing her. Was she pleased?

Then her Grandma Sophie spun her the other way. "There's something you need to know, Maddy." Her grandma leaned close to her ear. "I've been—"

"Come on, now," Owen said. He still had her right arm and gave her two tugs until she faced him again. "I want you to meet Pete."

"Who's Pete?"

"A friend of mine from college. He's not only an accountant but an ordained minister. He can marry us. I checked it out. It's all legal. Great news, isn't it?"

The man he'd been speaking with, the one she didn't know, grabbed her hand, and shook it with enthusiasm. He was dressed in a dark blue suit with a white shirt and a tie specked with little red balloons. "Hi. Nice to meet you, Maddy. I've heard a lot of great things about you. I'm honored to officiate your wedding."

Maddy may have said hi. She wasn't sure. There was a mild ringing in her ears, and her life took on a sort of strobe-light vibe. Moments were not flowing but clicking by in bright flashes with blank spaces in between.

Then Rachel was there with a dress draped over her arm. A white wedding dress with puffy three-quarter sleeves, an enormous bell skirt one flounce short of the Victorian era, and a bodice with enough lace to drape half the windows in their house. As if the dress wasn't already sufficiently hideous, the waist was adorned with a white bow large enough to top a car.

"Maddy, I did the best I could on such short notice. This was the closest they had to your size, off the rack. Go try it on."

"No time," Owen said. "Put it on over your T-shirt and shorts." As he was saying it, he was doing it, maneuvering the dress over her head. He got her arms through. But the dress bunched around her head and shoulders, forcing her arms upright, as if raised in surrender.

The fabric smashed against her face as he shifted and twisted the dress. Maddy struggled to breathe, though she didn't know if was because of the dress or the situation. *Snap out of it, Maddy! Think. Take action.*

"Give her time to go inside and change," her sister said. "I bought shoes and white stockings, too."

Owen's response was immediate. "Not necessary."

"She can't get married in sneakers!" Rachel said.

The strobe blinked faster. She waved her arms, still stuck up in a surrender position.

"The dress is long enough, so her shoes won't show," Owen said. "It doesn't matter anyway. Who cares about her shoes? We're getting married!"

Like a final stitch, the strobe light of time stopped. Maddy caught her balance. Her thoughts clicked into place, as did her spine.

"Owen, stop," Maddy said. Between all the chatter and her head still buried inside the mass of fabric, she doubted anyone heard her. They would, though. Meek Maddy was breathing dust. Mad Maddy chewed on nails.

When her head popped out of the fabric, her father was there. The lines on his face appeared deeper. His eyes had a sadness to them she only saw when she caught him staring at the wedding picture of her parents they kept on an end table in the living room. Dad wanted her to marry Owen and was thrilled about it from the start. Why would he be sad?

"I'd like a moment with my daughter," he said to everyone in the vicinity.

Before they walked away, Rachel said, "Wait. Here, I found this, too."

Her sister removed a silver loop out of her shopping bag, like a tambourine without the jingles. Long, white lace hung from one side. It was a veil. A wedding veil. Rachel placed the veil on Maddy's head, adjusted and pinned it, and handed her the shopping bag.

"Take this, Maddy," Rachel said. "The shoes and stockings are in here. Make Owen let you go change."

Let me?

Maddy took the bag and walked with her father through a lather of charging thoughts.

The dress was too big, and she had to lift the skirt to keep from tripping over the voluminous fabric. Her father led her a few feet away from the small crowd with his hand between her shoulder blades. It was as affectionate as he ever got, and it raised her concern. They stopped near the back of the house, next to the lilac bushes.

Her father stared at her for a moment before shifting his head toward the small crowd in their backyard. The three people who had dragged in the wagons were setting up the pedestal tables and placing the vases of tulips on them, creating an alcove of sorts in front of the umbrella tree.

"I always thought *I* was the one taking care of *you*," her father said.

It wasn't even close to what she expected to hear.

"What?"

"I covered the bills except for your personal expenses. I take care of the yard, the household repairs."

"You've always been great about all that stuff."

"Those couple of days you were gone…"

His farm-weathered face tightened. "What, Dad?"

"It was so natural, the way you slid into the role. I guess I never thought about how much you do around here. How much you've done since we lost your mom. Your grandma was right. Damn, I hate to admit such a thing. It'll light the woman up, for sure."

The acknowledgment was a hug to her heart. The nod to her grandma made her smile. "Thank you. I appreciate hearing that."

"After Owen called this morning to tell me about this surprise wedding, tell me how you wanted it. I took a good long look at that picture in the living room."

"Your wedding picture on the end table."

Her dad nodded and then glanced at the house, at the fragrant lilacs. "You know, I keep the lilacs there because your mother loved them."

"I remember."

He was still staring at the lilac bushes. "She sang, you know."

"Mom used to sing when she did things around the house, especially in the kitchen. I remember her singing. She had a pretty voice."

"No, I mean, when I met her, she wanted to be a professional singer."

"Really? I never heard anything about that."

"She was good enough. But so are a lot of people. I thought it was a silly dream. I…I didn't take her seriously. I regret it now."

"Dad, she was happy here in this house. I know she was."

"I know. She loved you girls with all her heart. This house, too. But when we were young, before we settled down, I should have cheered for her. Not brushed it off the way I did. I've been thinking about her a lot these past few days, more than usual. What I'm saying is, you're a good girl, Maddy. A deserving girl. And, well, there's more to you than what I let myself believe."

These were more words than she'd ever heard him say at one time, and all of them in her favor.

He nodded toward her chair beneath the umbrella tree. "I've seen you out there, drawing your designs. I always thought it was just a hobby. I didn't realize it was so important to you."

"In fairness to you, Dad, I never talked about it like it was important to me."

"Why not?"

Maddy's shoulders lifted in a slight shrug. "I couldn't say it out loud. It seemed so…far-fetched."

"I guess some of that is my fault. Like with your mother's singing, it was too dreamy. Nothing against the arts, but I need to know there's a steady paycheck."

"I can understand your viewpoint," Maddy said. "Especially when you have a mortgage, a family to support."

"You don't have those responsibilities. At least not yet. I know you've missed out on a lot of things your sister had. I'm thinking, well, it's not too late for you."

Maddy stared at her father for a moment. This turnaround was huge. "What changed your mind?"

"Done some thinking the last couple of days. A lot more since Owen called this morning and told me you wanted this. Maddy, you deserve to be happy. You deserve to chase your dream. It's what your mom would have wanted for you. I already screwed things up for you a couple of years ago. For the life of me, I can't get this parenting thing right."

"You've been a great father. Wait, are you talking about when I moved out?"

Her father nodded. "I should have never forced you to move back home after that guy broke into your apartment. But it scared the hell out of me."

She smiled and touched her father's arm, gave him a little squeeze. "I handled it."

"Handled it damn well. I bragged about you to the guys at work."

"You did?"

"You bet I did. Chasing him away with knitting needles." He chuckled, then his weathered face sank. "I was so worked up, I overreacted, dragging you out of there like I did. What I'm trying to say is you should go your own way."

"Are you saying you don't want me to marry Owen?"

A pained expression crossed his face. He took a deep breath and let it out. "Owen is a good man. He's got a good job, a nice house. You'd have security and a fine life with him."

Maddy stared down at the toes of her lavender sneakers poking out from the dress. "I know it would make you happy if I did marry him."

"It would. I'd worry less. It's why I was pushing for this marriage. See, I never thought about you as being out there in the world, all on your own. It didn't fit with the way I'd always seen you. Especially after that break-in. I'm sorry, Maddy. Maybe it was selfishness on my part, thinking I couldn't move on until you did."

"Even if I got married, I'd still come over and take care of things around here for you."

"That's not what I mean." He scratched his head through his thinning hair. "I'm not so good with words."

"You're doing fine, Dad."

The slight smile tugging at his face said he knew better. "What I'm trying to say is, you can take care of yourself, with or without a husband. You're a grown woman. You were grown long before you should have been. I'm ashamed to say I never saw you that way."

"It's not all on you, Dad. I could have pursued a career a long time ago. I chose to stay here."

"Well, you don't have to, not anymore. You follow your dream."

"Thank you, Dad. It means a lot to me to hear you say the words. Hey, wait. Are you and Hal going to take your RV adventure?"

"We are. I'm ready to retire, Maddy. It's time. Me and Hal, we're going to do some traveling. We're gonna hit some places and pan for gold."

"Pan for gold?" Maddy chuckled. "People still do that?"

"You bet." Her dad grinned. His eyes held a bit of childlike excitement. "People make some money at it, too."

She had trouble picturing her father in a river panning for gold. But, why not? He's retiring. We all have our dreams.

Maddy smiled at her father. "It's kind of sweet, you know?"

"What is?"

"We were both so worried about each other that we put our own lives on hold."

Her dad smiled back and nodded. "The love of a family."

Although they'd never been an affectionate family, Maddy hugged her father. He wrapped his arms around her and gave her a squeeze.

Her dad took a step back. "When Owen called me this morning, he said you wanted to get married but didn't want to deal with all the hassle of a wedding. I take it that's not true."

Maddy curved a slow glance toward Owen. There was no reason she couldn't have a husband and a career. In all fairness to Owen, like with her dad, she'd never told him this was important. He was a good guy. He just didn't know.

"Maddy, could I see you over here, please?" Pete said. He waved a hand toward the alcove of flowers.

"All I want is for you to be happy," her father said. "To be okay."

How happy would Dad be if he was worried about me all the time? What if I go on for years as a failure? In time, would it take a toll on his health?

"I'll be happy, Dad." *Maybe the toll would be worse if he thought I was living a secure, but unhappy life.*

Or maybe she was tossing around excuses. She needed to make a decision here and fast. Wow, when had life gotten so complicated? Not long ago, her biggest decision was what to make for dinner.

Maddy gave her father a kiss on the cheek. "Thank you, Dad." She lifted her skirt enough to not trip over it on her way to the developing alcove of plant stands and vases of tulips.

"So," Pete said. "Owen told me to keep it traditional, no writing of your own vows or anything. Since it's a surprise wedding, I don't suppose you wrote vows anyway."

"Um, no." She glanced over at Owen. She'd never seen him look happier. Did she make him this happy? Did she have that kind of power? He caught her looking at him, and he trotted over to her side.

"Are we all set?" Owen asked Pete. His eyes were full moons, and his smile was so big it was cartoonish.

"Almost," Pete said. "I just have one question. Most couples take obey out of the ceremony. Where do you two stand on the word?"

"Obey?" Maddy said.

Pete looked at her. "Is it a tradition you want to keep?"

"Oh, yes," Owen said. The man was joyful beyond reason.

Maddy gaped at him. And it all fell on her like confetti made from cut-up pieces of her future, crushing her down to the bottom line. She blinked. She breathed. Then she surfaced, emerging wobbly, but anew. No, she did not want to marry Owen.

Without leaving a second for debate, Owen faced the small crowd. "Come on, people. Let's gather now. It's time to begin."

All right. Her brain plucked through the debris. Where was that spine? It was here somewhere.

Say the words. Say them!

Maddy shook her head in two quick swishes. It stirred up everything inside her. Ah, there was her backbone, beautiful and strong. "Owen. I can't marry you."

"Yes, you can. Just repeat what Pete says." Owen laughed. It was a bit on the hysterical side. "Repeat what Pete says. Hey, that's funny. Repeat Pete." He sobered then. "Okay, Pete, let's get this show on the road. People, get over here."

As the small crowd moved in, Maddy said, "Owen, you're not hearing me."

"I'm hearing your nerves. Don't worry, Maddy, I'll walk you through this."

He didn't think she was reluctant. He thought she was incapable. Feeble-minded, even. "Walk me through it?"

"Yes. You don't need to worry about a thing. Not anymore. Come on, Pete. Get on with the blah, blah, blah."

"Owen," Maddy said, then stopped. "What's that sound?"

"I don't hear anything," Owen said. He made a rolling motion with his hand toward Pete. "Pete. Let's go."

At first, she thought the buzzing might be coming from inside her head. Who could blame her? Owen was doing his best to railroad her into a marriage. But the sound was real. Others heard it, too. She could tell by the way conversation faded and everyone looked around.

The buzzing, mechanical sound, too quiet for a lawnmower and too loud for a cell phone grew louder and closer.

The small crowd in her backyard shifted around to face the driveway. What was that? Then they saw it.

Rolling up the driveway was a yellow toy dump truck. *Tyler Toys* was stamped on the side. In the bed of the truck, facing forward, sat one of Joel's dolls. She was dressed in one of the outfits Maddy had made, jeans and a purple T-shirt with pink lace around the scoop-neck.

The toy truck rolled onto the grass, its battery working harder over the rough terrain. The doll's right arm was reaching out and up with an envelope taped to her little plastic hand. Maddy's name was printed on the outside.

The truck stopped at Maddy's feet. The doll teetered for a second or two, the envelope waving. Maddy bent over for a good look before peeling the tape. The envelope was only sealed at the tip, so it was easy to slip a finger under the flap and open it. She removed and unfolded a piece of paper.

Maddy,

There was a mix-up in the office, and the bosses didn't see the doll until late yesterday. They love the new look and want to start production immediately! We need more of these outfits from the brilliant designer. Those were their words, though I couldn't agree more.

Oh, and one other thing, Maddy. I love you.

Joel

Maddy raised her head. Joel was on the grass near the driveway, the remote control for the truck hanging from one hand.

He loved her?

She stared back at him. Joel wore a white, short-sleeved dress shirt with blue pinstripes tucked into his comfortably worn jeans, and new-looking white sneakers. His hair was combed, but a little wild, the way of its tendency. His smile was unsure.

It should be.

Joel wove through the small gathering until he stood a few feet before her.

"What the hell is he doing here?" Owen said.

They both ignored him, but Grandma Sophie answered. "I called him."

Maddy swung toward her grandmother. "How…Why did you call him?"

"I got his number at the motel after you walked out because, well, I had a feeling."

"What kind of feeling?"

"I saw the hurt in your eyes. You don't look like that unless you care about someone. He looked pained, too. And since you've been back, you've been pretty mopey."

"Grandma!" The last thing she wanted was to be humbled in front of Joel. What was wrong with her grandmother?

"Thanks for calling me this morning, Sophie," Joel said to her grandma.

"You're welcome," Grandma Sophie said. "Don't screw up."

Joel chuckled before turning his attention back to Maddy.

Maddy crossed her arms and gave a mock search over Joel's shoulder. "Did you forget your fiancée, again?"

Joel sighed. "You didn't take a very good look at the ring, did you?"

"It was an engagement ring. What else mattered?"

"The ring she wore was from a carnival she and I went to when we were kids. I gave it to her after I won it throwing darts at balloons."

"That's her engagement ring?"

Joel shook his head. "No. It was never an engagement ring. Roz had a rough childhood. I know because I lived next door. One day when I was thirteen, and she was eleven, her dad was smacking her around right there in the front yard. I was big for my age, feeling kind of cocky and heroic. I marched over there with a baseball bat and told him if he ever touched her again, I'd fix it so he *couldn't* raise a hand to her ever again."

Maddy's arms slid to her side. "Wow, no wonder she fell in love with you."

"Roz isn't in love with me any more than I am with her. We're friends. She…worries about losing my friendship. You're not the first one to see the show. Roz finds out I'm seeing somebody, and she puts on that old carnival ring. She shows up at a restaurant, a movie theater, wherever, and tells the woman I'm with we're engaged. Sometimes, she just goes looking for me, like that day at the motel."

"Sounds pretty stalkerish."

"She can be annoying, but she's gotten a lot better in the last year or so. It's partly my own fault anyway. I always let it slide because it never bothered me too much before."

"How could it not bother you?" Maddy asked.

"I wasn't out-of-my-head crazy for any of those women."

From somewhere nearby, Rachel said, "Aww."

"I took Roz out to dinner a couple nights ago," Joel said. "Her boyfriend wasn't too happy about it."

"She has a boyfriend?"

"Yeah. He gets a little jealous. I think Roz gets a kick out of it. They've been together almost a year now. Anyway, we had a good talk. I promised her she wouldn't lose my friendship just because I fell in love with someone."

Her smile must have been silly. Couldn't be helped.

"In love, huh?"

"You read the note."

"When did you know you were in love with me?" It was shameless fishing for more, but why not? She loved it. Besides, this was the year she was making up for lost time.

Joel grinned at her, dimple and all. Oh, that adorable grin! It made her heart skip and her bones all melty.

"I think it was when I saw you hitchhiking in a wedding dress. Or maybe when you worked so hard to make my creation marketable." His smile faded. "I knew it for sure when you walked out of that motel room. I never felt such an ache before. I hope I never do again. It was like watching my heart march away."

Another "Aww," from Rachel.

Joel placed a hand over his heart as if he were making a pledge. "I never knew I could love like this. You own my heart, Maddy."

Maddy was so liquified she flowed to him rather than walked. She'd closed less than two of the few feet between them before Owen clasped her arm.

"Oh no, oh no," Owen said. "We're getting married right now." He spun her around to face Pete. "Come on, come on, let's move this thing along."

Pete raised his brows, hands, and shoulders at Maddy, asking her without words.

"Owen," Maddy said. She twisted her arm in an effort to extract herself, but his grip was like a manacle. "I'm not going to marry you. Let go of me."

From the corner of her eye, Maddy caught sight of Joel. He dropped the remote control and charged on them with an expression so fierce she tensed. Unfortunately for Owen, her grandmother was closer.

"Get your hands off my granddaughter!" Sophie said.

Owen jerked Maddy closer and shouted back at Sophie. "Give it a rest, old lady!"

Before Maddy could tell him not to talk to her grandmother that way, Sophie took action.

Her grandma firmed her grasp on the straps of her over-sized, zebra-striped purse, and whacked Owen on the side of his head with it. The hard clunk triggered a collective wince. Owen's eyes bugged. He stumbled and swayed before lowering to a slow sit on the grass.

Grandma Sophie jiggled her purse and said, "I'm so glad I grabbed my new can of hairspray instead of the one that's almost empty. I just had a feeling I might need the extra weight."

Maddy's stare traveled from her grandmother to Owen. She had to make sure he was all right. A full can of Grandma's missile-sized hairspray could take down a jet if she swung it hard enough.

Maddy helped Owen to his feet. "Are you okay?"

"Right as rain," he said. He sounded fine, but his eyes took a moment to focus on her. "Ready? Good. Come on, Pete."

"Owen," Maddy said. Her patience and sympathy did a quick fizzle. "I. Am. Not. Marrying. You."

Owen stared at her with a blank expression. Maybe he was getting it. Maybe he had a concussion from Grandma's blow to the head. After a few seconds, Maddy spun away from him. Joel stood a couple feet from her. His expression was grim as he glared at Owen.

The next series of events happened so fast they were almost one.

She'd taken a single step before Owen grabbed her

arm again. He jerked her around with such force the sleeve of her dress ripped at the shoulder. Maddy shoved away from him as far as she could with Owen's hands gripping both her arms.

Owen shook her hard enough to rattle her teeth. "You're not doing this to me again, you stupid little bitch!"

The small crowd sucked in a gasp so big Maddy could swear her hair fluttered. She stood frozen in shock. Owen had never spoken to her in such a crude, nasty way. Was this a result of his stress or the revealing of a part of him he'd kept hidden?

Owen bared his teeth and, was that a growl? He let go of her arms and grabbed for her throat. Half a second later, the situation shifted again.

In a single deft move, Joel had an arm around Maddy's waist, scooped her out of the way, and punched Owen hard in the face. Owen spun a half-circle and was struck again with Sophie's loaded purse. He twirled like a wobbly top before sinking back to the ground. Owen lifted his hands in front of his face just in time to catch his head.

Her father scowled down at Owen. "Maddy, are you all right?"

She gathered her wits quick, so her father wouldn't worry. "I'm fine, Dad."

Then her father shifted his glare from Owen to Sophie and Joel. "You didn't leave any for me."

"Sorry," Joel said. "Next time, you get first dibs."

After a brief pause, her dad gave Joel an airy laugh.

"Dad," Maddy said. "This is Joel. Joel, my father.

The two men shook hands.

"I take it you met my daughter when she was…out

and about."

"Yes, sir. I did."

"Joel gave me a ride," Maddy said. Her dad wasn't a fool. He knew there was more to it. She could tell by the way he quirked a brow at her. He let it be, though. She and her dad had a new understanding of each other.

Sophie still held her position over Owen, her purse clasped in both hands, ready to take him down again should the need arise. "I'll stand guard," she said. "Go on, you two. Get out of here. Your adventure is just beginning."

"Your grandma is right, Maddy," her father said. He placed a hand on her shoulder. "Go live your life."

Joann rushed over then. She hugged Maddy and spoke in her ear. "Go, Maddy. Be who you want to be. Be with who you want to be with." Joann squeezed her tight before backing away with a weepy smile.

"That's exactly what I'm going to do," Maddy said.

Joel held out his hand. Maddy took it and used her other hand to gather some of her skirt. The two of them ran from the yard and down the driveway, laughing like school kids out for summer break. The shopping bag Rachel had given her with the shoes and stockings still dangled from her wrist. It slid down and caught at her fist full of fabric.

At Joel's car, he opened the passenger door for her.

Maddy stopped at the wedged opening and spun around. She clasped onto Joel's upper arms; arms so firm with muscle she was melting again. If this kept up, she'd have to travel in a bucket.

"Your bag is in the car," Joel said. "All your stuff is in there."

Maddy glanced through the window and into the

back seat. There sat the paisley travel bag she'd left at the motel. His bag was next to it. She faced him again, one brow raised.

"I was being optimistic," he said.

She used her own muscles to squeeze Joel closer, almost close enough to kiss. He smelled all clean, with a masculine musk. His face had a fresh shave. The ocean blue of his eyes glowed in the morning sun.

"I love you," Maddy said.

Joel lowered his face until it was close to hers. He spoke through a broad smile. "I love you back."

"Good thing. I'd hate to sic my grandmother on you."

Joel was still chuckling when his mouth lowered to hers.

Epilogue

Carl and Phyllis Morris were having a blast driving along old Route 66 in their classic retro kit car. It was candy-apple red, built by Carl and their two adult sons last summer to celebrate Carl's retirement from the accounting firm he'd been with for forty years.

The sun shone unfettered, but not too hot. The road was fairly clear. The trip had been a good one. The show they were catching on their ride treated them to a string of laughter while they played guesses at what was going on in the car in front of them.

First, two white dress shoes, ladies, with low heels, flew out of the front passenger window. They bounced along the road and off into the desert. Next was a pair of white stockings. They caught an updraft and danced away. Then, a woman's hand, holding a bridal veil with long, white lace, hung out the window. The lace blew back for a few seconds before she released the veil.

Just when they thought the show was over, there was one more act.

A full, white dress bulged out the window. It looked to be a wedding dress, all lacey and billowing. The garment swelled in different places as the woman kept shoving. At last, it popped out the window.

The thing puffed up in the air like a sail catching wind. It snagged on their own hood ornament for a moment, blowing like an extravagant windsock, before it let go and flew away.

A word about the author…

I lived most of my life in the wondrous city of Las Vegas, Nevada. For a while I lived in an R.V. with my husband and I was fortunate to see every state in this amazing country. Now I live in beautiful Michigan, where I've learned about layering clothes and that boats don't have brakes.

Visit Micki at:

Facebook:
https://www.facebook.com/mickimillerwriter

Twitter: @millermwriter

Instagram: micki.miller

TikTok: www.tiktok.com/@mickiwriter

YouTube: @mickimiller1474

Thank you for purchasing
this publication of The Wild Rose Press, Inc.

For questions or more information
contact us at
info@thewildrosepress.com.

The Wild Rose Press, Inc.
www.thewildrosepress.com

www.ingramcontent.com/pod-product-compliance
Lightning Source LLC
LaVergne TN
LVHW020535100826
845148LV00010B/1465

* 9 7 8 1 5 0 9 2 5 2 7 0 1 *